Little One

ALSO BY OLIVIA MUENTER

Such a Bad Influence

Little One

A NOVEL

Olivia Muenter

LITTLE, BROWN AND COMPANY
New York Boston London

Little, Brown and Company

Hachette Book Group

1290 Avenue of the Americas, New York, NY 10104

littlebrown.com

First Edition: February 2026

Print book interior design by Taylor Navis

ISBN 9780316594561

LCCN is available at the Library of Congress

Printing 1, 2025

LSC-C

Printed in the United States of America

For Jake

Her woods had no mirror, but she learned the shape of herself, anyway. Each morning, she woke alone and was soothed by assessing her body's needs and strengths, its hunger to endure. She was alive. There was nothing but this. She was lost to the world but she was not, for once, lost to herself.

From *Lighthouse* by Marion Earl

Little One

CHAPTER 1

Now

Push, yells the virtual trainer's voice as it spills out of my headphones and into the center of my skull. *Push forward. Now. Go. One more mile. Feel your feet hit the pavement.*

I try to concentrate on the rhythm of my stride, the repetition of my toe-heel strike against the concrete, but my stomach gurgles with hunger instead. The eight-mile run to pick up the cake had seemed like a good idea this morning, something that would make me feel better about the sugar, the day itself. I had pictured myself on the cab ride back, eyes closed in satisfaction, hands carefully clutching the thing I had earned. But seven miles in, all I feel is empty and weak, like the center of me has been carved out with a spoon. I'm caving in on myself.

Come on, the virtual trainer shouts again, *one more mile now. It's going to be so worth it. I promise you. That's right. Give me one deep breath through your nose.*

I don't have to look at my phone to picture the trainer. I know her well enough by now. I can close my eyes and see her bouncing on the treadmill, her two space buns perched carefully atop her head, her forehead seeming to glow with effort instead of actual perspiration. I imagine the giant fan that's probably just out of frame, the one that keeps her cool enough to find the energy to keep yelling things like: *This is what self-love looks like.*

Is it?

And if you need to take a break, that's self-love too, y'all. I promise it is.

I almost laugh.

And yet, I'm so close to being done that I figure it can't hurt. I try it. I search for that kind of affection for myself, that kind of care. Anything to make this easier, to keep pushing. Instead, all I find is a gnawing, angry scream inside my chest, my lungs burning, begging me to stop, to breathe, to eat. Maybe, I think, Space Buns is right. Maybe taking a break is the answer, just this once. And it's that easy. Just like that, I've entertained the option of giving up.

You've given weakness a seat at the table, says another voice, one that seems to come from somewhere behind my eyes, trickling over the ridges of my frontal lobe. *And now you need to ask it to leave.*

I realize now that I've stopped moving, that I'm doubled over in the middle of the sidewalk, pedestrians grumbling as I block their path, slow their pace. A cramp rips through my side. My face is burning, my skin raw and bitten from the wind. I want to go home and run a bath, sit in it until the water goes cold. It sounds nice.

You know it's always going to feel easier to stop, the familiar voice says again. *It will feel so easy that you'll be convinced it must be right, that you really are supposed to give in, to take the easy way out, to do the one thing that everyone else is doing. The feeling makes you think that giving up is normal. But we're better than that, aren't we, Catharine?*

A high-tempo EDM song starts playing, synchronizing with the last big push of the guided run. The sound suddenly feels garish and wrong, the motivational messages childish.

Self-love. Please.

I rip my earbuds out and stuff them in the pocket of my leggings, silencing the virtual coach, the uselessness of it all. And then I keep moving.

Suddenly all that pain from before is something sturdy and knotted, a rope that works its way between my ribs. I reach down into the center of myself, find the thing I know I can always control, that ache I know so well, and I grab hold. I pull myself up out of the place where giving up is an option, and I push forward.

Later, I drag my finger along the edge of the cake, admiring it. I watch as I indent the soft icing just above the circular base and study the writing on the top. *Congrats on 10!*, it says, barely legible, the letters and numbers drawn on in chunks of thick, goopy icing. Lazy work, really. Like a child did it. I sigh. It will have to do.

Besides, I've seen worse. I can still picture the first one: a discounted, week-old carrot cake, the only thing I could afford. I remember sitting in my speck of a kitchen on the first anniversary, elbows scrunched together on a table that folded down from the wall because that was all there was room for. I had stared at the cake, sweating beneath a dented plastic cover. The messy, neon orange blob of a carrot drawn on top seemed to say, "This is your idea of a celebration? Really?" No, I wanted to respond as I stabbed a single candle into the icing. This is something else. A ritual. An assurance that I will not be sad on this day. I will not be angry. I will not be that person. A reminder of just how far I've come. Not a celebration, but an acknowledgment of how hard I worked to create this life.

This year, I splurged on one of those Instagrammable birthday cakes, the Funfetti-turned-cool types that cost the equivalent of a week's worth of groceries and are always more aesthetically pleasing than they are delicious.

"We don't usually do custom messages," the twenty-year-old working at the bakery had insisted earlier when I picked it up, seemingly exasperated at my request. "It's kind of basic."

I had smoothed down my baby hairs, all of them sweat-soaked and wild from the run. I knew my face was beet red, that I looked flustered, out of breath, and old to them, probably.

"I get it. I totally do," I started, then lowered my voice. "It's just...I'm ten years sober today."

A lie, sure, but why shouldn't I get something shiny and special for a decade of survival? I gave up something all those years ago, too.

The twenty-year-old sighed. "All right...but it won't be pretty."

I thanked them effusively and gave them a big tip. I'm not a monster.

"Ten years," I say out loud to myself in my apartment, staring at the cake. My mind charts all the things that have changed in that time. The career I have built. The apartments I have tolerated in order to find this place, a building with a doorman and a gym, a trash chute instead of a utility room full of garbage and mice. I should feel proud of myself, relieved to have another year of distance between me and before, but I don't. This year, it all feels harder.

It's just the number, I tell myself. The weight of it. Double digits. I'm twenty-eight now, and it feels impossible that a whole decade has passed. I close my eyes and picture the Scandinavian-accented voice from my running app guiding me through the moment. *Sit with your feelings. Listen to them. Meet them with curiosity, if you must. But never judgment. Breathe through the—*

Fuck it.

I finally lick the dollop of icing that's been resting on my finger, and my cheeks pucker at the sweetness. Already, I know what comes next. First, a thin tendril of an idea: What if I plunge my open hand into the cake? What if I shovel it into my mouth in giant gulps? I follow the thought down deeper. I imagine I eat it all, then clock how much time it would take to throw out all the evidence, buy a new cake, emulate the writing in just the right way and pretend the first one never happened. I am well practiced in reengineering the truth of things like this.

I push away the impulse as I reach into the cabinet for a plate, but I can already feel a panic attack building in my joints. My mind feels slippery, every thought sliding through its grip, instantly replaced by another only for that one to slither away, too. I picture a train barreling toward me, my shoe stuck between the tracks.

We don't do this anymore, Catharine, I whisper out loud, following the advice that a kickboxing instructor once screamed through ragged, exhausted breaths as Miley Cyrus's "Party in the USA" blared in the background.

"Talk to your anxiety like it's a two-year-old," they yelled. "A toddler throwing a tantrum. It might not listen to you, but it doesn't matter. *You* are in charge. You are calling the shots, ladies."

The whole class had erupted in cheers.

Occasionally, this strategy had actually worked for me. I would crouch down and meet my anxiety, note how small it was, how stupid. Couldn't it see that everything was fine? That I was as safe as I have been for the last decade? Safer than ever, maybe. But today, it doesn't work. I need a different strategy.

I force myself to move to the bathroom and splash water on my face, then dab it dry with a towel. I stare at myself in the mirror, gradually moving closer until my nose is nearly touching my reflection.

"Now?" I cock my head to the side, my strawberry-blond hair glued to my forehead with sweat. I know there is no point getting angry at myself for a panic attack, especially not when I can understand what caused it. This day is always a minefield. Still, there is something about the rage that feels good. "Really?"

For a moment, all I see is my mother.

I sigh, steadying myself on the sink beneath the mirror, my shoulders hunched toward my ears. My mind scrolls through what I do now. How I take care of myself. I close my eyes and picture a ten-slide infographic on Instagram, each one an example of an effective form of self-care. A bubble bath. An audiobook read by a narrator with a vaguely European-sounding accent. Light stretching. A long call with a friend. None of it sounds good to me. I have no interest in being gentle with myself. I want to push myself around, to bully whatever weak part of me I need to until it eventually makes life easier. I owe myself that. Tough love. A discipline.

I look back up, meet my own stare.

"Fucking pathetic."

Finally, I feel myself start to relax.

I throw the towel in the hamper and start to make my way back to the kitchen, remembering the cake still sitting there on the counter, sad and sweating.

I let my left hand drag along the exposed brick wall as I go, trying to feel the microscopic ridges of my fingers as they travel across each bump and groove. I've always loved the feeling of something rough in the city, something that could scratch you or catch on your shirt. So many of the apartments I looked at before this one were all clean lines. Shining, smooth elevator banks. Long stretches of seamless sheets of gray. Perfectly straight lines going up, up, up. But I liked the bricks here, the friction. Friction keeps you on your toes.

I take a knife from a drawer and look down at the cake again. It should feel good, like a reward. Instead, it feels like a challenge. I slice into it but hesitate before making the next cut, gauging the size of my portion. Before I can decide between a wedge or a sliver, my phone lights up with a new email. I put the knife down and scroll through my inbox.

There are dozens of new messages from editors and other freelancers, even more from publicists, all of them jockeying for my attention. Each of them is another reminder that I built this life myself pitch by pitch, story by story, byline by byline. Lie by lie.

It wasn't as difficult as you'd imagine. *Sure, I know all about search engine optimization,* I'd say in our ten-minute phone interviews. Obviously, I have a journalism degree from a respected, but not flashy, university. It's not like anyone was checking any of this, not for a freelancer.

I learned to fill whatever role someone needed me to fill. I could be the lightning-fast copywriter. I could be an expert interviewer, no deadline too daunting. I could be the no-strings-attached, mysterious one-night stand who lets you do that thing you secretly love, who doesn't expect you to stay the night or even want you to. I could be the friend who watches *The Bachelor* with you every week, who holds your hair back when you throw up after a night out, who listens to your secrets. It's not that I didn't enjoy the work, the sex, the camaraderie. I respected it, even, the steadfast vulnerability of these people. I would look at them during yet another interview or birthday dinner and marvel at it, the way they trusted me. I just didn't delude myself into thinking that it wasn't all transactional.

They needed someone who would turn in clean copy, meet deadlines, not complain about writing yet another story about the Best Fucking Amazon Finds Under $25. They needed good sex, no commitment, to feel wanted but not needed—never needed. They wanted to pretend that having brunch and paying $70 for bottomless, watery mimosas once in a while means we're really close. Best pals. That's okay. I needed things, too. Money. Sex. The kind of social life that doesn't make people wonder if something's wrong with me.

At first, the assignments paid almost nothing, but once editors saw how much money they could make from an optimized story about the best dog toys/mascaras/vitamins/vibrators? Then things started to change. And by that point, I could do that shit in my sleep. I've made a nice little career of it now, offering pristine copy on tight turnarounds as well as consulting services on editorial strategy. And most importantly, I can do it all on my terms.

I am about to put my phone down when I see the subject line.

Story about your childhood?

I feel a dampness start to settle on my forehead again, my stomach slowly cranking beneath my shirt. I open it.

Hi Catharine,

I'm a journalist who's writing a story about a little-known, now-defunct cult in central Florida — big in the early aughts, I think. Does this sound familiar to you? I'd love to talk.

Reese Campbell

Immediately, I lift my elbows from where they're resting on the counter. I stand up straight. I have the familiar sense that I need to leave everything right where it is, that I saw something I shouldn't have and in order for me to be rational about this I have to move carefully. I have to find the things I can control and sink my fingers into them.

I set my phone aside gently, then assess the mess in front of me. The drooping cake. The knife. I can smell the frosting now, the air thick with sugar. My stomach rolls again. And then I am moving.

I grab a black trash bag from under the sink and hold it open near the edge of the countertop, then use my forearm to slide the entire cake into the bag. I want it away from me. I need it gone. In minutes, it's out of my apartment, then down the trash chute. There is no possibility of changing my mind. I take the knife to the sink, pausing before I run it under the tap. I want to lick the icing, but know I won't. I let the discipline fill me up instead, the voice from my run echoing inside me again. It doesn't erase the email, the panic, the reminder of everything before, but it's something. It is solid and within my grasp. I'm grateful that after all this time, it's still as true as ever, maybe the most honest thing my father ever taught me: Hunger is a thing you can hold.

CHAPTER 2

Then

Even the hottest mornings were mine. The mornings with fog so thick it felt like mud, like each gasp of air might fill your lungs with a steaming, invisible sludge. The mornings where every plant was connected by spiderwebs as intricate as lace, sticky wedding veils thrown over everything at night. The mornings that felt so obviously built for tougher creatures, things with skin like armor, blood chilled. I made them all mine. I liked mornings like these the most though, hot before the sun had even crept over the horizon. The entire world set to a low, silent simmer and me, in the very center of it.

I walked through the tomato garden until it swallowed me up, parallel rows of scraggly, ruby-studded green stretching out on either side of me as far as I could see. I ran my hand over the leaves, fingertips brushing swollen drops of dew, then looked up. The sky had ripened with color, sapphire now instead of deep navy. People would start waking up soon. The farm would come to life, pulsing with chores and routine. I closed my eyes and inhaled, taking the deepest breath I could imagine, just like my mother had taught me.

"Imagine all that air filling you up," she used to say. "From your toes to the tippy top of your head."

I remembered being a child, maybe four, her standing next to me with her hands on her hips, elbows bent outward, face toward the sky. I had mirrored her stance, opening my mouth wide and gulping the air down, hungry for it. The tomato plants were still small that year, but the air was sharp with their fragrance. My father stood from where he was crouched next to us, weeding, and did the same.

"What do you smell, Catharine?" I heard him ask. "What do you taste?"

I considered the question seriously, eyes still closed. Even then, I knew the importance of getting these details right.

"Green," I finally answered, confident. It all tasted like green. This was exactly what the farm felt like to me, from the very beginning. So bright and vibrant that even when you closed your eyes, the color of it was there dancing.

I looked up at him, searching for approval. He nodded, face still turned toward the sun.

"Nothing is this good," he said, stretching an arm out and pulling my mother into him. She smiled.

"Everybody wants this, and then they forget. They lose sight of what matters. But not us," he finished. "Never us."

It was this memory I returned to almost every time I found myself in the tomato gardens in the years after, the image of myself next to those young plants seared into me, a measuring stick. It was a reference point for the way the garden had slowly spread around us year after year, until *garden* wasn't really the right word at all. It was a field, a forest of life. My mind would whir through all of these memories, the way the farm had flourished and grown exactly as he said it would and know he was right. Nothing is as good as this.

The words echoed through my memory to the present as I pulled a tomato from the vine and brought it to my nose, comforted by its familiar smell, sharp and summer-warmed. Instant comfort.

A sound from behind me then, someone walking through the garden. I spun around and saw my mother there, her forehead already shining with sweat, her face framed by a soft halo of red wisps of hair, courtesy of the humidity.

"You know," she started, a cup of tea cradled between her hands. "I always thought that teenagers were supposed to sleep in all day. Isn't that what everyone says?"

I shrugged. "I don't know."

I didn't bother stating the obvious—that sleeping all day was never an option at the farm, for any of us. If it were, how would anything get done?

She took a sip and studied me. She had been doing this more and more lately, looking at me like she was monitoring something. I hated it. Finally, she went on. "Early start today, remember?"

In fairness to her, I had forgotten. Sometimes, on the hottest days, we started classes early, when the sun had barely risen. It meant we could avoid having to sit in the stifling schoolroom during the warmest part of the afternoon.

"Right," I said, wiping my hands on the sides of my denim shorts, starting back toward the school trailer. "Thanks."

I had just stepped around her when she spoke again.

"You really love it out here, don't you?" she said, her tone neutral, like she had peeled the emotion from the sentence word by word.

"It reminds me of how much there is to be grateful for," I responded, forcing confidence into my voice.

"Ah," my mother said. "Right. I see."

I could tell by how her voice carried that she was still facing away from me, her gaze focused down the endless row of plants. I continued walking without looking back, the whole way imagining how things would have gone if I had answered her honestly and admitted the whole complicated truth. If I told her that I was beginning to suspect I had given myself too much space. Sometime during all those quiet mornings, my mind had begun to wander, questions building and sticking to my skin like dew. I knew they were wrong, but I found I couldn't silence them completely. I was that weak. I comforted myself with the commitment that they would remain safely within myself, but this only lasted so long.

My father stood in front of all of us, his hands gripping each side of a podium, a dry-erase board covered with scribbles behind him. I could still see the faded remnants of a thousand other lessons if I squinted, layers upon layers of his messy, cursive scrawl. Despite the early hour, the room was as hot as ever, the door propped open in a way that felt almost comical given the utter lack of breeze. But I never minded school, not even back when there were so many of us, everyone sharing desks, sweat-sticky elbows wedged together.

One-room schoolhouses had been a staple of rural communities for centuries, my father had told us. They fostered community and collaboration. Bonding. I had seen it firsthand, my sister, Linna, and I working out hours of math and geography and spelling questions side by side, puzzling through it all, laughing about everything. School came easily to me. I excelled in most subjects and beamed in the glow of my father's approval, a place where I felt safest. Maybe that's why I felt compelled to ask the question that morning. I had let myself get too comfortable, too soft. I forgot that there was still more for me to learn.

"What did you say?" my father said, eyes fixed on me, his voice light, but a half-note sharper than usual.

I took in his imposing figure as it moved closer to my desk. His long, freckled arms were perched at his sides like wings, his hands on his hips. His armpits were stained with sweat.

"Just wanted to make sure I heard you correctly, Catharine," he said, a sweetness in his tone. His voice was almost singsongy now.

What *had* I said? It was as if the words had been born out of my mouth instead of my brain, that they had fallen out like loose teeth, as natural as it was horrifying. This had been happening more and more lately, cravings and questions and actions springing forth without my permission.

Think, Catharine.

"I just don't get it," I repeated, my brain moving on autopilot, recalling my last utterance. "The beans. The same food, every day. There are so many other options..."

I heard Linna swallow loudly next to me. When I looked at her, her eyes were so wide, eyebrows so high, that the entire proportions of her face had shifted.

"I don't mean, like, anything crazy," I explained, attempting to course correct. I felt my shoulders inch upward in a shrug. I was trying so hard to convince myself that if I was light and easy about this, then maybe he would be, too. "Just something different. Like how it used to be."

He had to remember, too, I thought, that things weren't so bad when there were fewer rules. That we were happy.

A chair squeaked behind me, and I turned to find the rest of the class frozen and silent. Only Jessie had a small smirk on her face, like she was enjoying this. Of course she was.

When I shifted forward again, I realized my father had moved closer while I had been facing the other way. Now, he was standing right in front of my desk, so close that I had to sink down in the seat and angle my neck upward to see him.

"When things were easier, right?" he corrected. "That's what you want?"

I considered the question for too long. I could feel myself digging a hole.

"No." I focused my eyes on my hands. My fingers were swollen from the heat. It was the kind of humidity with no mercy, the air still and suffocating. I glanced toward the door, trying to remember my morning in the garden, the tomatoes, the beauty of this place and this life.

I knew I didn't want the easy way out. I wanted this. Exactly this. I wanted the open space and misty mornings. I wanted to sit in the treehouse with Linna at dusk and watch armadillos putter around the fields, their skin like tiny sets of chainmail. There were so many good parts of this place. There always had been. I wanted more of them, not fewer.

"Catharine," he said, his voice warmer now, even friendly. "It's okay. Really. You can be honest with me. With all of us."

I slowly raised my head, blinking at him.

"Remember, none of this works if we aren't honest about what we crave," he said. "This place? It operates on knowing your weakest self. If you can't be honest about those parts of yourself, none of it works. On a surface level, none of us want to adjust. None of us want to learn. We want what's comfortable. What's easy. We can't even fathom that maybe, eventually, after some work, other things will appeal to us more. That maybe our highest self really isn't met via a comfortable path. We all have to learn that the hard way."

I nodded, cautious.

He put a hand on my shoulder and squeezed. "We're on the same team here," he said, then gestured to the rest of the room. "All of us."

I felt my body start to relax. This was so much like an older version of my father, the one that was light and hopeful, supportive and warm.

"You're right," I said. "I think I was just hungry."

As soon as the word had left my mouth, I realized my mistake.

His eyes narrowed, and he cocked his head to the side, like he was waiting for me to go on. His expression said: Is that quite right, Catharine? Try again, Catharine.

We were halfway through a thirty-day moderation fast, something that we'd done together as a community since I was a child. At first, these fasts had lasted for a couple days at a time, but eventually they had turned into more elaborate events, complete with more and more rules. We had a massive garden full of spinach and carrots and tomatoes that we were still harvesting, selling, and preserving, but we weren't allowed to touch any of it for ourselves. For two weeks, we had eaten beans for every meal with zero exceptions.

I should have known by then that this was how it went. The first days of the fasts were always easy, with all of us feeling the benefits right away. We were less focused on our next meal than we were on all the things that brought us here to the farm in the first place. Most importantly, we were all in it together.

But then, the days stretched on. By the second week, I'd always find myself in the same place, thoughts of food occupying every second of my days. I fell asleep dreaming of eggs scrambled with fresh parsley, of warm sourdough, still hot from the oven. I fantasized about slicing a ripe tomato and sprinkling it with salt. And all of it served to remind me the fast was necessary, the work was necessary. The moderation, essential.

Because my father was right. What I was feeling wasn't *hunger.* I wasn't starving. It was something closer to laziness, an impulse I was still training out of myself. What I had was more than enough. I had let myself forget so easily.

"Sorry, no. That's not what I meant," I corrected myself. "I have everything I need."

He nodded, then winked at me. Bingo. I had said the right thing.

"We all do, don't we?" He shrugged. "And yet, temptation remains. The easy way out is as spectacularly appealing as ever, isn't it, Catharine?"

No, I wanted to say. He didn't understand. This wasn't me. I didn't want the easy way out. I wanted to reach inside myself and find the thing that kept doing this, hijacking my willpower, asking the wrong question, making the wrong choice. I wanted to kill it.

"I'm sure you all have some of these same questions, too, right?" he asked the rest of the room, strolling back behind the podium, mindlessly thumbing through piles of paper. "You know you can talk about it here. We're all human."

The room stayed silent. He shrugged.

"Suit yourselves," he said. "But actually, I think it's pretty admirable that Catharine voiced her most basic, raw craving—that she entertained the easier path for a second and admitted it. How else would we ever get better? How would we ever be able to make each other better? I, for one, am proud of her."

I heard Jessie snort from the back of the room.

"You know, I think that's all for today," my father announced before walking toward the door, pausing before he turned back at us. "Go enjoy the day. Class dismissed."

Just like that, it was over. He was gone.

"Hell yeah," Kent said before cracking his knuckles, the sound sending a ping of discomfort up my spine. I hated when he did that. "And it's not even lunch yet."

Kent was seventeen and deeply tanned, his arms roped with muscle from working outside, helping my father with the hardest parts of running the farm. He was also Jessie's twin brother, and though Linna and I were only a couple years behind them, it might as well have been decades. The age gap seemed to render us entirely invisible to Kent and make us a source of constant bullying from Jessie and her best friend, Maura. Maura was closer to our age at sixteen, but dutifully laughed at every joke Jessie attempted, no matter how stupid.

"Oh," Jessie exclaimed with a laugh, a sharp chuckle that eventually dissolved into a long, knowing sigh. "Just trust me. We haven't heard the last of that."

I rolled my eyes. "It was just a question," I said. "You heard him. It's fine to question things."

I could hear the desperation in my voice.

"Yeah, well," Jessie said, following Kent's lead and walking out the door, Maura following behind her, snickering. "We'll see, won't we?"

Linna stuck her hand out toward mine, pushing her thick-framed glasses back up her nose with the other. "Let's get out of here. I think the inside of my eyelids are starting to sweat."

I hesitated for a moment, Jessie's words and my own paranoia echoing in my head. But in the end, I decided that I was right. It was just a question.

CHAPTER 3

Now

"I don't know, doesn't it feel just a little cultish to you?" my friend Stella asks as she takes a sip of her oat milk latte. "Seriously. Think about it."

After barely sleeping last night, I texted Stella this morning to see if she wanted to hang out. We've been friends for years now—close friends, if you were to ask Stella. But I sugarcoated most of the details of my childhood when we met. And how close can you really be with someone who doesn't know the truth of your life? Not the big stuff, at least. Not the ugly stuff.

I considered, briefly, that this was an opportunity to finally get it all off my chest. I have the urge every six months or so, like my body needs to expel the truth, vomit it up, be done with it. But I know that once I began I wouldn't know where to stop, what to hold back.

"I mean, you pay, what? Thousands of dollars for the thing?" Stella goes on. "You wait months on end for it to arrive. You let this hulking piece of equipment take up precious, precious square footage in the middle of your living room, and for what? To feel like you're part of the cool girls' club and let some trainer-turned-influencer tell you you're a rock star? Only to then abandon it a year later and beg strangers on Facebook Marketplace to take it off your hands so you can afford your monthly spot at Pilates instead?"

She huffs out a breath of air, then takes a sip of her latte. Purses her lips. "I'll pass, thanks!"

I consider reminding Stella that it was she who had insisted I try SoulCycle a few years earlier, she who told me that Barry's would change my relationship with my calves. It was also she who had begged me to do sunset rooftop yoga because "savasana just hits differently during golden hour." But Stella is my friend, someone who fills an important slot in my life, so I keep these thoughts to myself.

"It's definitely a little intense," I reply, shrugging. "But, people love it. Whatever works, right?"

Stella lowers an eyebrow at me from across the table, a look that says, "Come on. I thought we were here to talk shit," but she knows she won't get it from me. This is part of our thing, too. Our dynamic. I am the friend who rises above, who deftly avoids snarky gossip and tiptoes around passing judgment, but, somehow, still manages to be fun.

What I'm thinking of now is my own stationary bike, sitting in the corner of my bedroom, covered in laundry I need to put away. I had abandoned it for in-person classes once again, just as Stella predicted. There was more accountability this way. I'm also remembering how I've tried all the green juices she has recommended, the leggings, the early morning wake-up calls. The meditative yoga flows. Gratitude exercises. Social media cleanses that seem to always require announcing said cleanse on social media. Hashtag breathwork.

I could act like I was above all of it as much as I wanted to, could laugh off the infomercial-like endorsements of meal planning I'd seen from a friend on TikTok. But Stella and I were weak in all the same ways. The only difference was I never talked about it, and Stella couldn't stop.

"Come on." Stella rolls her eyes again, pushing me. "Does it even really do anything for your body? I hear you burn more calories just from walking to and from the train every day."

"Who knows?" I shrug, allowing a hint of a smile. I imagine a halo hanging above my head, rather than what is really there, a running tally of how many grams of carbohydrates are in Stella's drink. It's a force of habit.

"God knows it certainly hasn't done anything for Ava," Stella says under her breath, referencing a mutual friend of ours.

"Stella..." I say, chiding her gently. She knows that this is where I'll draw the line. That I don't engage in body talk. I once told her an elaborate story about a track coach who monitored what I ate and commented on my body during practices, ultimately spurring an eating disorder that had wrecked my early twenties. It was such a familiar tale that I assume she often forgets, confusing it with similar stories from other friends.

"I'm sorry, I'm sorry—that was shitty," Stella says. "You know I'm just jealous. She looks fucking great."

And there it is, the thing I love about Stella, the thing that made me want to keep hanging out with her after we first met on a press trip to the Hamptons, hosted by a sunscreen brand. It had been an eight-hour day that included a free breakfast, a lecture on SPF, and nearly six hours of sitting in stop-and-go traffic which triggered her motion sickness. Stella had looked at me from across the aisle of the bus, barf bag readied in front of her, and shrugged. "Do you think their plan is to break us down enough physically that we'll give the product a good review out of fear they'll make us do this again?"

Stella's charm is her honesty, her stream-of-consciousness commentary on the world. No filter. No shame, either. She often showed up at coffee and opened with three words: "I'm a mess," then launched into a list of the things going wrong in her life, the things she hated most about herself that day. For a long time, she waited for me to echo her complaints, name what I hated about myself that day too, a ritual of shame that I'm sure she had engaged in with every other female friend she had. But I couldn't do it. I could relate to the self-loathing, sure, but I couldn't pretend that her complaints and mine were stemming from the same mostly harmless brand of insecurity.

When I looked at Stella, I saw exactly what the rest of the world saw: a beautiful woman with a near-perfect body whose mom maybe did SlimFast once, talked about it a few too many times, and gave her a complex. I told her this, of course. At least the first part. Every time the topic came up, I reminded her: You're gorgeous. You're perfect. You don't need to change a thing. But I was disgusted when she said it back to me. I was so sick of being lied to that I took the topic off the table altogether.

"Honestly," I say, steering the conversation back toward the original topic, answering her question about why anyone would buy a spin bike and promptly abandon it for something else. "I think people are just chasing the high of being a part of something, a community, a way of thinking. That doesn't make it a cult."

Stella nods, her lips pursing together as she takes another gulp of coffee. Brown gunk has accumulated in the corners of her mouth that she's yet to notice.

"Maybe. But all I'm saying is that the whole thing does sort of give me the same 'hey, want to join me for Bible study?' vibes that my roommate gave me in college," Stella says. "She acted like it was a totally normal thing she was doing, inviting me. Being friendly. Meanwhile I had just told her how my Hannukah was over winter break. It's like, hello? Not for me! No matter how great and fun it might be."

"And did you go?" I ask. "To the Bible study?"

"Hell no," Stella tilts her head slightly, stopping herself. "Wait, actually, no. That's a lie. One time she told me that the youth pastor was very hot, so I did go. Bad choice. A lot of closed-eyed singing. And every guy there wore the most aggressive V-neck. Like, do we really need to see your bare sternum, sir? No. We do not. Jesus never asked for that."

"Fair enough," I say, chuckling.

"Like you said," Stella explains. "Whatever works for people, right? It's harmless, I guess. I should focus more on my own shit."

I don't point out to her that I didn't say it was harmless.

"You'll be horrified to learn I am still literally losing my mind over Jeremy," she adds before I can reply. "It's a sickness, I swear."

Stella also fulfills the stereotype of being the friend whose choices in men make it very easy for me to stay off the apps and avoid long-term relationships altogether. Stella's latest love interest, Jeremy, told her that they were twin flames before moving to Argentina on a whim, explaining via Facebook Messenger that it was all good because they were destined to meet again in another life.

"Oh, Stell..." I say, softly.

She waves away my pity, setting her coffee down on the table between us.

"What about you?" she asks. "Are you seeing anyone? Or are

you still mastering the whole wildly independent-and-thriving thing, making the rest of us look bad?"

My love life, or the lack of it, maybe, is one of the topics that usually triggers my impulse to spontaneously blurt out the truth. It exhausts me, having to constantly explain why I only do casual, why I refuse to let Stella set me up with someone. It's easy enough to nod along with all her theories, all the reasons why I avoid commitment and connection. A bad breakup, she muses. Not quite. A fear of change, she suggests. Maybe. A complicated childhood, she asks. You could say that. It's easy, yes. But it gets old.

I smile, roll my eyes. "Still as boring as ever. Nothing new to report."

"Smart girl."

I check my phone for the time, then reach down to gather my bag from the ground. "Well, I should probably—"

"Don't tell me you're leaving me already," Stella cuts me off. "I haven't even told you about Hinge guy yet. Good news: Excellent Jeremy distraction. Extremely impressive biceps. Bad news: He smells like eggs."

"Hm." I process this information, nodding seriously. "Rotten? Or hard-boiled?"

Stella leans in. "What if I told you it's somehow...both?"

"Okay." I laugh, standing. "We'll get to that next time, I promise. I just have somewhere to be right now."

She raises an eyebrow, clucking her tongue loudly behind her teeth. "Look at this busy, mysterious lady."

"I have to go to the library."

Stella sighs, disappointed. "Of course. I should have known. I simply can't compete."

Stella has made fun of my deep love of public libraries since we met. "You do realize this isn't actually a Nora Ephron film," she had said to me once when I had asked her to meet me on the steps of the city's flagship library, its marble columns rising dramatically behind us.

"If this was a Nora Ephron film, I'd be at a bookstore," I told her.

"Oh, I see," she teased. "So you're the even *cooler* version of Meg Ryan in *You've Got Mail.*"

I just laughed. I had never minded the jokes about my reading habits. I always understood that for most people, the library was more a character than it was an actual place. To Stella, the library was whimsical, fairy tale rather than function. To me, it was a necessity. I went most weeks, to read or learn or simply calm myself down. To remember just how far I had come.

The public library system is what saved me when I first arrived in the city. It was my lifeline to people and a constant, bottomless source of information, a quiet place to watch the world where I knew that no one would ask a single thing of me. I learned how to be alive in libraries. I learned how to be alone.

Stella stands to hug me goodbye. "Thanks for listening to all my bullshit," she says. "You know it goes both ways, right?"

I squeeze her back, grateful that she can't see the look on my face as I remember the email again. Unease claws at me from inside my throat, and I make myself swallow it down.

I smile brightly as I pull away from her. "Of course. But I really do have to go now."

It's the truth. Today, I have things to do, I remind myself. I have things to learn. Things to fix.

I decide to walk the twenty blocks to the library, steadying myself. The whole time, I bite the inside of my cheek, thinking about how easily I could have corrected the half truths I've fed Stella for years. I know how it would go if I cracked. I know she would eat it up, drool over the intrigue of it. The drama.

"You poor thing. It's just like those docuseries on Netflix..." she would say, eyes wide as saucers as she leaned forward, hanging on my every word. She would give me the reassurance that I've always fantasized about, tell me I'm not broken beyond repair or royally, spectacularly rotten. You're a *victim*, Catharine, she'd say. But that's the thing. I couldn't stand that either. I couldn't bear to look her in the eyes and let her lie to me about that, too. Not when I know the truth.

CHAPTER 4

Then

If the farm was a body, the main building was its heart. The building itself wasn't much to look at. It resembled a giant, dilapidated, vinyl-covered box with smaller (and equally ugly) vinyl-covered boxes jutting off it, everything flecked with a lime-green mold. The handful of windows were all cracked or broken, the remaining glass perpetually dirty. Compared to the four gardens that surrounded it, each a two-acre plot of land bursting with life and color, the main building was an eyesore. But it was also our kitchen, our living room, our gathering place. It was impossible to imagine life without it.

The entire property, my father told us, had once been home to a camp for troubled children. It was part summer school, part discipline-instilling rural bootcamp, and eventually shut down in the sixties. Even then, it was primitive, but it had everything a community would need to be self-sufficient. It was exactly what my father had been searching for. When he bought it at an auction, it had been abandoned for almost three decades. The two hundred acres of farmland surrounding it were deemed largely useless, hopelessly overgrown and infertile.

No one could see its great potential, my father explained to every new person who came to the farm. No one but him. He looked at that massive, flat stretch of land and the rundown buildings that sat on it and saw something more, somewhere for all of us to gather and grow together. It all served to illustrate his greatest gift, that he could look beyond what the world had put in front of him and instead see possibility.

Our dining hall sat at the center of the main building, a space that was once a gymnasium-theater-cafeteria hybrid for campers. Now, ancient and weather-worn picnic tables lined the room, though the original basketball hoop remained in place (the net was long gone), the stage perfectly intact behind it, both always looming in the background of our meals.

Half a dozen rooms stemmed from the dining hall, most of which were former offices and storage closets that had been turned into highly coveted, private bedrooms. This was where my mother's and my room was, and where my father had been before he moved to the new cottage. Compared to the bunkhouse, where most people slept, including Linna, staying in the main building had its disadvantages. The rooms were dark and often damp, but they were also consistently ten degrees cooler than anywhere else thanks to the thick, cinderblock-lined walls.

The kitchen was my mother's favorite place on the property, where I would find her during quiet moments, in between chores. A low-ceilinged addition off the back of the main building, it was filled with sprawling stainless steel prep tables, stacks of perpetually stained, two-inch-thick butcher block cutting boards, and a walk-in fridge, complete with a lock on the outside to which only my father had the key. We couldn't have people constantly walking in and out of it, he explained, giving in to the allure of the cold air and wasting precious energy.

For Linna, though, there was no better place than the stage—still lined with velvet, moth-eaten curtains that she would often pull closed and pin up, creating elaborate, musty forts to read in during the endless rainy days of spring. Over the years, we had collected hundreds of books. When we were younger, my father would return from yard sales with boxes full of curling paperbacks and heavy, dust-covered textbooks in the bed of his truck. Linna and I took it upon ourselves to stack and organize them in the shadowy corners of the stage. Eventually, my mother fixed up a set of shelves for us, then two more. The library was born. From then on, whenever I couldn't find Linna, I knew to check the stage first. I couldn't even count how many times I had found her there flat on her back, arms stretched above her, a yellowing paperback in her hands.

Linna's love of books and being alone meant that people often assumed she was shy, or meek, but they didn't understand her. Linna was sharp and precise. She deliberately saved her energy for the things that mattered the most. She seemed to feel no need to perform her personality to the world, to prove herself. It was one of the many ways we were different.

To me, it was always what was outside that made our home special. The second you left the main building, you were surrounded by the four gardens, each divided by a long, grassy path that led to the schoolroom, the bunkhouse, the old barn, and my father's cottage, respectively. The layout meant that for most people, getting to a meal or a chore required walking through all that beauty, thrusting yourself into the center of it. Every day contained a moment where you'd look around and see only green, smell only earth.

My favorite days were full of moments like this, meandering afternoons spent outside, just like the one Linna and I had after my father dismissed us from class. There were plenty of chores to be done, like always, but plenty of time, too. Daylight seemed bottomless at that time of year, stretching on and on as Linna and I roamed around the farm. It was such a perfect afternoon that neither of us noticed it had turned into evening or that we were late. By the time we walked into the main building for family meal that night, I felt relaxed and loose, loopy from the sun. What had happened that morning felt a million miles away.

I smelled it first, my nose crinkling instinctively. Something rancid, rotten, laced with ammonia. Then I noticed the room was missing its usual mealtime din, that the only sound was a faint buzz above me, a fly looking for a meal.

I reminded myself that quiet wasn't always a bad thing, especially since Crystal and Bianca left. The couple had showed up last year with a two- and four-year-old. For six months, there was no corner of the property that didn't seem to echo with the children's wails, their whining. When the constant screeching annoyed me, I reminded myself that the four of them were bringing some much-needed life back to this place, building it up again. The rest of us were teenagers now and it was nice to see small footprints in the garden's dirt again.

My father had seemed so much like his old self when they arrived that I felt myself relax. I slept better. I worried less. But they had left two months ago, out of the blue. Bianca had relapsed, my father explained. We couldn't have helped her even if we wanted to; the pull of the outside world was too strong for her addled mind to resist.

Today's quiet was different, though. It was as thick as the smell, suffocating me. Instinctively, I started walking toward the long line of yellowed, plastic folding tables where we always served ourselves, buffet style. The usual bowls were there, but as I approached them, I saw there were no beans in any of them tonight. Instead, there was shit. Steaming, stinking shit. Heaps of it.

My eyes darted from the bowls quickly, stomach rolling, and my mother came into view. She was sitting at a picnic table in the far corner of the room, her hands neatly folded in front of her. I could practically hear her voice in my head: "What did you do, Rin?"

But she didn't say anything to me then. No one did.

I realized then that my father must have walked out of our classroom with this very moment in mind—he must have spent the afternoon skulking through some distant cattle farm just for this. I wanted to melt into the floor. And then I heard the door close behind me, his presence announced by three short claps, like always.

"Now this, family," he gestured toward the serving bowls. "This is what happens when you confuse hunger with greed. When you think you are better than true discipline, true moderation. Real restraint."

I turned to face him and blinked four times, as if that could magically will him away. But he just stood there, staring at everyone but me.

"During class this morning, Catharine asked for something different, and well . . . here we are," he announced, casually gesturing toward me. "No beans for the rest of the week. Just like you wanted."

It was only Tuesday.

"I'm so . . ." I started, scrambling as I realized what my mistake would mean for everyone else, my face burning with shame.

His head snapped toward me, tilting slightly. "Hungry? Isn't that what you said? That you were hungry?"

I turned my eyes to the ground, humiliated. I could feel Jessie and Maura's glares from their spot at the picnic table closest to me.

He stepped away from me, turning toward the rest of the room again. "Well." He shrugged, turning his palms toward the sky like he wasn't sure what else he could say. "Don't let me keep you all. Family meal is sacred, after all."

And then he was gone. I could feel everyone in the room still staring at me, the silence interrupted by hushed, indiscernible mumbling.

"I fucking told you," I heard Jessie say.

My father always had a flair for theatrics, for drama. It was part of why he was always able to hold our attention in class, to draw us into a lesson again and again. But this was extreme, even for him. He had been more unpredictable lately, his mood falling with each person that left. And it had been months since someone new moved in. Still, his punishments had always been a private thing before now. An opportunity for reflection rather than a public humiliation. This felt like something new.

I was just about to apologize to the room when I heard the door open again. I turned to see my father reentering in a light jog, laughing.

"Goodness, look at your faces. Of course, I wouldn't subject you to eating cow shit." He laughed. "I mean, there's no point in that when the only person with a lesson to learn here is Catharine," he added lightly, turning toward me.

"So, Catharine. This is your meal. Your responsibility. Your lesson. Though, perhaps we can all learn something from this today, can't we?" My father leaned toward me again, whispering now. "Let it build you up, little one. Let it make you stronger. You can do that, can't you?"

I saw Jessie's head nodding eagerly out of the corner of my eye. Even as humiliation pulsed through every limb, I knew that I deserved all of this. I needed it, even. It was the only thing that would help me learn self-control.

"Yes," I said. "Thank you."

It was then that I noticed Linna was standing next to me, fists clenched at her sides. She was so rarely angry, but when she was, it was obvious. She was almost shaking now. I knew she wanted to protect me, but didn't she get it? He had no choice but to create this moment for me, teach me this lesson. It was a type of pain that, one day, I would know was a gift.

She opened her mouth to say something, but before she could speak, my father started talking again. "And for the rest of you: A surprise outside! Discipline and willpower will always be rewarded."

He turned to walk outside and waved for the room to follow him. Everyone rushed out the door, thrilled by the possibility of a surprise and likely grateful to be away from the disgusting smell. It wouldn't be the first time he had done this, a reward for discipline. I thought of how good that first family meal after a moderation fast tasted, how much more I appreciated every bite and flavor. It wasn't just another meal, but something earned and deeply satisfying, a small glimpse into how good all of life would feel one day, if only we put in the work first.

I thought of those quiet mornings in the garden again, how lazy I had let myself get, how I had so easily listened to that poisonous, greedy thing inside me that clawed for more, more, more. No, it was never hunger I was feeling, not even once. It was always an empty hole where my willpower should be.

CHAPTER 5

Now

The second I walk through the front doors of the library and into the massive corridor, I feel my shoulders relax. As I turn toward one of the two marble staircases and run my hand along the railing, I stand up straighter. I settle. I am perfectly at home while being entirely anonymous. Even Stanley, the security guard who I've walked by at least once a week for a decade now, greets me with only a single, knowing nod. We've never spoken a word. I smile back at him, grateful.

As I make my way to the reading room, I see a couple in their sixties gawking at the giant slabs of marble that line the entryway, the woman running her hand over the smooth stone in hushed reverence. Tourists.

A warm satisfaction passes through me as I consider all the things I know about this place that they do not. They will probably walk out the front doors and through the park without ever knowing that beneath their feet is an underground labyrinth of knowledge, a football field worth of books. Millions and millions of pieces of information. Answers to any question you might have.

Librarians sitting dutifully at their desks, sending books back up toward Earth.

I told Stella about the underground stacks once and she marveled. "That's some Harry Potter shit." She wasn't wrong, exactly. The library did have a magical quality to it. But to me, it was more than that. It was power.

In my early twenties, I spent entire days poring over novels and magazines, studying how-to manuals that ranged from practical to obscure. I scoured bulletin boards for freelance gigs. I attended every single free seminar available, learning about taxes and gardening and poetry and, eventually, copywriting. I closely watched small social interactions and felt like I was crouching behind a locked door, squinting through a keyhole and silently marveling at the world. I watched people study with monklike concentration, no noise-canceling headphones needed. I saw others attempt it to no avail, their eyes flitting up at every minor movement or sound, any excuse to avoid their work. Eventually, I could chart their growing panic. The library, it turned out, was not the thing that would help them finally be productive. I watched librarians' eyes latch on to patrons who appeared a little too unkempt, or a little too nervous. I watched college students flirt. I saw men stare at women across the room until they looked up, then marked their surprise or delight or disgust. I learned when to stare back. I taught myself how to be.

Now, I go to the library to remind myself of that girl. I can see myself ten years in the past, sitting in the very same chair at the very same table. Look at who I was, I'll think. Look at how I had grown. I had everything I needed to survive right in front of me.

I scan the reading room for an empty spot and find none, so I walk slowly down the long, wide pathway in the center of the room, waiting. I watch as people look up or stay buried in their work. At a table in the back corner, I spot an exhausted-looking man about my age in a quilted vest, his brow furrowed as he stares at his phone and swipes at the screen. A dating app. At the library.

For a few minutes, I stand near him, browsing the shelves, just far enough away that he doesn't notice me but close enough that I have a decent view of his screen. Left for brunettes, right for blondes. Left for ass, right for tits. Simple enough. Something I can work with.

I walk over, then stop just behind him and tap his shoulder. "Hey, I was just wondering if I could use this spot..."

He tugs out one AirPod, annoyed, and grumbles a reply without looking back. "I'm working."

"It's just that I'm taking the bar exam next week," I try. "And I have so much studying—"

"I said," he repeats, finally turning toward me, "I'm...I'm working."

At the last two words, his tone softens. I watch him take me in. I'm not what he was expecting, maybe. I am, however, sort of his type.

He places his phone face down on the table. "Sorry, I just...I have a lot to do. I waited half an hour for this spot."

"Right," I say, looking down. "Of course."

I turn to go, but he speaks up. "The bar, you said?"

Turning back, I nod, sheepish. "Second try."

He smiles, then brings his voice down to a whisper, leaning toward me. "It took me three."

I bite back a grin. The vest said finance, but the bags under his eyes screamed first year at a soulless law firm. I force myself to look surprised. "That's...wow. That's actually really good to know."

I adjust my bag on my shoulder, waiting. Come on.

"I tutor now," he blurts out. "On the side. If you . . . if you ever need help?"

Because who wouldn't want instruction on how to pass a test from someone who failed it repeatedly? Ah, the confidence of a man. I beam. "That'd be amazing."

From behind us, someone lets out an aggressive, very direct *shhhh.*

At this, he stands up and gathers his things, then gestures toward the seat. "You need it more than me."

I mouth a silent thank you and enter a fake number into his phone and finally, thank god, he walks away. I watch him stride out of the room confidently, like he's won something.

I sit down and pull my laptop from my bag, then open the email from the journalist again, reading, dissecting it piece by piece.

Now-defunct cult.

Florida.

I've decided that it's how surprised I am by it that unsettles me the most. Rationally, I know I should not be. Not when every time I open my phone, every time I turn on the television, there's another exposé on a cult you've never heard of. Another documentary. Another podcast. I mean, my god, the *podcasts.* It was impossible that anyone could keep up with it at all, and yet the shows kept coming, kept taunting me.

Every time I thought people would get sick of it, that they'd grow tired of seeing the same storyline played out again and again, there was more. More, more, more. More stories about men who loved their community college philosophy class a little too much. More men who felt misunderstood. More men who had an idea once and decided they felt called and chosen and special enough to share it. Men with hair to their shoulders, men who grew beards, like it wasn't obvious what they were trying to do, who they were trying to look like. It's always so goddamn obvious. More stories about how it was fun, at first. About how they were just people who loved self-improvement, just people who loved god. People who loved the occasional game of midnight volleyball. And sex. There was always sex, too, wasn't there? And then the hook, the cliffhanger, the turn that absolutely no one would have seen coming, not from a mile away, they say: It all seemed beautiful and wonderful and safe and harmless. Until it wasn't.

It's clear what I should do with the email: Ignore it, block him, report it as spam. Never think about it again. For all I know, this guy could be a quack, a fraud. Some kid in a basement, wired after doing one too many whippets and convinced of an outlandish conspiracy theory that he's already forgotten about. I was probably worrying about nothing. But it wouldn't hurt to make sure.

I straighten my posture, loudly crack my neck side-to-side, and take a deep breath as I open a fresh browser tab. Across the table, a woman glares from where she sits reading, clearly triggered by the sound of my joints popping. I ignore her.

I type Reese Campbell's name into Google slowly, calmed by the knowledge that I am taking the situation into my own hands. I remind myself that in a second, I will probably discover I have nothing to worry about, and then all of this will disappear.

Except Reese Campbell is not some fancy made-up name, an elaborate character invented by a bored teenage boy who loves to browse Reddit unsolved mystery threads. Reese Campbell, as it turns out, is everywhere on the internet. An actual journalist, his photo is plastered on a dozen different social media platforms, a charming, casual, well-lit headshot in which he wears round-framed, tortoiseshell glasses and a cable-knit sweater. His hair is a shade of blond that's just dark enough to read as mature, his eyes a blue like the center of a deep lake. He's good-looking, a detail that only unsettles me more.

I imagine him in meetings with *The New York Times*. With Netflix. With *Dateline NBC*. With HBO. He's the type of attractive that's universal but unthreatening, the brand of handsome that gets him places.

But it gets worse. As I read article after article, I realize that Reese seems to actually be good at what he does.

He won an award for an investigative piece he did while getting his master's at Columbia Journalism School, a deep dive into the story of a group of undergraduate students whose study group gradually morphed into something verging on a sex trafficking operation. I read all six thousand words of it. It's nuanced but objective, warm despite the subject matter. The people he interviewed, the depth of their answers, what they shared with him. It's impressive.

My pulse starts to race as my brain recites the email again.

Now-defunct cult.

Florida.

I inhale deeply as I tilt my face upward, taking in the fresco on the ceiling, a view I have stared at a thousand times, soothing myself. Slowly, I remember where I am. Here, I could disappear into any world I wanted, any story I could imagine. How many times had I saved myself from a panic attack by sinking into a novel instead?

The question reminds me to check if the library has received my favorite author's newest book yet, a welcomed distraction. I had first discovered her work years ago, when my greatest joy was scouring the new and noteworthy shelves of each library I visited. Her first book, a short story collection, had won a literary prize and thus garnered a small but devoted readership. I read it on a whim at first, intrigued by the cover, but as soon as I finished the last page, I started it again. Every story centered around one specific, vast section of Maine forest, and different people who had gotten lost there over the years, from the 1800s to today. It was all fictional, but each tale felt fully realized, interconnected yet entirely complete. To this day, it was the only book I had ever failed to return to the library. I had lost it, I lied to the librarian, feigning embarrassment.

I could have gone to a bookstore and purchased a new one myself, but there was something about that exact copy that felt holy to me, too pure to part with. I saw bits and pieces of myself in every story. Each character fought for their survival. I knew what that was like. It was the rare type of reading experience in which your body crackles to life as you go, fizzing with delight. It felt like finding myself in the dark.

Years later, there is still almost nothing that comforts me as instantly as that book. I close my laptop and walk to the help desk.

"Hi," I whisper. "I was just wondering if you had Marion Earl's latest?"

Without speaking, the librarian begins typing. "Did you hear she's writing a memoir next?" she whispers, eyes still fixed on the screen.

A memoir? My breath lodges in my throat. I'm about to reply when I'm distracted by a buzz from my phone. I pull it out of my pocket to find a text from Stella. I open it and it's a photo, a screenshot of an email. I use my forefinger and thumb to zoom in on the text.

Hi Stella,

I'm an investigative journalist looking into a cult-like community that I think your friend Catharine West may have been part of as a child. Does that sound right to you? Would you be willing to chat with me sometime?

Thanks,
Reese

"It looks like her new novel will be here on—" the librarian starts to reply, but I'm already rushing down the corridor.

"Ma'am?" she says from behind me, but I am focused only on my phone. I am staring at it as Stella's accompanying text arrives.

Umm...??

This is the thing about men and their brilliant ideas. They can never seem to leave it the fuck alone, can they?

CHAPTER 6

Then

Linna hesitated as my father called her outside, demanding she join the rest of the group. I watched her stare back at him, her teeth working under her cheek, grinding.

"Go," I pleaded, nodding in the direction of the door.

She didn't move.

"It will just make it worse for me if you stay."

This seemed to sink in. Linna sighed, squeezing my hand once before she walked out the door, leaving me to deal with the mess, the stench.

I sat alone for fifteen minutes before it occurred to me that it would, of course, be my job to clean out the bowls. That was the real punishment. The flies had seemed to multiply, the buzzing growing louder, only interrupted by the sound of giggles and squeals over whatever special treat he'd revealed to everyone else outside.

I was about to pin my T-shirt over my nose and bring the bowls outside when the doors opened again, my mother walking through them. She looked at me sadly before gagging slightly at the smell, then steadying herself. Her eyes watered.

"I had to leave," she whispered. "If I had stayed, he would have—"

I cut her off. "I know."

"Are you all right?" she asked. "That was..."

"It's fine," I pushed. Why couldn't she just let me sit with what I had done? Give me time and space to let the lesson sink into my bones? She reached out to touch my arm, but I pulled away. I felt contagious.

"I did this to myself," I insisted, annoyed. "I get it."

"No, that's not what I..." she started, shaking her head. She looked around the room, then behind her, as if she was checking if anyone else was there. "I just want you to know that—"

A burst of laughter from outside interrupted her, and her thought seemed to vanish. Instead, she pointed toward a closet where we kept cleaning supplies: mops and brooms and old rags. "The bleach is in there."

I spent the rest of the evening scrubbing the dishes, washing them out with hoses then soaking them in bleach, repeating the process until my hands were so dry that the skin on my palms split open and bled. The only thing that made it bearable was the bandanna Linna had brought me when she had snuck back in, after the excitement had died down and people had dispersed.

"I put some lavender oil on it," she whispered as she tied it around my face, tenderly avoiding getting my hair in the knot. It was the first time in the entire ordeal that I had felt like crying. "It should help."

By the time I showered and changed into clean clothes, I was so exhausted that I could have curled up in a ball and fallen asleep on the ground, but my body was begging for fresh air, as much of it as I could get. It was dark now, stars blinking on above me. I made my way through the gardens toward the barn. I would see if Linna was at the treehouse, if she wanted company.

My father helped us build the treehouse years ago, a makeshift, spindly wooden box perched in a cluster of oak trees behind the old barn. It was a gift, he said, though I remember thinking it felt more like a distraction, a way for Linna to forget everything she had to be sad about that summer.

"A space for just you two," he said. "Sisters need that."

In a lot of ways, it was the treehouse that cemented Linna's and my relationship. It gave us the room to see just how much we needed each other. It was a world within a world, a sacred space that was only ours. My father was right. We had needed it. And though maybe we should have abandoned it as we got older and the space became more cramped, the wobbly, makeshift shelf in one corner of the room no longer big enough to hold all of our favorite books and treasures, we kept using it anyway.

Over the years we developed a system. There were two flashlights in the treehouse, one for each of us. If we found ourselves there alone and wanted company, we turned them both on. If we wanted to be alone, we used only one. It was a code we respected fanatically, with no exceptions, an insurance that we would know when and how to be there for each other, always. A safety net. I thought of how Linna had looked at me earlier when I had thanked my father for the punishment, the lesson, like she was both angry at me and wildly sad. Maybe she wouldn't want to see me tonight at all.

I exhaled audibly when I finally made it past the barn and saw the two lights shining, a reminder that I was not alone. Linna's hand appeared at the small entrance above the ladder, helping to pull me into the space.

I collapsed on the floor in a heap, my limbs starfishing out around me, resting on the familiar fabric of old quilts and ancient flannel sheets.

Linna clicked off one of the flashlights and my eyes adjusted to the near darkness, staring up at the small skylight.

"You know," Linna said, breaking the silence first. "For a second, I actually thought it was his own shit."

I stayed quiet, and then a small giggle burst out of me, building to a deeper, rolling laugh that just kept going. I couldn't stop. Neither of us could.

"I actually thought," she went on, her hands laced over her stomach, muscles sore from laughing so hard, "that he had left the schoolroom and just focused really, *really* hard for a few hours."

I knew there was nothing funny about what had happened, about how badly I had messed up, how much I had to learn, but I couldn't help it. It was much-needed decompression. When we finally stopped laughing, I closed my eyes, luxuriating in the feeling of the day being over and the relief of learning, of knowing you'll never let yourself go through that again.

"What was it?" I finally asked, my curiosity getting the best of me. "The reward?"

Linna mindlessly picked up a book, her eyes scanning the pages in front of her in a way that made it clear she wasn't reading at all. She shrugged. "Nothing that special."

I nudged her foot with mine. "It's fine, Lin. You can tell me. I'd rather just know before Jessie and Maura throw it in my face in class tomorrow."

She put her book down again and sighed. "Ice cream," she said. "Strawberry."

I nodded, taking this in. We had had ice cream before, years ago. It had taken me a very long time to stop thinking about it afterward, especially during the hottest months of spring and summer.

"It wasn't even that great," Linna managed, perhaps sensing my disappointment. "I mostly just wanted to dump it over my head. How is it so fucking hot already? It's not even June yet."

I smiled, warmed by her efforts to make me feel better. I decided that it was nice of her, really, to not point out the fact that I had earned every bit of the punishment. That I did it to myself.

"Besides, you know how it is," she started, her voice deeper, dramatically serious. "It's like he's always monologuing about: A treat isn't worth it if we don't catalog how we feel right after. If we don't recognize how sick it makes us, how it scrambles our guts, our brains. Even moderation has consequences."

I should have laughed, just like I did minutes ago, but something about her tone had unsettled me. She was mocking him, I realized. It was something I had never heard her do before.

An awkward pause hung between us.

"Honestly, my stomach does feel a little weird now," she went on, her voice back to normal, if a little stilted. "Not worth it at all."

I felt my body relax, gratitude flooding my system. I was so thankful to have her there with me, protecting and shielding me in her own way, both of us in this together, learning. I thought of the conversation with my mother earlier, the way she had seemed so uncomfortable around me, so unsure of what to say, how to act. I thought about how she had stopped in the doorway as she left, her body in something like a half shrug, three bright candy-pink drops drying on the front of her shirt.

CHAPTER 7

Now

It takes me the entire subway ride home to calm down, but when I do, I am sure of something. Stella's texts confirm to me what I should have known from the start. I will lie to Reese Campbell, and it will be easy.

I will lie to him just like I lied to Stella.

"Ugh, not this again," I had replied to her as soon as I was on the subway, my pulse ragged. "I'm constantly getting confused with this woman. Same name."

"Whoa, spelled the same way and everything?" Stella replied.

Catharine is a less common spelling, sure, but it's not impossible.

"Yup. My luck," I sent along with a shrugging emoji before changing the subject, asking about a gallery opening that was happening next week. And hey, before I forget—did she want to come? Get dinner before? What did she think of this dress for my outfit? How about with these shoes? I kept letting the text bubbles fill up my screen, message after message, until the word *cult* had disappeared altogether.

Lying has always been the easiest part for me, a way to diffuse the tension of what I hold secret. To take action, do *something.* In the beginning, I dreaded it the same way I did socializing, or grocery shopping, or navigating an iPhone. I thought it would feel clunky and unnatural. Instead, it was simple. Fun, even.

I attended free "mastering the internet" classes meant for the elderly and said it was part of a community service credit, taking notes and pointers for myself along the way. I grocery shopped by mirroring the women in the store who I wanted to look most like, copying their choices in the produce aisle, the deli, the bakery. I got through dates and meetings by memorizing a handful of quick talking points to make things easier on myself—all designed to invite the fewest questions, or at least the easiest ones.

"Florida-raised. East coast. Gated community. Palm trees. Only child. Single mom. Not close. Never were."

See? It's not complicated. You start with a little bit of the truth, a strong foundation, and then you build whatever world you want.

I draft different versions of my reply in my head as I move to my standing desk and open my laptop to do some work, my feet soon pounding the walking pad underneath. I'm writing about the best automatic water dispensers for cats today, emailing vets about their expert picks, all of us pretending like anyone actually cares other than the publication who will make their money off advertising in the end. Admittedly, it's the type of mindless story I usually love, the kind that allows me to have a show or podcast playing in the background while I type.

Today, I opt for the audiobook of Marion Earl's first novel. Released two years after her short story collection, *Lighthouse*, it didn't garner any awards, but that never mattered to me. I've still read it half-a-dozen times and listened to it even more, the words comforting background noise even when they conjure feelings and memories that I buried a long time ago. Just like *Lighthouse*, readers and critics have debated about the book's message. One prominent review had claimed it was about feminism and what it feels like to forge a path alone, against the headwinds of patriarchal standards, but I saw it as something else. To me, it was about what all her stories were about; it was a tale of loneliness and who we are when we lose the people and places who shaped us.

After one re-read, I furtively set up a Google Alert for the author's name, eager to hear her take on her own writing, convinced she would confirm what I felt. But Earl was notoriously private. Other than the occasional, extremely brief interview, the only information about her was what I could glean from dusty internet forums. Baseless speculation. *She lives out west*, someone had written. *On a small ranch. What are you talking about? She isn't even American*, someone else had said. *Doesn't anyone respect people's privacy anymore?* another had replied.

I had searched for information so many times that by now, I had memorized it all, along with her author's bio, the only thing about her that I could trust as fact.

Marion Earl lives and writes in the mountains.

Eight words. The restraint of it felt almost admirable.

With a jolt, I remember the librarian's question from earlier, how she had asked it so casually. *Did you hear she's writing a memoir next?*

Perhaps I could finally get some answers. Something to ground this woman who felt eerily familiar and altogether far too distant for my liking. I open a new tab and search "Marion Earl + memoir." Sure enough, the first result is a recent brief interview for a popular librarian's newsletter—the only place Earl ever gave interviews to.

***Libraries Weekly*:** You're notorious for your commitment to privacy. Do you ever see that changing?

Marion Earl: Perhaps. I've been writing a memoir on and off for years. Some days, I feel ready to share it with the world and others, it feels impossible.

***Libraries Weekly*:** How about today?

Marion Earl: Today? More possible than not. That's how it's feeling more and more lately. Inevitable.

I read it twice, dissecting the words and careful turns of phrase. It wasn't exactly an announcement, but it wasn't nothing, either. I click back to the search page and find a Reddit discussion on the interview. "What a weird interview," one user wrote. "Something is 100 percent off with this woman." "Come on," another replied. "Being private doesn't mean you're hiding something. It just means you're private." I consider the comment. They had a point. Except, how many times had I described myself this way, too?

I increase the speed on the walking pad and refresh my email to distract myself, hoping for the last quote I need before filing the pet story. But there's only one new email in my inbox. And it's from Reese.

I wanted to follow up on this. I have a source who's confident that you are the Catharine that she used to know. I understand that this is a sensitive topic, but I believe this is an important story. Your father needs to be held accountable for what he did. Please don't hesitate to let me know if you have any questions. I think this is a story that needs to be told, but whether or not your voice is part of it is ultimately up to you.

I stop the walking pad with a jolt, jumping to place one foot on either side of the treadmill belt. My breath is shallow and labored, and I hate how pathetic I sound, like some kind of cornered animal.

Blinking furiously at my screen, I read the email again. It enrages me from the first sentence, that it's not: "Sorry to bother you! Just wanted to quickly follow up on this! But no worries if you're busy!"

None of that. It's direct. Assertive. I bet he didn't even have to edit himself, didn't have to remove a single exclamation point or qualifier or apology. It's persuasive—ominous, even, depending on how you read it, but in a way that still sounds professional.

I know it's time to lie, to spin my best story and finally put this to bed.

But now, I don't know if I can. Apparently, he has a source. Someone who knows who I am and told him how to find me. After all this time. He has a source who knows who my father was, what he became. He has a source who thinks he should be punished for it.

Of course, it could all be a bluff. I know that. In fact, this whole "either way, it's getting published," thing could be a farce. I immediately picture some bedraggled-looking editor in an all-glass office somewhere in midtown shooting Reese down again. "No source, no story, bud."

But if that was the case, how would he have found me in the first place? And more importantly, what if it isn't? What if he's telling the truth?

If he is, then I know for certain that there is only one person who could be his source. And for them, I am willing to step into the unknown. I will make myself vulnerable.

I click on the reply button and start typing.

A few emails later, the meeting is set for the following morning. As nervous as I am, there is something about finally taking action that settles me.

No matter what, tomorrow morning I will talk to Reese Campbell. I will learn who he is, and soon I will know what he knows. I'll make sure of it. I learned a long time ago that you can only control the narratives you fully understand.

The meeting with Reese is set for 10 a.m. and for the first time, I am grateful that I scheduled a 6 a.m. Pilates class with Stella. It will be a way to focus, I decide. I need to go into this meeting clear-eyed and confident.

The classes were, unsurprisingly, Stella's idea. It's what really changes your body composition, she had said. No better workout in the world. "EmRata goes here," she had texted when she first sent me the link to the studio, as if we both didn't know that Emily Ratajkowski's body composition was less a result of exercise than it was a biological phenomenon. But I didn't say any of that to Stella. Instead, I thought about how good it would feel to carve those taut lines down the sides of my torso, to whittle them into myself through planks, a million tiny muscle tears a minute.

Afterward, Stella tries to get me to join her at a work event, a media brunch for a beauty brand she now represents.

"Come on," she pleads. "You still write about beauty sometimes, right?"

"I'd love to, but I can't," I say between sips of water. "Too much work. You know what it's like in Q4."

Even though it's not quite the truth, I remind myself that it's not a lie, either. This is who I am. I'm busy. I'm successful. I channel that energy so that when I sit down across from Reese, he feels the truth of it immediately. That's why it took me so long to get back to him, after all. It's my busiest time of year. Gift guides out the wazoo. Look, I have a whole career here. A whole life. Social events to say yes or no to. I am not whatever other person Reese is expecting, the one he thinks he knows.

I arrive home to a stack of packages, mailers from brands hoping that I will write about them in the coming months. What to buy your spouse. What to buy your mother-in-law. What to buy the person who has everything. I open them carefully, slowly, one by one, each a little victory because it represents the career I have carefully built. The seminars I sat through. All the books I read. The lies I told. Hard work, all of it.

I throw the items I don't want in a donation bin that I bring down to my building's lobby for people to sift through every month and take the rest to my office before walking into the bathroom. I peel off my workout clothes and stare at my body in the mirror, check all the same spots I always do, note what's changed. Study what's softer, what's sagging. But I can never trust my own judgment when it comes to these things.

I take my measuring tape from the bottom drawer of my vanity and wrap it around my waist, my thighs, my neck, and open my phone to record the measurements before rolling the tape back up neatly and carefully placing it next to the miniature sewing kit. No one's ever asked me why there's a measuring tape in my bathroom, but if they do, I have an answer ready: "Oh, it's for clothes. Reading sizing charts. It's the only way to shop online." And they'll think of the thread and needle next to it, the small pair of scissors and the selection of extra buttons, and be embarrassed that it hadn't been obvious to them.

It doesn't take a genius to trace the origin of my little habits and tics when it comes to my body. It's not like I haven't connected the dots myself, a million times over. It's taken me years to move on from the food stuff, and even that still colors most of my days. I drink a glass of wine and wonder how I'm poisoning myself, try to feel the mouth cancer latch onto my cells, then drink the whole bottle to ignore the feeling. I exercise until it hurts to walk, because then I can order a burger at lunch instead of the carb-free, dairy-free, sugar-free meal, the one that will make people ask me if I'm on a diet. It's so embarrassing, the idea of telling the truth. "Of course I am. Look at me." It makes my stomach churn, the neediness of it.

I know none of it is good, though. The body checking, the exercise. I've read all the books, listened to all the podcasts, followed all the experts. And ultimately, the best I can say is that it's safer than the alternative. There are things we must allow ourselves in order to survive.

I check the time. Nearly 8 a.m. now. Time to get ready. I step in the shower and let the hot water wash over me. I spend longer than usual shampooing my hair, then conditioning it, then repeating the process. By the time I get out, the mirror is clouded with steam, my body nowhere to be found in the reflection. I check the time again, making sure I'm still on schedule. An anxious voice tells me to re-read his last email again, to triple confirm the meeting details.

His last reply is buried under a dozen or so emails I had already received that morning, mostly press releases about the latest plastic surgery trends or how some C-list pop star is partnering with a body wash brand to promote self-love and themselves. I scroll through them, searching, then stare at the message for the tenth time.

See you at 10. -R

Four words and an initial. That's it. He probably sent it while he was on the toilet, taking his evening shit. That's how unimportant it was to him. Or maybe that's how confident he is about the whole thing, about me.

I look back up at the mirror, and the steam has cleared. The only thing staring back at me is now my naked reflection, and once more I spot every flaw, my chest pounding with the knowledge that the inside of me is somehow so much worse.

CHAPTER 8

Then

After making my walk back to the main building that night, I crept into the room I shared with my mother and quietly crawled into my small twin bed, trying not to wake her. I was aching for sleep.

"I'm up," she said, startling me.

"Oh."

She turned toward me, the movement sharp, like maybe she hadn't been asleep yet at all, or that she had been waiting for me, practicing what she was going to say. "Rin, what he did to you..." she started, her voice as low and quiet as possible. "You should know that it doesn't have anything to do with you. Not really."

I prickled. Of course it had been about me.

"It has more to do with him," she went on. "What *he* needs."

"I needed to learn," I insisted, exhausted. Why did I have to explain this to her? "Now I have. It worked. It's fine."

My mother shifted in her bed, only inches away from mine, the silence lingering before she finally spoke again. "When he senses he's losing something, he starts to spiral."

I thought of how miserable he had been for weeks when Crystal and Bianca had left earlier that year, lashing out at us at the slightest mistakes in school or the smallest misstep during chores. It's not that people hadn't left before, but there were only nine of us now. Five years ago, we had dozens more people living at the farm, new families arriving every other week. Life was too exciting to focus on the people who ultimately couldn't handle the work, who weren't disciplined enough to learn true moderation. Now, though, it was different. He was different.

"He's always been this way," she added, her tone darker now, a jagged edge to it that wasn't there before, as if she sensed my thoughts and needed me to know she disagreed. "I can see that now."

I shifted in my bed, my skin damp with sweat. I had gotten so used to my mother and father living separately that I found it hard to remember that at one point it was just the three of us here, together. A solid unit instead of something spliced. It felt greedy to have ever expected that we could keep him to ourselves, not when there was so much to do, so much to build.

"He just wants people to see what we see," I said, ignoring her reference to before. "How good it can be. How everything is worth the work. That's all."

I waited for my mother's reply, but it never came.

Beans were back on the table the next morning, and my father moved on as if the punishment had never happened. In fact, his mood seemed brighter than it had yesterday, more hopeful. I thought about what my mother had whispered to me and almost laughed. This wasn't a man who was spiraling. This was what happened when you took the work seriously. I could feel myself standing up straighter, my body strengthened with the pride of a lesson learned the hard way.

Thankfully, almost everyone else forgot about the incident too, as if the secondhand embarrassment was too much to bear. It was only Jessie who seemed determined to drag me back into the moment, the humiliation.

"Phew, what is that *smell*," she announced, wrinkling her nose as she walked up to Linna and me as we browsed the shelves of our makeshift library. "Did one of you step on something outside?"

I rolled my eyes, ignoring her. Linna did too. But Jessie kept going.

"It smells a little like... hmm..." She paused for dramatic effect, leaning in to sniff me. "Oh, yeah. That's it. Shit. It smells like shit. Or, well, I should say *you* smell like shit, Cathari—"

I was determined to ignore her, but Linna was already turning around slowly, deliberately, walking toward her until she was so close that it forced Jessie to step backward and stumble a bit. Their noses were almost touching. "This is it, huh?" Linna asked, her voice steady, ice cold, almost a whisper. She was smiling. "I mean, this is really the best you can do, isn't it? The lack of creativity is astounding."

Jessie's eyes went wide for a second, filling with shame. But then she was smiling, her face breaking into a wide grin, then laughing. "Fucking weirdo."

Linna just smiled at her, then turned to leave, gesturing toward me. "Let's go, Rin."

We were almost out the door when Jessie started talking again. "It's like my mom always says. Girls with no mothers grow up to be weird, angry, ugly women."

Linna froze. It had been eight years since Linna's mother died, and the subject was still something even I tiptoed around. But she didn't react to the taunt, and instead kept walking, her hand reaching for the door. This was how Linna was: Fiercely defensive of me, but quick to ignore any jabs that had to do with herself. For a long time, I thought this was because nothing got to her. She was stronger than I was, made of tougher stuff. It only made me want to defend her more.

I channeled some deep, chilled pool of confidence within me and strode toward Jessie, who still looked amused, pleased with herself. It was exactly what I needed to push me over the edge, to snap something into place within my chest.

"You want to talk about mothers, Jessie?" I asked when I was right in front of her, watching goosebumps prickle her neck. "That's fine. We can do that. We can talk about how everyone here laughs at yours. You know that, right? You must know. You must see the way she's followed him around for years, desperate for him to want her, never understanding that he finds her pitiful. I mean, we all do."

Jessie's face had gone completely blank, her eyes now shining with tears. I almost wanted to pull back and apologize, but then I remembered how Linna's body had tensed a minute ago. I thought of her at six years old, her nails digging into my hand as my father sat us down and told us what had happened.

"But you want to know the saddest part?" I went on. "You do it, too. You beg for the attention. And your mother sits there looking at you like the competition, as if she has a shot at all. Like she's disgusted by you."

I felt electric, vibrating from the cruelty of what I had just said. For a moment, it felt startlingly similar to when I had questioned my father the day before, a siphoning of emotion I hadn't known

I needed. It was a relief to be so mean, like fresh air pouring into a stifling room. I felt, to my surprise, lighter. A tear quivered on Jessie's lower lashline.

"Poor thing," I said, putting a hand on her shoulder. Linna was right next to me now, and I saw her flinch at the movement out of the corner of my eye. But Jessie didn't react to it. For the first time since she had moved to the farm six years ago, she had nothing to say to me.

Just then, a triangle sounded from the kitchen. Time for family meal. Jessie quickly blinked back her remaining tears as people filed in through the double doors, turning her face away from them. I followed Linna to our usual picnic table, and when I sat down across from her, she was staring at me with a mix of pride and shock.

"Are you okay?" I asked.

She lowered her chin, her eyebrows shooting up. "Are *you*?"

I shrugged. "I'm fine. She's been asking for that for years."

Even as I said the words, I realized I had probably gone too far, been too cruel. The matter of Jessie and Kent's mother, Rhonda, was something most of us had avoided for a long time. She was a yoga teacher, one of the few adults who contributed a skill to the community that wasn't farming-related. She was quiet and kind, and led yoga class every other day, just before dusk—a practice that brought calm, joy, and structure to the community.

But there was a tragic, pleading edge to her, too, especially when it came to my father and Jessie. But acknowledging that meant talking about my mother, and Linna's mother, and the many forms of charm that my father had used to build this place. And not many people wanted to talk about that, especially not me.

I had been four years old when Linna and her mother first moved to the farm. We were still in the early days of building everything then, and new people were exciting. There were only five of us when they arrived: my parents and me, plus Ben and Bertie, an older couple who had moved to the farm after two years on our own. They were the first people beyond the three of us to really see my father's vision for it all. Bertie kept me entertained while my mother worked in the kitchen, and Ben, a former construction manager, helped my father with the biggest projects on the property—building repairs, irrigation systems, plumbing. They'd been like surrogate grandparents to me and I loved them dearly, but after years filled with only adults and imaginary friends, the possibility of a friend my age felt like the most thrilling thing that had ever happened to me.

I had been watching my mother, Ben, and Bertie peel carrots together over the sink when I heard the low rumble of my father's ancient blue truck in the distance, returning from picking up our new arrivals. I sprinted out the door as soon as the car came into sight, my mother yelling behind me about helping them clean up. I ignored her. Couldn't she see that this was more important? The truck sputtered to a stop at the end of a long, mostly dirt driveway, and the most beautiful woman I had ever seen climbed out of the front passenger seat.

"Wow," I said quietly, my neck craned up to stare at her, her long honey-brown curls illuminated by the sun.

I turned briefly as I heard my mother walk up behind me, wiping her hands on a dish towel. "Wow is right," she said under her breath before exhaling a long burst of air. I saw Ben and Bertie watching us through the kitchen window. I wondered why they hadn't joined us, too.

And then I spotted the little girl, one giant toffee-colored eye poking out from where she was hiding behind her mother's legs.

"C'mon, Lin," her mother whispered, her voice sweet and warm. "You never do this. Just look at how beautiful it is here."

"Lin," I echoed, almost yelping, as I looked up at my mother, then back at the girl. "That's just like me. I'm Rin. Well, sometimes."

It was a nickname my mother had given me. The world had enough Katies and Kates and Cathys, she said. I would be different.

"Catharine," my father corrected as he walked around the truck from the driver's side.

"Rin for short," my mother clarified.

I looked up at her, curious. Her voice sounded different than usual, clipped.

Linna's mother nodded. "Nice to meet you, Catharine-sometimes-Rin. I've heard a lot about you and your home," she said, smiling at my mother briefly before glancing around the lush gardens in the distance. It was the beginning of April, and our best harvest yet. Everything was a deep, delicious shade of green. The air smelled like honeysuckle and the fresh baked bread that was finishing in the oven.

"It's your home now, too," my father explained. "All of ours."

"Right. Of course," she said, looking a little embarrassed before crouching down so she was at Lin's and my level. "Catharine, this is Linna."

"Linna," I said back to her, getting used to the sound of it. I had never heard the name before, not in real life or in any of the books my mother read to me, nor in the bedtime stories Bertie made up. I decided I liked it.

Linna took a deep breath and then stepped out from behind her mother, like she was preparing for something. Finally ready to be brave. She had a pair of wire-framed glasses perched on the bridge of her nose, too big for her face. She pushed them up toward her forehead. "Hi."

"Hi," I said back, mirroring her hesitation before I remembered that there were things to do, things to see.

"Can I show you the gardens?" I said. "And the stage in the dining hall?"

Linna looked up at her mom, cautious.

"As long as it's all right with Catharine's mom," she said, then quickly went on. "And her dad, of course."

"Of course it's all right," my father said, answering for both of them, beaming. "Why do you think I made this place? You girls go play, and we'll go meet Ben and Bertie."

I grabbed Linna's hand and dragged her through the gardens, running the whole way. I nearly tripped over my own feet as I named every vegetable, then all of the pests that would eat them if we weren't careful. I was thrilled to have someone to show all the things I loved about my life, from the giant cabbage we had grown that year to the barn cat that I had named Orange.

"This is all yours?" she said, hands on her hips as she took in the gardens, the barn, the fields, Orange walking figure eights around her ankles, purring lazily. "All . . . everyone's?"

"Yup," I said, proud. "Cool, right?"

She stared up at the setting sun, the cantaloupe sky. "It's just like my mom said it would be."

I felt so happy, more whole than I ever had in my life. I knew that my parents would grow busier and busier as new people arrived. Linna's arrival was assurance that I would never have to be alone.

"Rin," Linna said, waving a fork in front of my face. "Earth to Rin."

I shook my head. "Sorry. Just zoned out."

She nodded, smiling kindly, like she understood, or maybe she knew how much the confrontation had taken out of me. "You know you don't have to do that for me, right? I'm fine. She's been gone for a long time."

"I know."

She pushed around a mealy mound of beans with her fork, mashing them until they were a thick, dark paste. Her eyes quickly flashed up at me. "Thank you, though."

Now it was me nodding, the adrenaline from the interaction finally starting to taper off. I smiled back at her. "You and me, right?"

"You and me," she replied, but she was already looking down again, eyes fixed on her plate.

CHAPTER 9

Now

He's late. Later than the polite fifteen minutes that I had calculated and forced myself to take so I wouldn't arrive first. I'd intended to be just delayed enough that I would seem too busy for the meeting to take precedence in my calendar, my mind. I wonder if this was his goal, too.

I had played through the scene in my head earlier as I circled the block for the fourth time: I'd walk in the door and scan the café, spot him in the back and politely smile, not to charm him, but as an acknowledgment that we're two professional, mature adults. My cheeks would be flushed, and maybe I'd wave the waiter over right away, make sure to get my order in quickly. I only have an hour, I'd say as I glanced at my phone—well, a little less than that now.

Instead, he's almost half an hour late now, and I'm still sitting here waiting. Already, he has the upper hand. I should leave now, maybe, consider this a sign from the universe that this was a mistake, but I give myself fifteen more minutes. Fifteen more minutes, and if he's not here after that, I'll leave.

I order a second cappuccino after gulping down my first, a decision that I know I will regret, but I make anyway because I've planned to be drinking this exact thing when he arrives. Whole milk. Full fat. No oat milk or skim or almond. I want him to know I'm no nonsense. Not like the other girls—a phrase that elicits a particular type of scorn, I know, but this is what men like Reese respond to. They want women who don't make things more complicated than they need to be. It's sexism, sure, but part of me wonders sometimes if men's willful ignorance is based in jealousy, too. Like deep down, most of them know that they could never hold all of those calculations in their heads themselves. That they would be crushed under the weight of them.

My coffee grows cold as I wait for Reese. I twirl my spoon round and round, the long, skinny sugar packet on the plate beneath it left untouched like I didn't even notice it there.

Then, twenty-seven-and-a-half minutes after the time we'd agreed on, Reese arrives. He looks completely unflustered, not panicked or rushed in the least. He's tall, much taller than he seemed from the photos I found online—well over six feet, definitely. He's wearing a forest-green quilted jacket with a corduroy collar over a crewneck sweater. Khakis and well-worn sneakers. And those tortoiseshell glasses, the same ones from the photo. He pushes his hair off his forehead only for it to bounce forward again almost immediately. It is the type of volume most women chase for years. I am almost offended by the ease of it. He scans the room but doesn't spot me, then repeats the action. I realize I'm probably hidden from his view thanks to the large coat rack near the hostess stand, that I can see him but he can't see me. I know I should stand up and reveal myself, wave him over, but I'm enjoying this moment. A blip of vulnerability.

Eventually, he starts walking toward the back and spots me in a booth, hesitating for just a moment—not like he's unsure if it's me, but like he's pleasantly surprised. What was he expecting, exactly? Someone in a tie-dyed kaftan who doesn't believe in deodorant? Come on.

Today, I opted for something classic. I'm wearing high-waisted trousers with a whisper-thin cashmere sweater that's well-fitting but not obscene, just tight enough that someone who knows their way around lingerie would guess I was wearing lace underneath.

I remember how I stood in front of the mirror this morning and stepped into four different pairs of shoes before choosing my new Adidas with the gum sole. Leather boots felt too harsh, heels too try-hard, flats too juvenile. Sneakers say that I'm busy, unbothered. That this is just another day to me. Just as I think of my shoes, my foot starts to itch under the table, and I have the urge to tear off the sneakers and throw them across the room, scratch the arch of my foot until it bleeds. But there's no time for that.

He strides over, confident, and for a brief moment I wonder how he recognized me so quickly. The avatar I use for my email is an illustration, an abstract cartoon that looks like me in only the vaguest of ways. An editor asked me about it once, and I told her that I viewed the internet more suspiciously than most, that I didn't believe in having any social media presence at all aside from what I absolutely needed for work. "That's actually really chic," she had said. Men liked this, too, always oohing and aahing when I would tell them that there was no Instagram to follow, no photos to scroll through and send to their friends. "That's so badass. I hate when girls are too obsessed with all of that, anyway," they'd say before they picked up their phones without even thinking about it, scrolled mindlessly, insisted I look at some hilarious video of a raccoon or otter or squirrel they had seen.

But as soon as I begin to get paranoid, to wonder if he's somehow stalked me before now, I realize I'm the only person sitting alone. It's just process of elimination.

"Catharine?" he asks politely as he reaches the table, but he's already taking off his coat before I can even finish nodding. "I'm Reese. So sorry I'm late. Train was delayed. And I miscalculated the commute, if we're being honest. It's my fault. I apologize. I swear I'm usually fifteen minutes *early* to interviews. Anyway, thanks so much for getting back to me."

The word 'interview' feels formal, loaded. It makes me nervous.

"It's fine," I say, hating myself for it as soon as it comes out of my mouth. Shouldn't I have told him that I really don't have much time now, that I'm in a hurry? "Nice to meet you."

"Same to you," he says, stuffing his coat into the space in the booth between him and the wall.

He takes a moment to get situated and rolls up the sleeves of his sweater, exposing tanned, muscular forearms. A prickle of attraction crawls up my neck against my will, a biological reaction to bare skin and proximity that I resent immediately.

He must work out. Something like tennis or rowing, probably. A sport that requires a club or a membership fee, that he picked up during his semester at Oxford or some shit. Really more of a social thing, he'd probably say, like the resulting physique is just a happy accident.

We sit there for a second as he settles in and orders his drink—an iced latte with almond milk, he says, no simple syrup. I wait for him to explain himself, to give the disclaimer. "I just can't do dairy anymore," or "I can't trust myself around sugar, I swear to god," but he says nothing.

"So," he finally says, placing both of his hands flat on the table and lowering his chin in a way that's serious yet friendly, charming, even. It doesn't feel like the look you give someone whose secrets you know, but maybe he's better at this than I even thought. Maybe he knows how to give nothing away.

He stares up at me from behind his glasses. His eyes are just as dark blue in person as they had looked online, but there's a hint of green in them, too, I realize. Of course there is a hint of green.

"So," I say back to him, forcing myself to keep staring at him.

"Thank you for agreeing to this," he says, repeating himself in a way that makes my skin crawl.

"What is it I've agreed to, exactly?" I ask too quickly, my tone sharp. A wave of regret floods my brain.

I should have waited to let him fill the silence. He needs to tell me what he knows first. The sooner I say something, the sooner I lose the upper hand, I had told myself in the mirror this morning. Now, I look defensive.

But he's blushing now, a flash of red crawling across his cheeks, the color so intense that it almost embarrasses me, too. "I mean, agreed to meet me, at least," he stammers, then steadies himself. "That's all this can be right now, if that's what you want."

I stay quiet this time and wait for him to go on.

He waits for a moment, too, to see if I'll talk first, but I keep my mouth shut and let it linger, raise an eyebrow as if to say, "Okay. And?"

Good girl.

"Like I said in the email," he starts. "I'm researching a community that was based in central Florida in the early aughts and even a little bit beyond that, I think."

I blink, my face unchanged, a challenge.

"This is a place that started as a sort of a... crunchy, health-focused, grow your own food, homeschool your kids, everything is everyone's kind of... you know, compound, from what I can tell," he explains.

I prickle at every adjective. Crunchy. Health-focused. Everything is everyone's. I'm not sure whether it irritates me because of how much I want to tell him he's wrong—that it was both more complicated and simpler than what he's saying, that he could have never understood it. Or because maybe he's right. I had spent so long telling myself the story of where I grew up and how I left that I realized I may have rewritten it a dozen times, no one there to tell me what was or was not accurate.

"It's all so reminiscent of those videos you see everywhere now," he went on. "The ones that are like, 'Ever dreamt of buying a fifty-acre plot of land and moving there with all your friends? Getting some chickens? Raising your kids together?' This, like, cottage core, return to the land, off-grid lifestyle that sounds so good in theory. Anyway, that's all part of why I think this story is so timely. That it's so relevant to the world right now."

I force my face into something neutral, timing my blinks so they're not too frequent. I take a sip of my now-cold drink, swallow.

"Groundbreaking," I say, my tone deadpan.

He seems startled by my sarcasm for a second, thrown off. But then he chuckles, the sound coming out like a "huh," smiling so wide that a dimple pops up on one of his cheeks. "I'm sorry?"

My heart is racing now, my ego boosted that I was able to surprise him, to throw him off ever so slightly. It feels exciting, full of promise. I shift my tone to something measured and practical.

"I don't mean to offend you," I offer. "I'm just wondering how your story is different from the thousands of other stories about not-cult cults that are plastered all over the home page of every streaming service? Sounds fairly derivative."

He sits back in the booth, staring at me, trying to stifle the smile that is somehow still there. He looks impressed. Or intrigued, maybe. Some primal part of me responds positively to this, his expression tightening something deep in my stomach. But the rest of me is just annoyed now. How smug, I think.

"Well." He shrugs. "Maybe it is. There are always a lot of similarities when it comes to extremism. That doesn't mean people's stories should stop being told."

I want to laugh. I couldn't even count how many of these documentaries I had watched, how many of the articles I had read. In every single one, a woman tells her harrowing tale and I recognize some part of myself. And yet I couldn't tell you even one of their names now, couldn't remember a single distinguishing feature about them. It was only the most salacious details of the saga that stuck in my memory, the detailed portrait of the monster in charge of it all.

"Ah, right," I say instead, twisting the mug around in my hand. "Yes. The stories."

"The thing is," he goes on. "This place in Florida...this community...it did exactly what it proposed to do in the beginning. For a good chunk of time, it seemed pretty harmless. A little extreme in some ways, sure, but not dangerous, necessarily. I've talked to a ton of people who recall living there and liking it, who moved in and then out in the early aughts and chalked it all up to a phase, something you do when you're young and rebellious, or bored, maybe."

I try to recall all their names, the people who came and went. I was almost a teenager during those good years, not a baby. I should remember, at least some of them. But I find I can't name one.

He laughs, the sound garish against my thoughts. "I mean, I interviewed more than one person who spoke about the place like it was the one that got away or something. They'd wax poetic about how they should have stayed, that they would be...I don't know, thinner, healthier, happier if they did."

His laughter is gone now, his face more serious, his eyes searching my own expression for something. I wonder for a moment if he expects me to start crying now, to break down at the smallest reference to how bad things got, what he might know.

"If I didn't have my original source pushing me so hard, insisting that the whole thing had been more sinister than that, I honestly would have dropped it years ago."

Did he say years?

My heart jolts, a palpitation from all the caffeine, probably, but it makes me feel unmoored. I didn't expect him to say years.

"It's their story you want to tell, then," I offer, distracting myself by twisting a paper straw wrapper between my fingers, rolling it into a tiny, compact shard. "Your source."

"It's a hell of a story," he admits, then pauses, as if deciding whether he wants to say more. A moment passes before he does. "They're a hell of a storyteller."

A surge of something bright bursts in my chest at this small nod to who his source could be, but I steel my expression. "And you believe them?"

"I do," he nods. "But I want to tell your story, too. Your side of things."

My side of things, as if we might be opposites. Shame uncoils in my stomach like a snake, twisting and stretching.

He watches me take this in. "If you're willing."

I know I must look at least a little like I feel now, fear and desperation bubbling to the surface. I know that doesn't help me.

"I'm actually kind of impressed you found me," I say after a beat, the smallest possible curve of a grin on my lips, so slight he will wonder if it's there or if he's imagining it. "I don't make it easy."

His eyes light up at this. He must have known when I agreed to meet him that he had found the person he was looking for, but this is the first time I've confirmed it in some way. He looks delighted, as if I've revealed something without realizing it. It reminds me what is important here. It's all a picture I'm carefully painting. I'm cagey and sarcastic because I'm scarred, obviously. Bitter and jaded from a hard childhood. Distrusting of men. I'm flattering him because I am just that impressed, because he's just that good at his job, at asking the right questions, making me open up to him. I just can't help myself. I'm here for the same reason. After all this time, all these secrets, I need someone to talk to. I crave it. I can't resist the opportunity to unload it all. If I play my part well enough, this is what Reese will think. This is the person he will see, and then, eventually, he will lead me to his source.

"Why is that, Catharine?" he asks. He's leaning slightly across the table now, his body angled toward me like I have his whole attention. I suddenly feel warm, in need of water.

I scoff, brushing off the intensity. "I don't know," I manage.

I don't know?

The stupidity of my response eats at me. I keep doing this, swinging from carefully chosen replies to sounding like someone who is unsure of themselves, unsettled. I hate it. It's not like I didn't know what he looked like before now. The attraction, primal and plain, has surprised me, made me clumsy. The first years I spent in the city, I developed silent crushes constantly. It was as if my body had stored up all the hormones I should have been experiencing as a tween and supercharged them as they lay dormant. I was insatiable. But I was never like this, unsure of myself and off-balance. I know what I'm feeling now is the attraction, yes, but something else, too. Something new. It is the very first time I have ever sat across from a man who might know some sliver of me that came before.

I take a deep breath and a blip of a memory floats to the front of my mind: *Attraction is nothing but power, Catharine,* a familiar voice says. *It's like gravity you can control.*

"I'm a private person, Reese," I course correct, mirroring how he had used my name. I can hear the confidence in my voice returning, and it turns me on again, though this time the warmth is different. It is specific and controlled, something I am wielding instead of a thing that is happening to me.

At this he blushes again, just for a second, and I wonder if this is what does it for him. If he's ever slept with a source, sat across from them at a café just like this one and played this game while he's hard under the table the whole time. If he's promised that this has never happened before as he fucks them in the bathroom of a dingy coffee shop. That he never does this, that he's usually a total professional but god, he just couldn't help it.

"It makes sense," he responds, his tone matter-of-fact, pulling me out of my thoughts. "I guess I would be private too, after growing up like that."

I don't react.

"Or maybe I just miraculously resisted the siren song of Instagram," I say, my voice light, verging on playful. "The first millennial of my kind."

He laughs. "Sure. Maybe."

The laughter seems to relax both of us a little.

"It's funny," he starts. "They kept saying that you would be like this."

I tense. "They?"

"My source," he answers. "They said if you were still anything like your father, you would make sure I was intrigued. Hooked. That you'd be running the interview before I even realized it was happening, if I wasn't careful. They said it was inevitable."

The word clinks against something in my mind, but I frown, offended. "That's ridiculous."

He shrugs.

"You think I'm running this interview?" I push. "Come on."

"I thought this wasn't an interview?"

I don't flinch. "It's not."

He just smiles.

"I don't understand why you even need me," I press, irritated by the comparison to my father, the reminder of him. The word *still.* "If you have this other source who knows so much, then why am I so important?"

I think I know the answer to this, but I have to ask, regardless. He is an all-knowing wealth of information, and I am the eager woman sitting across from him. I am nothing but questions.

He cocks his head to the side, like this question surprises him.

"Because," he says. "You were there until the end."

I stare at my empty mug, the brown ring of residue left inside.

"Weren't you?" he presses.

I take a moment to catalog all he has said, everything he has revealed and held back. I know there is more. I know that in order to keep talking, I have to give him something, too. For most of my life, this would have been unthinkable. But for this? For her? I would find a way. I would show him enough of the darkness that he will assume there could not possibly be more.

I make eye contact for a moment longer than feels comfortable, then let my gaze fall to his mouth. Just for a second, and then I'm back to meeting his eyes. His pupils are slightly dilated. Good.

"Yes," I say. "I was."

CHAPTER 10

Then

If I didn't know her so well, I might have missed Linna's crush on Kent entirely. It had grown quietly, like a vine. A small weed of a thing at first, harmless, then something larger. By the time we were both seventeen, it was covering everything.

It had been a year since the confrontation with my father, and I felt more focused than ever. The discipline had made me feel heavier, like I was a thing that could not be swayed. Linna, however, was the opposite, avoiding chores and rolling her eyes during lessons. I could feel the dissatisfaction radiating off of her. But her growing attraction to Kent had distracted her, made her brighter and less serious. At first, I was almost glad for it. Eventually, though, there wasn't a single conversation that didn't loop back around to him, no matter how hard I tried to avoid it.

"Just be nice," I muttered to myself as I climbed the ladder to the treehouse, trying to remind myself that this was just a phase. A teenage rite of passage. She'd realize soon enough that Kent wasn't interested, and things would go back to normal. I knew she tried not to talk about him around me, that she'd dodge the subject entirely until there was a lull in the conversation. But then

I'd watch her get antsy, clearly itching to talk about him, the questions soon bubbling out of her. Had I noticed how he laughed at her joke earlier today? How he held the door for her? His freckles?

It wasn't like I didn't understand obsession. We had been down a million rabbit holes together over the years. Every few months since we had both become teenagers there had been a new book Linna and I would discover and re-read together a dozen times, a certain character or writer becoming the center of all our discussions. For weeks, we would speak of nothing else. And then we'd move on, suddenly enamored with something new, happily falling down that rabbit hole together again. The exact subject of our fixation wasn't the point as much as our shared love of it, the collective energy behind the obsession. That was where the joy lived.

I could see a similar energy in Linna now, a different but familiar brand of giddiness. I knew it made her happy. And, of course, I wanted that for her. I just wanted her to be happy and to be herself, the person who saved her focus for only the things she deemed most important. And Kent? This pining? It was exactly the opposite of important. It was how I knew it wouldn't last.

I hoisted myself into the treehouse to find Linna scribbling in a notebook, her eyes narrowed in concentration. It was a scene I had stepped into a million times. At some point, I knew Linna would stop writing, silently flip to the beginning of the notebook, smooth the pages back, then hand it to me. I was always her first reader. In the beginning, she was too shy to watch my reactions as I read, but now she seemed her happiest when I'd smile or laugh at a scene or repeat a line that I loved out loud. I felt lucky to be the first eyes on her words, to chart the exact ways they got better and better.

I said a quick hello and threw myself dramatically onto the quilts, letting out a long burst of air.

"Hi yourself," she chirped, her voice light and playful—a sign of a good day. "Where have you been? I haven't seen you since school this morning."

I had been working most of the afternoon, handling my mother's chores for the second time that week as she dealt with yet another migraine. They had been happening more and more over the last year, manageable at first but more frequently devolving into something debilitating. She needed total darkness during these episodes, my father had explained to me. He had created a detailed healing regimen for her, and though the headaches kept coming, I could see how much the dark helped, how much more quickly the pain seemed to subside then. I knew it was my job to pick up her slack while she healed. "That's how community works," my father had told us, so many times. "Someday it might be you who needs help."

"It was a long day," I answered Linna. "Another migraine."

She set down her notebook, like she was trying hard to focus on what I was saying, the seriousness of it. "I'm sorry."

I shrugged. "It's fine," I said. "The more she rests now, the sooner she'll get better."

Linna didn't reply, but it looked like she wanted to. The silence scratched at me.

"How was your day?" I asked, changing the subject. "Better than mine, I hope."

"Oh, it was okay. Good, I guess. Good."

She was being weird. Her face looked pinched, like she was trying to keep something in. A smile, maybe. A laugh.

"Uh huh..." I said, my tone suspicious.

I glanced down on the floor, the notebook she had been writing in when I got to the treehouse still open. I picked it up. "What are you working—"

She snatched it away, interrupting my question.

"Whoa," I said. "I'm sorry. I didn't know it was..."

I paused, considering my words. Private? Secret? It had been many years since Linna was guarded about what she was writing. These days, there was always a story she wanted to tell me about, a poem she wanted to recite. Her writing was like anything else she did—decisive, intentional, precise. By the time the words made it to the page, she seemed to be completely sure of them, her confidence unwavering.

"It's nothing," she said, tucking the notebook behind her.

"Oh, come on," I said, sitting up and craning my neck to try to catch a glimpse of a paragraph, a single word. "I already know whatever it is is incredible."

"I said it's nothing," she insisted again, her voice laced with tension.

This wasn't like Linna, to be so cagey. Especially not around me. It was the best thing about our relationship, I always thought, that we could count on complete and total ease around each other, never a drop of the awkwardness or shame that seemed to bubble up when I found myself around Jessie or Kent or Maura, or my mother, even. We were safe around each other, always. That was the rule.

"What?" I teased. "Is it a love note to Kent or something? A sonnet?"

I was laughing. It was the kind of thing that Linna should have found hilarious. A ridiculous notion. Something she would never do. But Linna looked stung, hurt.

"Wait," I said. "Is it *actually* a love letter..."

"No," she muttered, drawing her knees toward her chest and hugging them. I could feel the "but" lingering. The thing she was holding back. I bit my tongue, waiting for it.

"It's just a letter," she added. "Some thoughts on a page. Whatever."

My heart had started to race.

"A letter to *him*, though..." I clarified, imagining her taking a piece of paper lined with her deepest secrets, folding it up, and hiding it under his pillow for him to find when he went back to the bunk building at night. I cringed, picturing how it would be when we saw him the next day, how he would have to tell her that he was flattered but didn't feel the same. How we'd have to see him every day after that, too.

Kent had recently graduated, meaning we didn't see him in school every day anymore, but there were plenty of responsibilities to keep him busy. Sometimes, even with just nine of us, the farm managed to feel crowded, everyone's business overlapping in ways that felt suffocating. Other times, it felt logistically unmanageable. There was always so much to do, to stay on top of. I could tell it pained my father to keep us in class, away from chores, especially when most of us were old enough now to be genuinely helpful. But he always said that us staying in school until we turned eighteen was important. Education was a fixture of our community that made us different from other places. What's more, he wouldn't have anyone accusing him of something as absurd as abuse. Child labor. The world didn't understand the value of hard work anymore, he explained. "They have all managed to rebrand discipline as some sort of cruelty," he said of the rest of society. "No wonder every child enters the world soft as dough, ready to be flattened."

All of this meant that there was no break upon graduation. Instead, Kent was busier than ever, darting from garden to garden, project to project, my father's new right-hand man. I thought of how word would get back to Jessie and Maura about the note, how they would tease us...

"Listen, Linna," I started, injecting as much empathy into my voice as I could. "I don't know if that's such a good idea. It could make things awk—"

"It's not awkward," she interjected.

She was sitting up straighter now, avoiding eye contact. I played her words back in my head: It's not awkward. Present tense. As if maybe she's already sent the letter. As if this isn't the first of them.

"What do you mean?" I asked.

"Kent and I," she said, shrugging. "We talk. Write letters when we have free time. It's not a big deal."

"You talk," I echoed, incredulous. I could hear how shocked I sounded, how panicked. It was humiliating, really. I searched every memory I had of the last year. Had they been flirting, all this time? Had I somehow missed it all? When had we stopped telling each other everything? When had she decided that the rules had changed?

"He's not as bad as you think, you know. Nothing like Jessie," she added, like I hadn't grown up side by side with them, too. Like I couldn't gauge their differences myself from the last six years of living together, of sharing the farm with them. "He's... deep. He has ideas."

God.

"Deep," I said, nodding. "Right. Okay. Cool."

She didn't say anything, but I could feel her watching me react.

"So this is, like, a thing?" I pressed. I sounded so deeply bothered by this, so incredibly uncool that I was almost disgusted with myself. "You and him?"

"I don't know, Rin."

I laughed, and the sound was high-pitched, sour. "I mean, it sounds like you know. You're writing each other love letters. Not exactly casual. Honestly, I wasn't even convinced he could read, so I mean good for him, I guess..."

Part of me expected her to laugh, but, of course, she didn't. It only reminded me of just how much had changed, just how much I had really missed.

"This is why I didn't tell you, you know."

Her voice was quiet, cautious, like I was a fragile thing.

"I don't care who you write letters to, Linna," I scoffed, scooting to the front of the treehouse, letting my legs swing forward so they were halfway out of the floor opening, the breeze prickling my skin. "Sounds... fun. Really. Enjoy."

"You don't have to do that with me, you know."

"Do what?"

"Try to act like you aren't..."

And there it was, the thing I had dreaded. I looked down from the treehouse at the murky ground, the dozens of hardened knots from the oak's root system jutting out of the dirt. I wondered how many thoughts I could have before I hit them, if only I just nudged myself a little farther off the ledge. I didn't want to hurt myself, I just wanted to be anywhere but right there. I wanted to get this part over with. Our first real fight. "Like I'm not what, Linna?"

"Jealous."

The word shot through my chest like a barb, catching on everything as it went. But I laughed, dragging the sound into the world by its hair. "Trust me, I'm not jealous."

"Not of him," she corrected. "Maybe it's not even jealousy. Maybe you're just scared of being left behind or something. Things changing."

I wanted to cry but I laughed again instead. "I have my own shit to worry about, Linna. I don't need to hang out with you 24/7. I'm a big girl."

"That's not what I mean."

"I get it," I insisted. "I know what you're trying to say. You think you've graduated to this higher level of adulthood and I'm still left here waiting to experience it all."

I could have stopped there, but I wanted her to know that I had perspective, too. I saw the way she acted around him. I saw it maybe more clearly than even she did. "How will I possibly understand you if I don't know what it's like to follow some guy around for a year until he finally tells me I'm pretty, right?"

I blinked away a tear, twisting myself back around to climb down the ladder, facing her as I did, desperately trying to ignore how hurt she looked.

"I bet you feel special, right? That he chose you," I said, the words spilling out of me. "That he looked at the—what? Two other eligible girls here and chose you. Me, you, or Maura. Wow. Remarkable. One in three odds. Congratulations. Sounds like true love to me."

Her mouth opened slightly, and I wasn't sure if it was because she was going to reply or because she was shocked. But then her brow settled into an angry line. "That's not true."

"I don't know, Linna," I said, perched on the ladder. I was almost shaking, panic thundering through me. It felt like I was watching my sister fade away from me, like fear, but I found that anger was the only thing I could reach. "Look around. I'm pretty sure it is."

"No," she said, her voice cool and steady, so much calmer than mine. "He said he doesn't even consider you a girl, really, just an extension of your father. He looks at you and only sees him."

At that, I finally propelled myself down the ladder, missing the last few rungs and landing on the ground with a jolt, my ankle twisting at an odd angle. I groaned at the impact, tears finally pouring out of me. A moment passed before Linna's voice carried out of the treehouse, softer now. "Are you okay?"

The sound made me spring to my feet and start limping my way down the long path back to the main building. I knew Linna's concern was an olive branch, that I should have taken it and moved on. Told her I was fine. That I would be fine. That we would be fine. But I couldn't bring myself to do it. I wanted to stew and rage and be exactly how I felt, wildly and hopelessly alone.

* * *

I arrived back at my mother's and my room to find her awake, sitting up in bed and reading. This had been happening more and more, her having one of her episodes during the day only to be wide awake at night, busying herself with something. I was hoping she was still asleep this time, though. All I wanted was to close my eyes and forget about the evening, to not talk about it. I started to change into my pajamas silently, not bothering to greet her.

"Hello to you, too," she said after a minute or two.

"Hi," I muttered. "I'm tired."

I pulled on a pair of sweatpants and winced as I shifted my weight onto the twisted ankle.

"Are you hurt?" she asked.

"It's nothing."

"Looks like a very swollen nothing," she said. "I'll get you something."

I was too tired to protest, too sad to push back.

She returned a minute later with a cool rag, gesturing for me to sit on the bed so she could wrap it around my ankle. It wasn't ice, but it felt good. I thanked her.

"What happened?"

"I fell coming back from the treehouse," I said. "Just an accident."

"I mean with Linna."

I bristled. "We're fine."

"And this has nothing to do with Kent?"

My eyes cut her way, my pulse beating angrily under my skin. How was it that everyone seemed to know more about the state of things than I did? Was everyone paying more attention? Was I really that naïve? That stupid? I didn't reply.

"I saw them a couple times," she explained. "Sneaking around at night. When I can't sleep, I go outside and practice my breathing exercises.

"He's always seemed sweet to me," she added. "Smarter than he lets on."

I rolled my eyes. "God. Not you, too."

She smiled. "I get it. Firsts are hard when it's not you."

This again. Why did everyone think I was so angry about falling behind? Why did no one get that this was about my sister and best friend becoming someone different? Why did no one seem to care about that part at all?

"It happened with my sister and me, too," she said. "We were so close in age that people thought we were twins. Attached at the hip. But she was a little older, and when that first boyfriend came around when she was thirteen or so, oh... it changed things. The first night she and Scott Klein went to the movies together and I had to stay home... gosh, I think I cried for hours. When I finally came out of my room, my mom had made me popcorn and set up a pillow fort in the living room. She painted my nails, braided my hair. She had it all planned, like she had seen this coming. Now, I realize she had probably gone through the same thing, too. She knew how hard it was."

It had been so long since I heard my mother talk about how she grew up, about her life before the one she had here with us. I knew the basics of the story, that her only sister had passed away when she was in high school, leaving her an only child of two parents who seemed more interested in drinking than raising her. It was a story I thought of often when things were hard here, or a fast was challenging, a reminder of what this place had to offer that the rest of the world didn't. "All my parents knew how to do was numb their pain with more. More alcohol. More work. More food. More, more, more. Nothing was ever enough," my mother had explained once. "I wanted something different for my family. Something better." I wanted that, too, I remembered thinking.

It was new, though, to hear my mother talk about her family like this, with such lightness and affection. I scanned through what I knew about her childhood, her story, and I realized that everything I knew was filtered through a lesson. A consequence of gluttony and greed. This was something different.

I tried to picture her sister, her parents, if they looked like me. If my father had met them, if they knew how wonderful it was here. I thought to ask her all of this, but I felt something in me rise and steal the words out of my throat, protective. I remembered Linna, the way she had revealed everything to me, how stupid I had felt. I couldn't bear the idea of realizing I had been wrong about someone else, too.

"It gets easier," my mother added, filling the silence. "My sister and I got over it. We both adjusted. You and Linna will, too. You just have to be patient. One day you'll find someone who looks at you like Kent looks at her. I promise."

I grimaced.

I knew what she was trying to do, to assure me that all of this was survivable, that there was documented proof of it, but I felt irritation bubble up like acid. I hated the way she assumed being a teenager was a standard experience. It made every emotion that pulsed through me feel unoriginal, a copy of a copy of a copy. It invalidated everything I felt until there was not a single thing about me that was special, not even inside my own head. Even worse, it implied that she and I were the same. We were not the same.

"Right," I said, staring at the ceiling with its grid of yellow, faded tiles. "That patience really paid off for you, huh?"

I didn't dare look to see her reaction, but I heard her adjust in bed so she was lying down, too, likely staring at the same ceiling, the same grid. I wanted to take my comment back, to explain that I didn't know why I had poked at an old wound. My parents' divorce was an unemotional thing, really. Easy. Practical. My mother agreed to it for the greater good of the community, to ensure that Linna and her mother could stay here and be safe, both of them fully, legally attached to my father.

It was what my mother wanted. It was what was for the best for everyone. And yet I had made it into something ugly, a reminder that she was technically alone now, discarded.

For the first time in months, I remembered the way I had questioned my father in class the year before, the desire to push back welling up from a place inside me that I couldn't point to. But I had learned my lesson then, hadn't I? I was so sure I had learned. The fact that it was happening again had only one explanation, something I was beginning to think I had always known. There was something in me that was broken, dark and unfixable.

Apologize, said a voice in my head that I didn't quite recognize. I felt like a future version of myself had nested inside my body, that it was screaming at me that one day I would regret this. One day I would replay this scene and wish it had gone differently. I pushed it away almost immediately. Instead, I wished that my mother would fight with me, jab back with something just as mean, but she stayed quiet.

I turned off the lamp next to us, a signal that this conversation was over. This night was over. Please, I thought, let this be over.

My mother's voice cut through the darkness gently. "Being a teenager is a monstrous thing, Catharine, isn't it?"

I paused, taking in what she had said, considering all the words I could throw her way in response. In the end, though, I just said good night. I would never have been able to explain to her that she was wrong.

Being a teenager wasn't the monstrous thing, I was.

CHAPTER 11

Now

The day after our first meeting, I spend ten hours straight in the library. I decide to learn everything there is to know about Reese Campbell.

I am naturally inclined toward obsession. I know this about myself by now. It is a part of me that has never changed, a characteristic I can recall clearly from my childhood, even when other memories remain foggy. When something feels deeply interesting or important to me, I am a dog with a bone. Jaw locked, teeth bared. I do not let go until the thing is ripped away from me, or I find something else that holds my attention in the same way. It's a trait that's served me well. It often means I am the person in the room with the most information.

With Reese, the dynamic is different. We both know that he has access to information that I do not. But we also both know that he needs me. If he didn't, then there would be no waiting for my side, as he so generously alluded to. There would be no moralistic desire for fairness. Journalistic integrity. Please. He wouldn't be able to help himself, not after years of research. That's what he had said. He's been at this for *years*. He's smart enough to know that the world isn't asking for the perfect cult story as much as it is for another one as soon as possible, please. In other words, the story doesn't exist without me. And if I need to use that to get in front of his source, after all this time? Well, I will.

The social media stuff is the easiest to parse first. I spend hours cocooned in the whispered hum of the library, reading his tweets from high school (idiotic, but not offensive). I find his college girlfriend on Instagram (pretty) and then soon know her name (Megan) and the names of her current husband (Charlie) and their new baby (Lily), then google their old wedding website, assess their taste in cookware (disappointing). I go as far back in his tagged photos as I can go, until I find images of him with acne, wearing a polo shirt and posing with a copy of his first article in his undergrad paper ("Recycling on Campus: Is It All a Sham?"). I look up his Spotify account, figure out what kind of music he likes and listen to his latest public playlist. It's titled, "For S," and I imagine that S is Sarah or Sadie or Savannah, some girl from an app who he hooked up with once, or is trying to. Though I can't imagine he has to try very hard. There must be so many women.

Average-looking men thrive in New York City. It's what I learned almost immediately when I first started going on dates, hungry for experience and the feeling of bare skin on mine. It was all new to me, totally foreign, which embarrassed me until I realized that certain men—most men, really—liked it. It was like they could smell the inexperience on me. They could teach me, they said over and over again, like it was supposed to delight me, to comfort me. Even when I had lived here for years, when I had slept with dozens of men, when it should have been so blatantly obvious to them that I knew exactly what I was doing, they took this as a sign that they had done something right. That they had unlocked some untouched yet innately sexual miracle woman. A pristine hidden gem among the filth. I let them believe it because I didn't care. And in the end, this worked for me, because usually I was as insatiable as they were. Not for any particular man, or any particular sex, but for options.

I understood how men were all fueled by the notion that if they settled down they would lose out on the millions of other single women in the city, millions of other possibilities. They were scared to limit themselves. Or to be vulnerable. Or to miss the perfect lay. They wanted to wait for something that didn't exist yet, a person who can sense what they want or need without ever having to ask for it. I understood because I was the same.

But Reese is better than average-looking. He probably isn't even on the apps. He doesn't need to be. The "S" from the playlist is probably someone he met at a CVS while buying toothpaste, both of them laughing over the absurd length of the paper receipt. And yet, I feel the need to confirm this. To know for sure if he's on Hinge, or Bumble. It's not that I'm jealous, though I admit that I'm curious to know whether I'm his type.

I keep thinking about the moment he stood up to leave at the café. He had reached his arm into the sleeve of his coat and the hem of his sweater lifted a bit, his waistline level with my eye, inches from my mouth. Soft blond hair trailing down. I wanted to hook my fingers into his belt loop and pull. I thought of those words again. *Attraction is gravity you can control.* So I had simply tilted my eyes upward. "Bye, Reese."

"Talk soon," he had replied.

I had laughed. "Maybe."

I'm sure he's spent hours on his laptop doing the same thing, that he's dug and dug and dug for every fine thread of my story he could gather. He probably searched until he had enough intel to feel confident sitting across from me—until he felt like he could predict how I would be, how I would react, what I would want.

Maybe he searched for my dating profiles, too, and when he found nothing, he somehow tracked down a guy I had met in a bar, bought him beers until he told him what I liked, what he knows.

"Dude, she was..." the guy would start, shaking his head, unsure if he should kiss and tell but eventually just going for it, because it was casual, and so is this. "She was nuts. Best sex of my life."

I smile, imagining this little interaction. Was Reese turned on then? Was he thinking of this when he sat across from me, drinking his coffee?

He was just trying to build a better picture of me. I'm sure this is what he would say if ever asked about the interview, how my sex life was really relevant to everything. He was just trying to understand exactly how I got from point A to point B, he'd say. Nothing out of line about it. Sure. Well, then, maybe I'm trying to do the same. I'm trying to build a better picture of him. My father used to say if you really wanted something from someone, you had to understand them first. You had to be able to crawl inside their head and get comfortable. So that's what I'm doing. I'm getting comfortable.

I'm getting so comfortable that when he eventually introduces me to his source, it will feel like his choice. He won't even question it. And finally, for the first time, I will have the chance to sit across from my sister and apologize.

I click out of Reese's Facebook profile, most of it untouched for years, and open another tab, then type in a familiar name. It's a nervous tick of mine now, searching for information about Marion Earl, especially since Reese's email. I am newly convinced there is something else I have missed in the depths of the internet, even after all this time, all my previous searching. An interview. A photo. A decades-old article from a small-town newspaper. I know there must be something that will confirm or disprove the absurd theory that has floated to the surface of my life, once again.

For Christmas last year, Stella had bought me a signed copy of one of Earl's novels, presenting it to me over drinks at a casual happy hour. We hadn't planned on exchanging gifts, and when I saw what she had given me, I was almost relieved that I was unprepared. There is nothing I could have bought her that would have compared. The thoughtfulness of it hit me square in the chest, tipping me off balance. "I... I don't know what to say," I whispered.

Stella laughed from where she sat next to me at the bar. "Are you going to *cry*? Oh my god, I didn't think it was possible."

My breath caught in my throat as I turned to the title page and ran my finger over the author's signature, studying the curve of the letters, tracing the loops and slants, searching for something. Remembering something.

"Really, it's no big deal," Stella added. "I knew you were a fan. I browse eBay like it's my job. Boom."

"Thank you," I said.

Stella lifted her glass of wine in response, as if toasting to the moment. "You just really like her books, huh?"

How could I explain it to her?

"I see myself, I guess. In her stories. The way she writes."

Stella nodded, taking this in, then asked me which of her books I thought she should read first. I don't remember my answer. The entire time, all I was thinking was that I hadn't quite explained it right. I didn't know if I could ever convey the depth of what Marion Earl's words meant to me.

All those years, I had been convinced I was seeing myself in her books, but as I ran my fingers over her signature, I realized it was something bigger.

I wasn't just seeing myself. I was seeing my sister.

That night, I had come home and laid my palm against the book's cover, pressed down, and hoped for magic. I wanted the book to give me a sign, for the truth to travel from its pages to my body. After so many years of seeing Linna in crowds, and so many years of being wrong, I didn't trust myself anymore.

The next morning, I had woken up with the book still tucked between my hands. In the light of day, I felt ridiculous. I wanted so badly for Linna to be alive that I had let myself get stupid. Of course Marion Earl wasn't my sister. What kind of a person tells themselves such a preposterous story? That's what the theory sounded like. A story. It was a way to soothe my own guilt, not a logical conclusion. It was pathetic, I thought. I was just a person clawing for absolution wherever I could find it. Maybe it was enough, I told myself, to find a book that spoke to me, a character. Maybe that was magic in and of itself.

In my core, though, I knew that it wasn't sufficient. That nothing would be. It's why Reese had crashed into my life with such violent efficiency, why I had made myself so vulnerable. I had barely even hesitated.

I think of the interview, the mention of a memoir. I think of the word *inevitable*. I think of Reese's emails. His source. Is it such a coincidence that all of this had launched into the world in the very same week? Into my world?

They're a hell of a storyteller, he had said.

They were, I thought. She was.

Maybe she still is.

CHAPTER 12

Then

Linna and I made up for the same reason we always did: We shared too much of our lives not to. My father taught me that everything in life is more manageable when everyone is on the same page, in the same boat. The sooner you get back to that, the better.

"I overreacted. If you're happy, then I'm good," I told her as we hung laundry on the line to dry. "I know people can't stay the same forever."

Linna didn't reply right away, instead reaching down to grab a damp towel, then busied herself with pinning it to the line. She looked pensive. Frustrated, even.

"That's the thing, Rin," she eventually said, pushing a tightly wound curl behind her ear. "You think this makes me so different. I'm the same person. Just because what's happening outside of you and me is new and different doesn't mean our friendship is."

Of course it does, I thought. It changes everything. But I knew what she meant, and I didn't want to fight anymore. The week we had spent giving each other the cold shoulder had left me feeling miserable and disoriented.

"I know," I said, hanging up a sheet between us so she couldn't see my face, or guess I was lying. "You're right."

"Listen, I know change is hard," Linna said as she leaned down, grabbing another towel, and I rolled my eyes as she looked away. Because this was it. This was the thing that had changed. Couldn't she see it? Couldn't she hear herself? The way she talked to me like she was a few rungs above me now, reporting back on what she'd learned about life? "This place only makes it harder."

This manner of speaking about the farm was new, too. It had been happening for a while now, I realized. But it was subtle, something you might only notice if you had spent as much time with her as I had, the kind of thing only a sister would see. The farm had become *this place, this thing.* Something impersonal and cold.

I looked to my right at the sprawling cut flower gardens, color and texture pouring out of the ground, spilling into the path next to it, bees buzzing from bloom to bloom.

"Does it?" I asked her, keeping my voice measured, casual.

"Sure. I mean," she gestured around. "What has really changed in the last ten years in this place? It's like everything is frozen in amber."

"I don't think—"

She interrupted me. "What has changed for the better, I should say."

I knew what she meant. Around the time Kent, Jessie, and Rhonda arrived, the farm had been thriving. My father seemed to be in his element, with fresh ideas every day. He was rarely moody and was intensely focused, positive, and determined. There were new projects going on in every corner of the property—fields cleared for crops we had never grown before, renovations that we'd talked about for years finally underway. Moderation fasts were sporadic, challenging but always manageable.

Then there was Maura and her mother, Stacy, a single mom and master gardener. Stacy was quiet but managed to make every corner of the property sparkle, using native plants to landscape even the most hopeless patches of dirt. A year after they arrived, there were nearly thirty-five of us, ten kids, my father teaching all of us. Everyone seemed to bring a new skill to the community, a new set of knowledge.

Then, the heat wave happened, a series of weeks with temperatures so high that ten people left in one summer, unable to stomach the lack of air conditioning, no matter how many times my father explained that it was better for their immune systems. Every person who left seemed to set off something in him, inflaming a desire to make sure the people who remained were completely committed.

Moderation fasts became a more regular occurrence, with the rules of them changing every few months, then every few weeks. Sometimes, we cut out foods that no one was really devastated to see go—green beans, Brussels sprouts, spinach. It was less about the food itself, anyway, than the ability to exist beyond it. One less thing our bodies would crave, my mother reminded me at first. An opportunity to build our strength and willpower, a dedication to one day meeting our highest selves. But over time, the rules became stricter.

Soon, it wasn't just Brussels sprouts and green beans but bread, then grains altogether. Then eggs. Then honey. Eventually, the eliminations were no longer temporary. My father was learning more about nutrition, about what our bodies needed most. Of course he wasn't going to reintroduce things into our meals that he knew were harming us. Increasingly, the rules were met with dissatisfaction, unsettling some people and confusing or even angering others. I had struggled with it, too, obsessing over the foods I was missing until they consumed my thoughts and clouded my judgment, just like that day when I had questioned him in class. But that was just it. The unhappiness only proved his point. With every thing we gave up, it only became more clear how addicted to indulgence we had become. Our discomfort with the change was the surest sign of all that we needed to eliminate it altogether.

I felt my brain fixate on the food that was now off-limits, and I knew in my core that I was exactly as weak as he said, that the only way to pull myself to something greater was to concentrate on the weakness more than I did the need, the want. And as much as I sometimes yearned for those easier, lighter days, there was also something about our numbers dwindling that gave me a small, secret thrill. A lightning bolt of energy in knowing that someone else had given up, but I hadn't yet. That I had been willing to do the work and they had not. That I was stronger. I wanted the community I had once known, the buzz and laughter of people, everyone in it together, but sometimes, especially when the rules and changes felt suffocating, I wondered if I had needed the edge that this gave me more, the quiet knowledge that I had fought harder.

And deep down, I was grateful that there was someone out there to manage it all for us, to sift through everything and find the truth. But the rules weren't for everyone. Discipline wasn't for everyone either, my father had explained during his lessons.

And so people started to leave, disappearing from the property as quickly as they had arrived. Fewer people meant fewer projects were completed, renovations were left in limbo. The bunk building still only had one functional bathroom, renovations for the rest delayed indefinitely. In a narrow, clipped view, I knew how it looked. I knew what it would mean if someone else left, how unsustainable life on the farm would become without the additional sets of hands. But this was part of the process. It required trust. Patience. Grit. This was how it worked.

In some ways, it reminded me of my earliest memories of the farm—when it was just my parents, me, and Ben and Bertie. The feeling was the same then, the fears the same, too. All that land for so few of us, the promise that one day there would be others. But we stayed focused on the work, and eventually, there were Linna and her mother, then everyone else. There was an ebb and flow to it all, and it was best to weed out the people who weren't invested in this life. I wanted to help Linna remember this, too.

I took a deep breath, the smell of lavender soap and wet, sun-soaked grass filling my nose, then exhaled. "Well, the gardens have never looked better, for one," I offered. "I haven't seen them this healthy since we were kids."

"Right," Linna nodded. "And how much of that food do we even see? Even the flowers don't stick around long enough to make it to the table. Not ours, anyway."

I knew she was talking about the farmers market business, how my father had started selling all the produce we didn't eat to small-town markets across the state. Over time, the share that was left over for us became a smaller and smaller portion of the crop. But we knew now about the inflammation and arthritis that nightshades like tomatoes and potatoes caused, the painful bloating that came from eating broccoli. We knew better. If other people wanted to bury their heads in the sand and expose themselves to all that, my father said, so be it.

"These women stand there with their gigantic, artificially flavored coffees and their swollen bodies and ask me if it's all organic," he told us once, laughing. "None of them are looking for real knowledge, real truth. They're looking for an image. To fit into some box. Meanwhile, they can't face the reality of how addicted to it all they've become. How soft and round and sad.

Same as everyone out there. Sheep. Far be it from me to turn away their money when I can use it for something good."

So they got the honey from our bees, the flowers and tomatoes and broccoli from our gardens. And we took their money, pouring it back into the farm, the rest being saved for bigger projects, like the bunkhouse and the old barn renovation. Even though they'd stood unfinished for years, there wasn't that much more work that needed to be done. Six months, my father told us. A year, tops. Then there would be an art studio; after that, a greenhouse. There were even talks of a pool.

A dozen times, I had considered telling Linna that I understood her urge to rebel, explaining to her what it had been like when I questioned my father in class, the dissatisfaction that I had let fizz out of me, the greed. I knew what that burning, restless energy felt like, how easy it was to mistake it as meaningful in some way. But I understood now how much better it felt to know the rules and the boundaries of life, to follow them relentlessly. I imagined being that out of control again and all I felt was dread. But understanding wasn't what Linna needed, I decided. I knew exactly what happened when someone you loved validated your unhappiness. I had watched enough people leave to know.

"Where is all of this coming from, exactly?" I said gently.

"Nowhere," Linna sighed, exasperated. "It's just... don't you ever get tired of waiting around for it?"

I picked up the empty laundry basket, balancing it on my hip. "For what?"

"To be better. Your higher self. For whatever we're working toward to finally arrive. I mean, after all this time, all this work. Shouldn't we be there by now?"

I turned, walking back to the main building and the former

janitor's closet that was our laundry room, a mop sink serving as a washing machine. Linna followed a few steps behind.

"Ben and Bertie always said the hardest part isn't the work itself. Not the rules, either," I offered, eyes fixed ahead. "It's the trust. Day in, day out, you have to trust that it will pay off. Even when it's hard—especially when it is. It's the biggest part of all of it, they said. The only way it works."

"Do you think it was worth it for them?" Linna asked.

I closed my eyes and pictured their faces, deeply tanned and carved with wrinkles. Bertie's signature hot pink lipstick stark next to her long, white braids. I remembered how Ben would hold Bertie's hand across the table at family meal, even as they both were eating. They had died when I was seven, Ben from a heart attack and Bertie soon after, from the stress of losing Ben.

They had been like grandparents to me and then, to Linna, too, especially in the year after her mother died. Bertie had set up an art studio for us in the barn and French braided our hair. Ben had made us mint tea during chilly nights, taught us how to play HORSE in the dining hall. Both told us how lucky we were to be there, together, again and again. It was part of the reason I always trusted the power of the farm and my father. That Ben and Bertie had endorsed it and him only made me believe in it more.

"Of course," I answered. "They loved it here. They chose it. How many times did they tell us that?"

We had heard the story dozens of times over the years. Ben and Bertie had been true hippies in their youth, living on a commune in the Pacific Northwest for most of their twenties. But when they tried to get pregnant and couldn't, Bertie became obsessed with finding the best fertility specialists and treatments. "None of those involved living out of a school bus and juicing wheatgrass, it seemed," Bertie would tell us, Linna and I gathered at her feet in the garden. "At least, that's what everyone told us."

She and Ben moved back to a major city, closer to hospitals and doctors, and got real jobs with real medical insurance, all things Bertie said the experts had recommended to make the whole process easier. But by the time Bertie had reached her mid-forties, she and Ben had all but given up on children, the life they had once known on the commune seeming impossibly far away, too. "Part of me thought I had dreamt it," Ben would chuckle to us, telling us about the camper vans they had lived in, the community garden. So they let go of their dream of children and that place, and they worked until they could move somewhere else, eventually landing on a retirement community in Florida, a sprawling, monotonous suburban entity in the middle of the state.

And then, one day some years after that, they showed up here, each of them with a single suitcase. "I had an epiphany," Bertie would tell us. "I wasn't going to spend the golden years of my life lining the pockets of some rich man somewhere, pumping myself full of pills and potions, was I, Benny?" Ben would beam back at her. "You certainly weren't, honey." Here, they had what they had always wanted: a quiet, different type of life. A family.

"They loved us, too," I reminded Linna.

Linna had propped herself on the counter next to the sink, her long legs dangling down, swinging nervously. "They did," she agreed. "I miss them."

I felt my shoulders relax into my spine. Finally, I thought, there we were again. The same page. The same boat.

"Me too."

It was only then that it felt safe enough to tell her the idea that I had been stuck on for the past week, something I had turned over and over inside my head until it made perfect sense. I had been watching my father and the way he would hurry from place to place, task to task, mapping how erratic he seemed and how exhausted he looked. He needed help. And then there was Linna, with that thing behind her eyes glowing and alive, hungry for rebellion. I knew she was convinced that I couldn't possibly get it. But I did. I remembered it. I needed to make her understand that I still saw her, that I understood just as much as I always had. I didn't need to fuel her unhappiness and questions, to amplify them with my own. Instead, I needed to distract her, to give her something that made her believe we were still on the same page, after all this time.

"I have an idea," I announced, crossing my arms as I leaned against the sink.

She seemed surprised. "Oh?"

"I think I should get my license," I said.

She blinked once, slow and hard, her brow creasing. "I'm sorry, you think what now?"

"I think that I should get my driver's license. He needs the help," I replied. "And I think I need some space. The open road, whatever."

I tried to make this sound as casual as possible, while still emphasizing that this was about me. Maybe Linna wasn't the only one changing. Maybe I could surprise her, too.

Linna took this in, like she was skeptical. But then she was smiling. "Even if he lets you..." she started, serious again. "What makes you think he'll let me go with you?"

I shrugged. "It's like you always say."

She looked confused.

"The only person you ever met who was more persuasive than him..." I start, letting the second part of the sentence hang between us, waiting for her to put the pieces together.

Then it clicks. She nods, remembering, a smile growing wide across her face before finishing my thought. "Is you."

CHAPTER 13

Now

The second time I meet with Reese, he suggests a bar. I start planning my outfit immediately.

I settle on a cornflower-blue silk slip dress under an oversized brown sweater, worn off the shoulder. Knee-high suede boots. Together, the colors and textures are perfect. It's warmer today, unseasonably so for November, so I opt for a chunky scarf instead of a coat, something to take off when I sit down, to slowly unravel so all that's eventually left is my bare collarbone under a thread-thin strap. I wondered if it was a little much, but it's only one shoulder. One small patch of skin. It's casual, really, just like my outfit was the last time we met. I'll admit it's sexier, too. Softer and warmer. But hey, he chose the time, the day. It's a Friday at 4 p.m. Maybe I have somewhere to be after this.

I'm the one who's forty minutes late this time, on purpose, of course. I take my time as I walk in the door and situate myself. I know where Reese is sitting before I even get past the hostess stand, having spotted him through the window as I crossed the street. He's at the bar, his posture annoyingly perfect in a way that somehow reads as regal instead of forced. He must have heard the bells on the door when I came in, but he doesn't look over, and I don't beeline for where he sits, either. Instead, I move in slow motion, studying the decor, even though I've already seen most of it online. I've walked by this place before, often on my way to meet Stella after a date gone wrong. Her go-to place is next door, an old-school Italian spot. "Remember going-out tops?" she had asked me once. "The thing you'd wear with jeans *every single* Saturday night in college because why fix what isn't broken? That Italian place is my going-out top. It works. I don't mess with it."

I had never been inside this bar, though, and as I look around, I know why. Nothing about it is blatantly offensive, but that's exactly what makes it stiff, lifeless. I'd rather be in the kind of place where there are dollar bills glued to the ceiling and my shoes stick to the floor, smacking as I walk through the crowd. Still, this is a bar, and come 1 a.m., I imagine it won't look that much different from anywhere else you'd find yourself at that hour in the city. No matter which way you slice it, this is not the place you bring a totally platonic source for a totally professional interview. But then again, this isn't an interview, not quite yet. That's what I told Reese when I agreed to meet again.

"Sure," he texted back, almost instantly. "We'll just talk."

Right, I had thought. I've heard that one before.

He's still working on his laptop when I walk over, just like he was when I saw him across the street, staying busy. A mug of black coffee sits steaming next to him despite it being nearly 5 p.m.

"Hey, Chris, can you grab us another coffee?" Reese asks when he briefly glances my way, directing the question to the man drying glasses behind the bar.

Chris nods and grabs a mug.

"Thanks, man," Reese says, as if this is his scene and Chris, simply a supporting background character.

This guy.

"Coffee's fine, I'm assuming?" he asks, closing his computer, finally turning to look at me head-on. "And hi, by the way."

I wonder if he ordered for me because he's trying to avoid us drinking alcohol together, or if this is all some charade to show me what kind of journalist he is. That he's a regular at this place, always here on Friday afternoons. He likes the quiet and how it's not at all trendy. He wants me to picture him moodily typing on his laptop, fueled by endless cups of coffee and the knowledge that in a few hours he'll switch to beer, or meet a woman at his own nearby, go-to date spot.

"Hi," I say. "And yeah, coffee's fine."

I should probably tell him that drinking coffee after noon makes me jumpy and paranoid, more prone to the panic attacks that I hate so much, but it's an admittance that makes me feel sensitive and out of control, like a child whose mother warns them about how they react to sugar.

I arrange myself on the barstool next to him even though it feels awkward, like if we turn to face each other at the same time our knees will bump together. The bartender sets a thick white mug and bowl of plastic, single servings of creamer in front of me. I thank him as I tear one open and pour it into my coffee, focusing on how the milk cuts through the murky liquid as I feel Reese's eyes on me, waiting.

"So you wanted to talk," he starts, ignoring how late I am, like he was working too hard to notice the time. Touché.

"Off the record," I remind him, flourishing the statement with a pointed finger. My manicure is fresh, my nails short and neat, painted bright red, just barely poking out of the too-long sleeve of my sweater.

"Off the record," he nods. "For now."

I raise an eyebrow toward him and drag the wooden stirrer through the coffee, making figure eights. "I can't promise that will change."

"That's fine with me."

A lie, obviously.

I tap the stirrer on the edge of the cup then bring it to my mouth. A splinter catches on my tongue, and I ignore it, even as I taste blood. Reese watches me the whole time.

"Where did you grow up?" I ask, still staring at the coffee as he stares at me.

"Upstate," he says in a way that sounds automatic and practiced, if not a bit surprised. "Near Hudson."

I picture him young, wearing the kid version of those same glasses, running through fields, or farms, or maybe climbing mountains. Sitting by a fire sipping hot chocolate. Isn't that what everyone does upstate?

"Rural?" I ask.

"Sort of," he says, a little awkwardly, like maybe he doesn't want to keep talking about himself, or about this. "My parents were professors, not farmers. NYU."

Ah. This makes sense. A city kid who spent summers at a farmhouse with a saltwater pool, who doesn't like to claim he mostly grew up here because he knows it makes him instantly less relatable to the rest of the world. He probably thinks this improves his odds of connecting with me, skirting around the full truth like this. I think it makes us a little bit the same.

"Hmph," I say, laughing a bit as I bring the mug to my mouth, my sweater-covered hands cradling it like a precious thing. I'm all soft edges today. "My father was both of those things, I think."

Reese sits up instantly straighter then. His wheels are turning. I'm finally giving him something real. Something specific.

"Oh?" he says after a beat, trying to seem casual, like this doesn't thrill him.

I set down the mug, tapping my nails on the side of it, letting them fall one by one.

"He was good-looking," I start. "Not vaguely attractive like the men you usually see in those documentaries. You know the ones, commanding the interest of all these people, luring them in so effortlessly, and you think... really? This guy?"

Reese has slowly swiveled toward me. I can feel his knees pushing into the side of my chair, resting centimeters from my hip. His boot is balancing on my barstool's footrest, and it feels intimate. I glance sideways, and he's rapt, waiting for whatever I'm going to say next. I have his full attention.

"But my father was handsome. He had this ability to make people slow down and pay attention. And that was before he would start talking. He was a magnet, always pulling people in and holding them there. Holding their attention. It was one thing I always admired about him, tried to emulate, I guess. Maybe that's what she meant," I add. "Your source."

I glance over to see Reese's jaw flex for a millisecond. Otherwise, his expression stays the same. "I never said it was a woman."

It was worth a try. "Right. My mistake."

I expect him to say more now, but he stays quiet. Waits.

Maybe he's given himself parameters for this conversation, too. Mine are simple, easy to memorize and abide by. Everything that came before that last day is safe to share, each story an opportunity to get him to trust me.

"Was he always that way? Even before? As a kid?" Reese asks, and I shoot him a look that must read as annoyed, because he backtracks. "Sorry, I just—of course, your memories are essential to the story, but the origin of everything matters too. Is a person like your father born with all the pieces in place, all the ingredients for—"

"Becoming a cult leader?" I say with a burst of easy laughter. It sounds light and airy, which is intentional. He needs to know how ridiculous it all sounds, how much it's all a story that everyone's heard before. It's nothing special. Neither am I.

He does something between a half shrug and a nod. "I just think the psychology is fascinating."

I scoff. Of course he does.

I once watched a documentary about a beloved new age therapist who rose to fame by curing people of addictions through hypnosis. People came in as sex addicts or pack-a-day smokers, and after one session with this man, they were healed. They owed him so much, they said, so they stuck around. They said they would follow him anywhere, and then they did.

Years later, the man oversaw a community of more than seventy-five people living on a sprawling property in Hawaii. He was leading a group of hypnosis sessions every week, convincing each and every one of them to transfer their life savings to him, or have sex with him, or both. There were people in the community who had been raped, who had lost everything they had spent their adult life working for, who had stolen money from their family members just to give it over to this man. But what did the documentary focus on? What were the majority of the expert interviews about? The psychology of it all. Of him. Of how such a smart, talented, pleasant man became such a monster.

"The only beginning to his story I know is the one that starts with my mother," I say. "He was a community college professor. Food Science. She was a student. They fell in love."

I repeat the facts, running through them one by one, ignoring the tide of sadness that rips through me at the thought of my mother. Sometimes I think of her and it feels clinical and distant. Other times, there's just anger. And occasionally, like now, there is only grief, so acute it feels brand new.

"TA," Reese quips, interrupting the emotion.

I blink at him. "What?"

"He was a TA," he says, sipping his coffee between replies. "Teaching assistant."

"What?" I say again, realizing how stupid I sound. I clear my throat. "What do you mean?"

"He was never actually a professor," he says. "Not as far as I've found."

I feel my shoulders hunch as I realize he's one-upped me. I should have done the math by now, I realize. I should have known that it was impossible my father would have already had an important job at such a young age. I should have known that I would never be finished adding to the list of things he had lied to all of us about, everything he had manipulated and weaponized.

"Ah," I say, like it's not a big deal, like it doesn't make me uncomfortable that Reese knows things about my father that I don't, like I'm not wondering now what else he knows that he isn't sharing yet. "Makes sense."

"Tell me about your memories there," Reese starts again, his voice softer, like maybe he feels bad for me, that I apparently didn't know this small, yet still somehow important, detail about my father. "The beginning. The good years."

I take a deep breath, my mind filling with the smell of summer as I remember those afternoon thunderstorms, sheets of rain followed by blistering sunshine, everything steamy and sparkling in the aftermath.

"Well," I begin, but a shout from the other side of the bar cuts me off.

"Catharine," the voice says again, and I feel myself freeze.

"Holy shit, that *is* you," it says again, and I turn to see Stella walking toward us.

Shit is exactly right.

I wave, my smile stretching so unnaturally wide it almost hurts. "Stella! Hey!"

I watch her look from Reese to me and back to Reese again, and I know exactly what she's thinking.

"Didn't you have a date downtown tonight?" I ask, trying to shift my face into something neutral to hide my anxiety.

She shrugs. "Yeah, but it's a blind date. I freaked out last minute and asked to move it up here to that place I like next door. So here I am. Early. Weirdly nervous. I came in here to do a shot for liquid courage. I don't know why I even agree to these things, I swear. I start sweating almost immediately."

I nod, smiling again now trying to figure out how to avoid what I know is coming, knowing I should say something before—

"I'm Reese," he interjects, extending his hand to her.

Shit.

"Stella," she says slowly, her eyes narrowing like something about his name or face has tickled her memory.

I can see her scanning her brain and wait for her to land on the email that he had sent her days ago. I know she must have googled him.

"Wait, wait, wait..." she says, her hands going to her hips. Bingo. "Reese. Like from the email. Cult Reese?"

Reese and I laugh, though his sounds casual and mine sounds high-pitched, hyena-like. Jesus.

"Yeah," Reese starts. "That's me, I guess."

I cut him off before he can keep talking. "Yeah, well. He may have had the wrong Catharine West, but as it turns out he is very charming over email, so here we are."

My back is toward Reese now, and I don't dare turn to look at him and see his reaction.

"Well, well, well," Stella's eyes light up, like this is the best thing she's heard all day. "Talk about a meet cute. My therapist is going to love hearing about this after my months of insistence that people don't meet in person anymore. It's like a movie."

"*Just* like a movie," Reese says, and I can hear the grin in the lilt of his words.

The bartender pushes a tequila shot with a wedge of lime toward Stella, and she thanks him before thrusting it in the air toward us.

"To love," she announces, before tipping it back, wincing as she swallows.

I chuckle a bit and, to my horror, give her a double thumbs-up in response.

Oh my *god*.

"Well, I've gotta run, but we'll talk later, babe," she says with a wink, her voice so sweet it's syrupy. "It was nice to meet you, Reese. I hope you find your cult lady in the end."

"You know, I hope so, too, Stella," Reese says, and I keep my back to him as she walks out the door.

When I'm sure she's gone, I slowly swivel my stool the opposite way, so we're both now facing the bar top.

Reese breaks the silence first. "Charming, huh?"

Even out of the corner of my eye, I can see his grin, the way he's stifling it by biting his bottom lip and failing miserably.

"Hey, Chris?" I say, ignoring Reese, trying to get the bartender's attention. "Can I get a glass of pinot noir?"

Reese laughs.

"I had to say *something*," I finally sigh, explaining the interaction, the lie.

"I mean, hey, don't get me wrong." He shrugs, the stupid grin still there. "I'll take charming."

"Your emails were not charming, trust me."

"Ouch." He laughs. "Though I wasn't really going for charming, I don't think."

The glass of wine is in front of me now, and I take a sip. "What were you going for then?"

He waits for a beat, peeling off the label on the beer bottle in front of him.

When the hell did he order that? When I was so focused on Stella? Or is he just that much of a regular that at 5:30 on the dot, Chris just places it in front of him without asking. It's such a small detail, but I don't like it. I feel like I am existing in a script he has already written.

"Convincing, I think?" he finally says with a bashful half smile, like this is some radical moment of vulnerability and openness for him. Please.

"Is there really a difference? Isn't the end goal the same?"

He considers this, and I take another sip of my wine, strum my nails on the stem.

I get impatient, turning to face him, and now it's my knees that are grazing his hips, my foot on his footrest. "I mean, here we are."

He smiles and nods. "Here we are indeed."

Then there's a longer pause, a charged moment where it's clear things could turn into something else. The bar is half full now, people trickling in after work or before dates. Music hums in the background. It's Friday night. Anything is possible. For a second, I'm convinced he's going to lean into the moment, move slightly to the right so his leg is touching my knee, but he doesn't.

"She doesn't know anything, does she?" he says instead, softly. "She's your best friend, and she doesn't know anything about who you really are? About any of it?"

I consider lying, but in the end I realize that maybe the truth is safer. "No."

"Does anyone?" he asks.

I feel the strap of my dress slide off my shoulder, the movement catching his eye. I don't fix it. "You tell me."

He chuckles, the sound low and gritty in his throat, then tips back his beer. "You're interesting."

I roll my eyes so hard it almost hurts. It's such a boring compliment. "I promise, I'm really not."

"No?"

"A less than perfect childhood doesn't make someone interesting," I quip. "It makes them human."

He doesn't reply immediately but I can feel his eyes traveling over my face, studying me. When I meet his gaze, I expect him to look chastised, but instead he looks challenged. "So it's that simple, huh?" he asks. "A hard childhood. A new, fancy life."

I shrug. "Maybe it is."

"If that was true, I don't think you would be here."

"Who knows?" I say, raising my wineglass to no one in particular. "Maybe I just really love drinking in places that look like they appeared on the 2007 season of *Bar Rescue*."

At this, he really laughs. It's a pleasant sound, like sunlight. It glows.

"I should go," I say. I know I should.

I reach to pull my wallet out of my purse and my library book falls out in the process, landing softly on Reese's tote bag. The room is almost full now, every seat at the bar occupied. Between the chatter and the music, he doesn't even notice.

CHAPTER 14

Then

Linna and I spent weeks rehearsing what my father might say when I brought up the license. I knew I could be convincing, maybe, but he had become increasingly unpredictable. I worried about going to him on the wrong day or meeting him in the wrong mood, how quickly it would be over before we even got a chance to ask.

"You've got this," Linna said, coaching me through the plan one evening in the treehouse. "He listens to you now. More than anyone else here, maybe. You know how to talk to him in a way that means he hears you, like you speak his language or something."

"I don't know about that," I said, brushing off the compliment, then wondering if it was a compliment at all.

She was right, though. Something had changed in the last year. I had become finely tuned in to what my father needed to be happy, what I needed to do to be praised, to be safe. I felt like I had momentum. Every time I got through a moderation fast without complaining, every time I managed to use any discomfort I felt as fuel, letting it buoy me along instead of sink me, I felt powerful. I could feel my father's eyes on me constantly, like he was assessing all of this, charting my dedication. I could feel him trust me. It was part of why I thought the plan about the driver's license might work.

"We'll run through it again, okay?" Linna offered. "I'll be him. Ready?"

I nodded.

"Don't do any of this for me," she bellowed, imitating my father's precise intonation. "Do it because you are better than your most shallow impulses! Because you see yourself in ten years and you want that person to be someone who had the wherewithal to say no to all the things the rest of the world says yes to!"

I laughed at her impression to hide how uncomfortable it made me. I didn't know how to explain that I *wanted* to be that person, the one who said no. That I worshipped that future me, that I did everything in service of her. I'd fall asleep at night tiptoeing into the future, eventually stretching so far that I'd feel myself split in half. If I had to choose one of us, I'd choose her, the me in ten years. I knew that to push myself harder meant discomfort, but it was a welcomed ache. It was proof of improvement. Life was nothing without it. The license was a loophole, a way to satisfy Linna's need to push against the rules and mine to thrive within them.

In the end, it was my father who suggested it. I chose to talk to him after school on a particularly good day when he'd been chipper and alert through lessons, his smile wide and unflinching. "Was there anything I could help with around the farm?" I asked, eyes wide and earnest. I wanted to do more.

He ran his hand across his chin, the sound of his five o'clock shadow rubbing against his palm like sandpaper. He was thinking.

"Well, I could really use some help with farm store pick up and drop-offs," he offered. "It's such a long drive and I can't be leaving the farm for so many hours at time. There's too much to get done here. But we wouldn't want to raise eyebrows. You'd have to get a license—"

"If you think it's a good idea," I said lightly, shrugging. "Plus, it may be good, you know, for the rest of us to be seen out and about. Didn't you say Mr. Crandell asked some strange questions the last time you saw him?"

My father had been paranoid lately, convinced our closest neighbors were watching us, despite the fact that their property was miles away. They knew my father, though, from his trips off the farm, and remembered our family from when we first moved in, when it was just the three of us.

Once, years earlier, my father had let it slip during lessons that the Crandells had originally assumed we were some rural evangelical Christian family. A religious homestead. They were god-fearing people, too, it turned out. He never corrected them, and as far I could tell they had never bothered us beyond the occasional polite hello to my father, normal questions about how the family was doing. Now, though, these were things that seemed to send him spiraling downward, making him suspicious of everyone and everything.

"Your mother could go with you, I guess," he said, like he had just remembered her existence. "She needs fresh air, anyway. I keep telling her... Vitamin D is nature's salve."

My mind flashed to how my mother had looked when I saw her hours earlier, the way it had taken her double the time it should have to complete the usual garden chores, how her breath had sounded labored and shallow as she pulled weeds. She had been sick for months now, the headaches that had plagued her for so long growing more and more frequent. I knew that my father was doing research all the time to fine-tune her healing regimen, but none of it seemed to be working. It wasn't the first time I had wondered if she was following any of it at all. When was the last time I had seen her meditating outside? Doing her breathing exercises? Sticking to the raw diet he had outlined for her? I couldn't remember.

She still had as many good days as bad, though, moments of lightness interspersed between all the fatigue and headaches. There were stretches of time where she seemed like herself again, enough to feel like she was clearly improving. It would be healthy for her to be outside instead of curled up in that twin bed, breathing in stale air.

"Great idea," I said, looking up at my father.

"I'll talk to your mother about it," he said. "Give her some guidelines about where to go, and when."

"Thank you," I said, my body buzzing with excitement.

"Of course." He smiled. "You've earned it."

It was like he always said. Discipline reaps rewards.

My lessons began the next week.

For almost a month, my mother taught me to drive every Tuesday and Wednesday afternoon for an hour, my father often watching us from the old barn.

I climbed into the driver's seat like I was going to work, doing my duty. I was stoic, never cracking a smile. My father needed to feel confident that, for me, this wasn't about escape or fun. This was about contributing to the farm, my family, keeping things going.

For the most part, my mother matched my energy, her mood serious. But every so often I would see the facade fade, joy crackling beneath it. On one of the last weeks of lessons, my father was nowhere to be found. He was busy, and he trusted us to handle it on our own, she said. Her face broke out in a smile so wide and unexpected it almost scared me. She was more energized than I had seen her in months.

There wasn't much left for me to learn at this point, but I stayed focused. Studious. We were at the farthest point from the main building when my mother finally spoke.

"You know this was my car, right?" She laughed. "Still is, I guess, not that I can remember the last time I drove it. But when we first moved here, it was mine. I named it Patsy. After Patsy Cline."

I blinked, lost.

"You know," she nudged me. "She had that song, 'Blue'..."

I stared at her. I had never heard this story, nor of that song. There was some music at the farm. My father had a CD player and a stack of classical albums he kept in the main building. The music would drift over the gardens as we did chores or ate meals. But it was something that he controlled. There were no CDs in the library for us to choose from ourselves. By now we knew better than to complain.

"I used to love just driving around in this thing, singing it over and over. Pure bliss."

I nodded. "Sounds fun."

She studied me for a moment. "This was your idea, right?"

I kept my eyes fixed ahead, acting like I didn't know what she meant.

"The license?" she pushed. "The driving?"

"I just wanted to be helpful," I said, feeling suspicious of her question, then began to turn the wheel, taking the familiar route back to the barn.

"Stop, Rin," she said. "Just park here for minute. We're in no rush."

This was new. We had never paused our lessons before. I did what she asked, slowly, unsure.

"You didn't want to drive, then?" she pushed. "Didn't want a little freedom, maybe?"

The question made me uncomfortable. I shifted in my seat, adjusted my seatbelt. It was cutting into my throat.

"I mean, the driving part seemed fun," I admitted. "But I don't need freedom. I mean, where would I go? Everything I need is here."

"I get it," she said, nodding. "It's like satisfying an urge to break the rules without actually breaking the rules."

I looked in the rearview mirror instinctively, searching for my father.

"What?" I said. "No. It's not like that."

"You really never think about leaving? Just for a few hours, even?"

I shrugged. "That's not against the rules."

She looked at me, her eyes full of something like sadness, or maybe disappointment.

I forced myself to keep talking, to make her understand me. "The door is right there," I said, quoting the phrase my father always used when he talked about leaving the farm. "Same as always."

"You think that?" she said. "That he would just let you leave? Let Linna?"

My heart raced. I replied without thinking. "Of course."

I thought about the month earlier, when I had walked into our room to find him crouched by her bedside, stroking her sweat-soaked hair. "You can always go get a second opinion," he said. "No one is stopping you, beloved." It was a gesture so intimate that I had to turn away for a second, uncomfortable with seeing the two of them so close. It was the most time I had seen him spend with her in years. But she'd just looked at me in the doorway and then back at him. No, she said. Her voice gentle, but resolute. No. This is where I need to be.

"This is good," my mother said, slicing through the memory. She sounded like she was convincing herself of something. "This gives you options."

I turned to face her and she was staring in the rearview mirror now, too, watching. "Options," I echoed.

"If you need something one day, you can get it. A job, a doctor's appointment," she said. "Now you'll know."

"Everything I need is here," I repeated, feeling like a child, stubborn and uncreative. Was that the only thing I could think to say? "That's why you haven't been to the doctor's either, right? You have him. You have this place. You don't need anything else, either."

She swallowed, then turned her face so she was looking out the window, the only thing beyond it acres and acres of knee-high weeds. "That's different."

"How?"

"You'll understand when you're older," she answered.

But this wasn't an answer, not really. It was a platitude, a clichéd phrase that meant nothing. I felt a familiar layer of rage rise in my stomach, a sludge that I knew would travel up and up until I said something horrible. I had learned to control it around my father so well, to push it down, down, down until it settled, but with my mother I had less say over what it did. It always spilled out of me, in the end. I wasn't scared enough of what would happen when it did.

"I promise you, Catharine," she said before I could lash out, her voice some unfamiliar, shaky mixture of adrenaline and grief.

"Life changes your mind about things whether you want it to or not. It just happens."

I rolled my eyes. "We can't all just give up."

She sighed. "What is that supposed to mean?"

"The healing regimen. The vitamin D protocol. You don't even try anymore," I said. "You don't even care enough to try."

I shifted the car back into drive wordlessly, my eyes welling with tears. We were back at the barn before she spoke again.

"It's not true, you know," she said, unbuckling her seatbelt. "It's all I've ever done. With you, with him, with this place. Try is all I've ever fucking done."

She climbed out of the car and shut the door before I could reply.

CHAPTER 15

Now

"Can I just say," Stella says when I open my front door, hand outstretched in my direction, holding a green juice. "Only you would find that gorgeous of a man on accident."

It's early Saturday afternoon and I've agreed to a post–Friday night debrief on my couch.

"Hi, Stella." I laugh, gesturing for her to come inside. "Welcome. Nice to see you, too."

She steps out of her sneakers and walks to the small kitchen, making herself at home. Stella has a gorgeous apartment on the Upper East Side, but she has roommates. My place, she says, makes her feel calm, grounded. Like a real adult.

"And can *I* just say, once again," I add. "That we were just talking."

"Right," Stella says between sips of juice. "And fucking."

"We're not." I laugh, putting my hands up. "We're friends. It's friendly."

I realize it feels true as I say it. Reese and I had talked like friends, joked like friends. New friends maybe, but friends, nonetheless. My mind flashes to the moment when I left the bar last night, my fallen book unacknowledged. I have another meeting now, anyway, he said, and I had looked around the crowded room and laughed. "A date, you mean?" I asked. "Not a date," he said, smiling, like something about the way I had asked the question had amused him. It felt playful, when I focused on single moments, split seconds of banter. But then I zoom out. I remember how it felt when I got home later, the way I had paced around my apartment, fixating on the conversation.

It was subtle, the way he had played his hand. The teaching assistant detail was, I'll admit, a surprise. A successful way to throw me off balance, if only for a moment, and to remind me of all the other potential information he has gathered over the years. But it was also a deliberate, indulgent way to stroke his own ego. To flaunt that he was in more control of the situation than I was.

So, no. We are not friends.

"Mhm," Stella nods, plopping herself in a love seat by the window, tucking her ankles under her. "Sure looked friendly."

"How was your date?" I ask, glad to change the subject.

"Well," she starts. "He spent the first half of the night talking about cryptocurrency, and the second half talking about his mom, and there was a not-so-insignificant portion of overlap in between."

She sucks down the dregs of her green juice loudly, then gets up again and crosses the room to the kitchen, tossing the empty cup in the trash.

"Good thing you took that shot I guess," I offer.

She laughs. "Oh, you have no idea."

She's halfway across the room when she stops abruptly, her eyes fixed on a shelf near the entryway. She takes a step closer, her vision zooming in on a selection of framed photos.

Shit.

"Whoa," she says, picking up a photo in a thick wooden frame. "Is this you?"

I control my breathing and stand slowly, walking over to her and then pausing, both of us staring at the photo in her hands. It's my only photo from the farm. In it, Linna and I are standing outside the old barn, the two of us in paint-splattered, adult-sized, button-down shirts that had been turned backward. Makeshift smocks. Ben and Bertie are behind us, Ben's arm wrapped around Bertie's bony shoulders. Linna and I were almost seven that summer, and it had rained almost ceaselessly, the most precipitation the state had seen in years, my father said. We were restless. Bertie had put together a makeshift art studio in the old barn, helping us create whatever we wanted. My mother had snapped the photo, inviting Ben into the shot as he came by to say hi to Bertie, stealing a quick kiss. I look at the photo and can feel my skin, sticky from humidity and paint. I can smell the soil, warm earth soaked with summer rain. It has been so long since I let myself remember those early days.

The photo was one of the few things I kept from the farm, an item that I tucked away years ago. In the time before I met Stella, I displayed it only to punish myself—a daily visual reminder that I had made mistakes, that there was a reason I was alone. Eventually, I hid it away because it made life feel more survivable to forget. But after yesterday's meeting with Reese, I came home determined to find it, to put it in the frame again. I had dug through my closet and found it tucked inside a notebook, then ripped a generic photo of a sunset out of its frame. I had told Stella it was a shot from a favorite childhood vacation, but really I had found it in a thrift shop. It was someone else's sun-soaked memory. The second I had replaced it with the photo of Linna and me and put it back on the shelf, I had felt myself regain something.

"Yeah," I reply, taking the photo from her and bringing it another inch closer to my face. She cranes her neck, still studying it.

"And who's that?" she asks, pointing to Linna, who is mid-laugh in the photo, a thick slash of blue paint across her cheek. I am standing next to her, holding up my paintbrush proudly.

I consider telling Stella she's a cousin, but somehow even that feels too close to the truth. It's easier if she thinks Linna is no one to me; there will be fewer questions that way.

"An old friend." I shrug. "I don't even remember her last name now. But I loved that summer camp."

"And them?" Stella asks, pointing toward Ben and Bertie.

"Counselors," I answer. "Art camp."

The lie stings as it leaves my mouth.

"Wow, artsy Catharine," Stella says, shrugging as she walks away and tucks herself back into the chair. "Who knew?"

I'm relieved when I hear my phone buzz across the room. I speed-walk over, but Stella is closer and has already reached for it. She glances at the screen before handing it to me and her face breaks into a wide grin. "Well, well, well... would you look at that."

REESE CAMPBELL is scrolling across the caller ID.

Took him long enough.

"I have to take this," I tell Stella, walking toward the front door and opening it.

"Of course," she says as she slips on her shoes and saunters into the hallway, already waving her fingers in a goodbye gesture. "What's more important than privacy for calls with completely platonic friends?"

I laugh, closing the door behind her, then answer. "Hi, Reese."

"Library girl, huh?"

I scoff loud enough that I make sure he can hear me.

He tries again. "Library . . . woman?"

"Just a woman who goes to the library, Reese," I say. "It's safe to assume it is *you* who has my missing book, then?"

"Yours truly."

"How'd you find this number?" I ask.

"I guess I could say through hours of painstaking investigative research," Reese muses. "But it was probably the 'return to reader' customized leather bookmark with your contact information that did it."

I smile. I had paid $100 in rush shipping to have the custom bookmark mailed overnight. "And to think I once told my ex that that was a completely useless gift."

I expect him to linger on the mention of an ex, the most subtle of nods toward my sexuality, but he doesn't.

"Look, are you around today?" he says. "I can meet you in the park with the book in, say, two hours?"

I hesitate for a split second to consider the best reply, and in the pause, he answers for me. "Great. I'll drop you a pin. See you then." Then he hangs up.

After the call, I pace the apartment, anxious. He hadn't mentioned anything about the book. Not the title, nor the author. Had he even looked at it? Had he somehow not noticed? And if he did, but still didn't make the connection, was it because he didn't know that his source was actually Marion Earl, or because I had imagined the entire thing? Paranoia pokes at me, a popcorn kernel slicing into my gums. I consider, once again, that maybe all of this has been a bluff. My father was only a teaching assistant. What else had I missed?

It occurs to me that maybe I am willing to believe anything, no matter how far-fetched, if it means that my sister is alive. My desperation had made me lazy, soft.

I walk over to the photo of the four of us again and stare. Referring to Linna, Ben, and Bertie as people who were barely more than strangers to me had been painful. They all felt like family. Ben and Bertie were the only version of grandparents I had ever known. It was why I changed my last name to one of theirs when I moved to the city. Catharine West felt like an entirely plausible version of me. Clutching the photo in my hands, the memory seems to sharpen in my mind's eye—the timeline, the exact series of events. They all feel more important than ever. I make myself remember.

CHAPTER 16

Then

The next time I showed up at the barn for a driving lesson, there was no one there to meet me. The old truck was parked inside. I waited for half an hour before I realized no one was coming. I wasn't sure if this meant my lessons were done, or if maybe something about the fight with my mother had taken the possibility of a driver's license off the table altogether. But I was so close. Four weeks of lessons, my father had said, and then I could go with him to the DMV and get my license, and soon after start making trips. This was meant to be my final week.

I checked the main building, searching for my mother in the dining hall, then the kitchen. When I eventually opened the door to our room, though, I was almost mad at myself. Of course, she was sick again—her body curled into itself on the bed like a dog trying to stay warm. I winced at how small she looked. I kept having moments like this, where I'd instantly realize just how much worse she had gotten. It made me feel disoriented, like I had somehow slept through entire days and years of deterioration. I tried to close the door quietly, but she stirred at the sound. I had woken her up.

"I'm sorry," I whispered. "I'm going."

Her hand went to her head. "Right. The lessons."

"It's fine," I started. "We can do it another day."

"Your father will take you out today, Rin," she explained. "I wish I could go, but..."

I felt a wave of guilt over the argument we had had at the last lesson, how cruel I had been and how quickly she had let it roll off of her. "Can I get you anything?"

"No, honey," she said. "I'll be okay."

The entire walk to my father's cottage, I tried to convince myself of this, too.

The long path that stretched from the main building to the cottage was lined with sunflowers. A few years earlier, he had decided that each of the four paths that stemmed from the main building would be accented with different types of flowers. It was a gorgeous idea, one that made everyone happy to imagine. We had started with the sunflowers, planting them too close together, all of them eventually growing tall and forming a sort of tunnel above the path. In the summer, Linna and I would sit in the shadiest spots and stare up, the wide blossoms bobbing in the breeze. In the end, this was the only path that had been properly planted. We had run out of manpower. There were so many other more important things to focus on.

Linna and I loved the sunflowers, but we'd only go so far down the path. It was a universally agreed upon rule that the cottage was off-limits for anyone except my father, barring an invitation from him directly. We all respected this because we knew what the cottage represented. There was a time when even watching Ben and my father build it together, piece by piece, had been thrilling. The cottage would be built first, they had explained, and then all the other big changes would follow. It was the symbol of things improving, the establishment of a headquarters for helping the farm run smoothly. We all stood out front on the day it was done and applauded as my father hung the final shutter on the windows outside. I knew there were times when my mother, or Linna's, had visited him there in the early days, but I hadn't been back to the cottage myself in years.

I knew it was risky to just show up there, but I was so close to being done with lessons that I couldn't wait. What's more, as I got closer, and the small, neat shape of it came into view, I found it hard to feel trepidation at all. It still looked exactly how I remembered it, like something out of a storybook, planted in the middle of a splash of wildflowers.

I took another deep breath as I approached the door, reminding myself that my mother had told me to seek him out. Hadn't she? Besides, this would show just how eager I was to help out, to start contributing to the farm in a real, concrete way. He trusted me now. That was what mattered. This is what I told myself when I knocked on the door.

It took at least a minute before I finally heard the lock click, something I'd only noticed because it had been so long since any other room on the farm had required a key. I remembered watching my father use a screwdriver to remove the locks one by one, collecting all of them in a plastic bucket. *Privacy only creates deception*, he had said. As he did it, I already felt less compelled to hide things. I concluded that he must be right. The cottage was different, though, I remembered, home to all the documents and systems that made the farm work. Obviously, he had to protect all of that.

When the door finally opened and I saw the look on my father's face, I considered that maybe I had miscalculated. He looked deeply irritated, more annoyed than I had ever seen him. His hair was disheveled, his eyes hooded and red. It looked like I had just woken him up, though that was impossible. It was the middle of the day.

I knew he trusted me now, but maybe I had gone too far. I was about to apologize and turn the other way when he spoke.

"Catharine," he said. "How can I help you?"

"I was just…" I started, stammering, my eyes shifting from his to the ground, back and forth. "My driving lessons. Mother isn't feeling well."

He sighed, an exasperated gust of air flying from his mouth toward me. Leaning on the doorframe, he crossed his arms in front of him. It was the first time I noticed he was wearing a thick knit cardigan. How was he not sweating?

Then, before I could say anything, he turned back inside and closed the door behind him, a burst of cold swooshing my direction. Seconds later, he emerged again, this time in his standard tank top. He locked the door behind him and started walking, seeming newly energized. "Come with me."

My spirit lifted, assuming that we were now on our way to my final driving lesson. But then he walked into the main building instead of going past it toward the old barn. I followed him into the dining hall and watched as he opened the door to a small closet near the stage. For years, the closet had been used to store gardening tools, extra rakes and shovels and shears.

I peered into the dark over his shoulder and was surprised to find the small space almost completely empty. The only thing left was a scale on the floor.

He stepped aside, gesturing toward the thing.

I stared at him, trying to make sure I understood. "You want me to get on?"

"Please."

This scale was different from the industrial kinds we used to weigh produce, measuring out orders for the farmers market, organizing pricing, tracking growth. But I'd never considered using those to weigh myself. I couldn't have even guessed what I weighed. I hesitated, confused. He had become more fascinated recently with tracking discipline, creating a scientific measure of whether or not we were obeying the rules and following the moderation fasts. A month earlier, he had instructed all of us to start journals and keep careful track of our food intake, with him then reviewing and signing off on the entries at the end of every week. I tried to tell myself that this request with the scale was something similar, but it felt different.

"Honestly, Catharine," he rolled his eyes. "You look terrified. It's not a big deal. It's something I'm testing out. A statistics thing, really."

His tone was casual, but the moment felt taut with something I couldn't quite place. Dread. Pressure. I craned my neck, peering into the dark, narrow space. The closet was so small, barely enough room to stand in. It made me feel claustrophobic just looking at it.

Then I reminded myself of what he had said. This was not a big deal. He knew what he was doing. I had almost summoned the courage to take a step forward when a voice chimed in from behind me. "Don't be shy, honey. I'll go first."

It was Rhonda, a dish towel thrown over her shoulder. She must have heard us from the kitchen.

"Rhonda," my father greeted her, his tone unenthusiastic. "Great. Be our guest."

She handed me the towel before stepping on. It only took a second before the number populated on the scale's small screen.

"How much?" my father asked, a question that struck me as

odd when the number was fully visible to all of us. He wanted her to say it out loud, I realized. She recited it, her voice almost proud, no doubt pleased with herself that she had given him exactly what he wanted.

My father clicked his tongue, recording the number down on a notebook that he had pulled out of his back pocket. "Worse than I thought," he muttered.

My eyes flashed to Rhonda, and she looked horrified. This was not how she had expected things to go. "Oh," she said.

My breath was getting shallower now, the realization that I had no idea what he was looking for setting in. This was a game I didn't know how to win.

"Better next time, yes?" he said to Rhonda. "Consider it a starting point, a place from which to improve. A built-in, biological discipline gauge."

Rhonda looked like she was about to cry, but she just nodded as she stepped off the scale. It was almost admirable the way she stayed upright, her chin jutting slightly outward. It was the unmistakable look of a woman who would use this to fuel her later. "Yes," she said. "A starting point."

Part of me hoped he had forgotten about my presence now, that I could quietly slip out of the room and disappear, but of course he hadn't. "Your turn, little one."

I took a deep breath and exhaled, like some part of me believed the extra air might add to the number, then stepped on the scale. The closet was even smaller from the inside. My father was standing directly in front of me now, his body blocking the view into the dining hall, his foot propping open the door. All he'd have to do was take one step back, lock the door and I'd be stuck here. I remembered how quickly the whole thing had gone with Rhonda. Just a few seconds, I told myself. I closed my eyes as I waited for the number to appear on the screen, only opening it when my father asked me to recite it to him out loud.

I read it out. It was less than Rhonda's weight, but I was so much shorter than her. Of course it would be less. I had no idea what was enough.

"Excellent," my father had said. "Beautiful."

So much pressure lifted off of me then, so instantaneously, that I felt I might actually float toward the ceiling. Up, up, up. It felt like all those times I had followed the rules but better, because now it wasn't just some abstract thing, my own belief I was good. Now, there was numerical proof of it. The relief of it was so overwhelming I could have cried.

"I knew you were following the fasts," he said, scribbling the number before slapping the notebook shut. "But it never hurts to be sure, of course. Accountability is everything here. You know that."

I nodded. "I do."

He beamed at me, his smile knowing, like he was about to bestow upon me a great gift. "Now let's go get that license, shall we?"

I couldn't believe I had been so worried before. I thought of all the moments that had shown me how deeply flawed I was, how hopelessly out of control. The question I had asked in class. The hungry thing inside me that pushed toward rebellion, danger. All that wrongness.

I closed my eyes and could still see the glowing number on the scale, my father's pride. All this time, I realized, I had been searching for proof that I was good. Finally, here it was. I had never felt better about myself.

CHAPTER 17

Now

By the time I leave to meet Reese at the park, I am bouncing off the walls. I decide to jog there to burn off some of my anxious energy. I look in the mirror before I walk out the door and I realize that, head to toe, I'm probably wearing a thousand dollars of gear, maybe more. The right shoes, the right leggings, the right sports bra, the right sweat-wicking, heat-tech shirt. The headphones that still let you hear the man coming up behind you with a snide remark, a wandering hand, a knife. I shrug. It doesn't seem like that bad of a deal, not really. A thousand dollars to shut off my brain for an hour, to make the next day of eating and existing that much easier. A thousand dollars to feel part of the club. Be a Person Who Runs. Money well spent.

I'm less than a mile in when I realize that today, my brain doesn't seem to be cooperating. Every person in the park reminds me of Linna, her name echoing in my head until I feel it turn into a shapeless mush, a sediment settling into my veins.

I turn my music up louder but all I hear is my own labored breathing. Everything about running feels hard today, and not in the way that makes me feel challenged, or proud. Rock solid.

Instead, it is the type of run where it feels like I've never done this before in my life, that I'm just a person wearing a thousand-dollar costume. A joke.

I slow to a walk, embarrassed as another Linna lookalike zooms past me, no doubt hitting the perfect pace in her fourth mile, her fifth. I stare at the ground and feel embarrassed, weak. I'm normally so good at this. I fly.

I stop at a bench and sit down, thankful I got here early enough to cool down before Reese arrives. There are two women about my age walking slowly down the opposite side of the path, leaning forward in unison to read the inscription on every bench they pass. The sound of laughter drifts toward me as one of the women places a hand over her heart, her mouth melting into a frown the way people's expressions sometimes do when they see something so sweet it makes them want to cry. I should smile at the scene, but my only reaction is to tap my foot. I'm antsy, anxious. I consider texting Reese that I'm here early, on the off chance that maybe he is, too, but I resist the urge. I need to calm down.

I place my hand on the back of the bench and twist at the waist, stretching my spine. As I do, I catch sight of the inscription on my own bench.

To Penelope. I would have sat right here with you forever.—Clark

Ah, Clark. Poor Clark. I wonder where he is now. If he spends his days seeing Phantom Penelope everywhere. If this comforts him or drives him mad. If he can't even look at this bench now, or if it's the only thing that keeps him going. Either way, I get it. I understand Clark. There's nothing more all-consuming than the knowledge that you would have gladly stayed with someone in one spot forever, if only it meant things wouldn't change.

My phone lights up. It's Reese.

"Be there in 10."

I react to the message with a thumbs-up and use my phone's front camera to check my appearance, smoothing down rogue hairs. I sit up straighter and sniff my armpits, just in case. Then I lean back and cross my legs, watching the two women walk away together, stopping at each bench, marveling at every message.

The first thing I notice is that Reese is not wearing glasses today, a deviation from what I've come to know about him.

"Are you wearing contacts?" I ask as he approaches the bench.

He sits down next to me. "No?" he says. It comes out like a question, like he isn't quite sure why I would be asking. I give him a second, and he figures it out. "Oh. The glasses are for blue light."

I stare at him.

"And, you know, to look older, if I'm honest." He shrugs. "I listened to a podcast once about how wearing glasses can make people take you ten percent more seriously."

There's something about this kind of bald-faced effort that I usually find so unattractive, at least when it comes to myself. I go to great lengths to conceal it, like it's a terrible rash, the first thing anyone would ever notice about me and the last thing they would remember. But with him, it reads as self-effacing. He wanted people to take him seriously. Most people would probably think it's charming.

"Also, hi," he adds. "I'm doing great today, thanks for asking, Catharine. How are you?"

"I'm fine."

He chuckles, then reaches into his bag and pulls out my library book.

I run my fingers over the plastic-wrapped cover, tracing the title and byline.

Lighthouse by Marion Earl. Her short story collection. I think of my prized personal copy at home, stolen from the very same library years ago. Maybe I would steal this one, too. I can feel Reese's eyes travel from my face to my hands, watching me.

"That good, huh?" He laughs.

I focus my eyes in his direction. "I'm sorry?"

"I've never seen someone look at a book that way."

I can feel my heart racing now, blood glugging through my limbs. He is acknowledging something. I can sense it. I try to stay calm.

I laugh. "I've only read the first story."

At this, he looks confused. "Really?"

I shrug. "I've been busy..."

My chest tightens as the words leave my mouth. The lie feels heavy and obvious. To not explain exactly what I love about Marion Earl's work to anyone who will hear it, to not make them pull up her website and order one of her books that very second, is a foreign experience to me. But I can't do that now. It would be too obvious. I need to see how Reese reacts, what he will give away.

I put the book in my small running backpack and lay it flat on my lap, then place my hands on top. I can still feel Reese's eyes on me the entire time, assessing something.

"Well, it's great," he finally says. "Pretty remarkable, actually."

Remarkable.

Every part of me wants to talk to him about the book, but I have to remind myself that this is just part of his game. That he is probably bursting right now, delighted by his distinctive upper hand, the fact that I am so close to his source without even knowing it. I gasp in faux horror, disguising my true reaction. "You read *my* library book? I think that's illegal."

He laughs. "*Definitely* not illegal. And for the record, I read it a couple years ago," he offers, then pauses for a beat. "And then again, actually, more recently."

I feel fireworks going off inside my head, but I sit perfectly still. His tone is more serious now. There is no mistaking it.

"Impressive," I say, keeping my voice even.

He ignores my sarcasm and leans closer to me, his voice a whisper. "Also, I hate to break it to you, but underlining and writing in the margins of library books is *also* maybe illegal."

Instantly, I realize my mistake. Somehow I had given him my original copy. I grip the book on my lap, hating myself for how careless I was. I don't know whether to feel grateful or patronized that he is ignoring my lie. It must be obvious now that I hadn't only read that first story, but he doesn't point out the dishonesty.

It's clear that he is playing with me. I should get up and walk away, collect myself and come back fresh, but I feel so close to the truth, so close to my sister, that I am frozen.

"How did you find me, Reese?" I blurt. "Really."

He seems taken aback by this. "I told you, at the diner. That first meeting."

I shake my head. "No, you didn't. You said I was a hard person to find. Not how you found me."

He adjusts himself on the bench, uncrossing then recrossing his legs. "You know I can't tell you that, Catharine."

"Because it will identify who your source is."

Because there is only one person who would know exactly how to find me, who would eventually guess exactly what name to type into Google.

He glances down, and his eyes go toward the backpack on my lap. The book. A silent message. I have to remind myself to breathe. For the thousandth time in the last decade, it's all I can think of: *I need to know or it will kill me. I need to know or it will kill me. I need, I need, I need.*

"What if I agree to go on the record?" I ask. "Give you a whole interview. The real thing."

He stares at me, considering the offer. I know I should stop there, but I can't. I don't care what it will mean risking.

"Would you tell me then?" I push. "Could I see her then?"

"I don't know if they're ready to see you, Catharine," he says. I notice he doesn't correct my use of *she*. "It's . . . a lot. They've been through a lot."

I know, I want to scream. You don't think I know?

"I will tell you whatever you want," I offer, the words leaving my mouth before I fully register them. I know how desperate I sound, but it feels cathartic, to voice my true feelings. All that want. "About all of it."

It is scary to offer him so much of my past, give him more access than I have to anyone else. But I remind myself that there is still a line I will not cross, one story I will not tell, and that comforts me. There is so much other pain and humiliation to serve up to him. So many things that would make his jaw drop, make his brain stir with possibilities and headlines. All of them are memories I'd rather not talk about, if given the choice, but it's beginning to feel like I don't have one anymore. The possibility of seeing Linna is too close, too all-consuming.

Reese considers this for a second, then gets up and pulls his phone from his pocket. "Let me make a call."

Twenty minutes feel like two days as I sit there, waiting. I watch Reese walk back and forth in the distance, one hand stuffed into his pocket. The idea that Linna might be on the other end of the call makes me want to run across the lawn and rip the phone from his hands, but I stay still. I wait. When he finally comes back, he looks tired.

"So?" I ask.

He pauses before replying, choosing his words carefully. "They're still processing a lot of what happened. It's not been a totally easy transition to the real world for them and now that they're happy, successful..."

I swear he glances down again then, in the direction of the book. I don't dare interrupt him.

"They value their privacy. I don't know if they're totally ready to give that up yet."

I nod intensely. Of course, they value being alone. Still, there was that *yet*. They're not there *yet*.

"I also think they're a little worried you'd be angry," he says. "That they exposed you to this. To me, I guess. Blew up your own happy, comfortable, private life. They've been considering sharing their own story for a couple years now. But yours... well, it's yours. They respect that."

It almost pains me how much this sounds like Linna. To think that, after everything, she'd still be considering my own struggles. It's exactly her.

I need to know or it will kill me.

I need to know or it will kill me.

"One question," I try. "Answer one question and I'll go on the record. Please."

Reese sighs, exasperated, like maybe I've finally broken him down. "One question."

"How did they know how to find me?"

He nods, silent, his eyes fixed on passing joggers for a few seconds before he turns toward me. "They told me about Ben and Bertie Abramson. That you three were close. She could barely remember them, really, but she said if I could find more information about them, that maybe I would find you. Bertie's maiden name was West. It wasn't exactly much of a stretch after that."

I knew it was risky when I changed my last name, that maybe someday it would allow someone to connect the dots, even if it was unlikely. Bertie loved to tell Linna and me how much she had regretted changing her name to Ben's, how we should always stick to our gut instincts. All these years, I had remembered it. It helped that West was such a generic surname. There were a dozen other Catharine Wests in the world when I changed my name, and thousands more Katherine and Kathryn and Catherine Wests beyond that. I knew a more generic spelling was likely a safer option, but I couldn't bring myself to change it. It was a name my father had carefully chosen. Every time I doodled a different version of it, my heart raced. In those early days, it felt like an act of rebellion so direct that it would immediately summon him from the shadows. Keeping my given first name and changing my last to something that reminded me of Ben and Bertie felt like a compromise I could live with. Besides, if there was anything I wanted to keep from the farm beyond Linna, it was them.

But the reason it ultimately felt safe was because of something else. Yes, Linna knew how close I was to Ben and Bertie, maybe more so than anyone else on the farm, but she was also the only one left who would have remembered them. Ben and Bertie died just before the busiest years, when new people came and went frequently.

Reese has angled himself into the corner of the bench now, so he faces me. I can tell he's watching me react. I can't imagine what my face looks like. It is the first time in years I have felt this. I am swimming in hope, trying not to drown.

I turn toward him, smiling weakly. "I knew it was her."

CHAPTER 18

Then

By the time my father suggested that Linna join me on one of the drives into town, almost a year had passed. The trips to pick up supplies or drop off produce had become a near-weekly occurrence by then. At first, my father insisted on going with me for each of them, like he had to see for himself that I could handle it. We would take the same route each time, turning out of the property onto a long, mostly empty country road and eventually turning again onto the highway, then driving in silence until we arrived at the familiar intersection.

He must have known I remembered the intersection, the place where we had turned left in the past so many times on the way to the big town. But now, I'd fix my eyes ahead of me each time we passed, ignoring the turn altogether, like I couldn't possibly recall the trips I took there as a kid.

When I was younger, it was normal for all of us to go into the big town once or twice a year. There were boxes that needed to be checked so people didn't pay attention to us, my father said. Checkups. Dentist appointments. Necessary evils, my father explained. As I got older, the appointments had become less and less frequent, but of course I still remembered. Linna and I would look forward to those days all year, discussing the details of what we had seen in town, what new things we had experienced. I could still recall the time a receptionist had offered me a lollipop at the end of my appointment. I had stared at my father, panicked, and he just laughed at me. "Well, don't be shy, Catharine," he said, as if that was the only reason I was hesitating.

We were only driving for a minute or two before he reached over and pulled it out of my mouth, the candy cracking loudly against my teeth as he yanked it away. I watched him throw it out the window and realized that my taking the lollipop had been checking a box, too.

But I never brought up those appointments on those early drives with him, never talked about the big town. Never stopped unless I was told to. I simply waited for as long as it took for him to speak first, to start pointing out the important parts of the scenery I was missing. The man at the gas station who was paying for mini bottles of Jack Daniels with quarters and dimes. The omnipresent drive-through line that wrapped around the Burger King. The elderly woman standing in the median, wrinkled fingers curling around a soggy cardboard sign, a message written on the front saying that anything helps. At the last instance, my father had rolled down the window and asked if she would prefer a few dollars or a few boxes of fresh produce. Without hesitation, the woman said a few dollars. He didn't even reply. Instead, he had rolled up his window, then turned to me. "See? This is what it's like out here." I was relieved that the light turned green a second later, that I could press the gas, determined not to look in the rearview mirror. I was even more relieved that the farm meant we never had to make those choices ourselves.

After a couple months, my obedience paid off. My father said I could make the trips with my mother, a loosening of control that I saw as the final step before it was Linna and I going ourselves. It was just an added benefit that the drives seemed to help my mother's now almost daily headaches, giving her a boost of energy that she badly needed. I knew she was still sick, that there were still stretches of time she spent in bed, but every time I'd see her in the passenger seat, I swore I could feel her getting better.

She didn't watch me like my father did, either. Instead, she'd close her eyes, tilt her face toward the sun, let the wind whip through her hair until it completely covered her face, not bothering to push it out of the way. For the first time in a long time, she seemed like herself, or closer to it, anyway. On one trip, after a string of particularly good days, I worked up the courage to apologize about how cruel I had been to her. It felt so vulnerable to admit I had been wrong, so dangerous, that I had to gather the strength to do it for weeks.

"You seem better," I started, cautious.

She smiled. "I do feel good today."

"I'm sorry for what I said..." I muttered. "Before. During driving lessons. I can tell that I was wrong, that you're doing everything you can, following the regimen...I mean, just look at you lately. I think it's really working...I should have known. I mean, he said it would take time, that healing isn't instant...I should have listened..."

When she didn't reply right away, my eyes darted from the road over to her, assessing her reaction. The smile had faded from her eyes. "It's okay, Rin," she said. "You don't have to apologize to me. I understood why you were upset."

We hadn't talked about the argument since the day it happened, not even once. For a long time, I interpreted her silence to mean she knew I was right. She hadn't been following the rules at all. It seemed like that was what she was trying to say now, but I could tell she was holding back. "You did?"

"I did," she said. "I do."

I hesitated, debating whether or not to push more. I wanted to be completely sure that we were on the same page. I wanted there to be no doubt. It felt like the only thing that would keep us both safe. Instead, I told myself not to spoil the moment and stared at the highway, the asphalt ahead undulating with heat, my father's words from that day on the scale echoing in my head. *Excellent. Beautiful.* I felt locked into something powerful, my commitment finally larger than my fear. I wanted to turn to my mother and say that I wasn't upset at all anymore. I was excellent. I was beautiful. I was good.

The strings of good days soon ended, though, and when they were gone, things seemed to take a turn. My mother was too sick to help me carry the supplies to the truck, then too sick to even get out of the car, and then, eventually, too sick to come at all. I told myself that this was just a bump in the road. She'd get better again. By the time my father suggested Linna join me for one of the trips instead, I had deluded myself completely. She would rest and get better. And in the meantime, finally, I would get to go on an adventure with Linna.

We had been spending more and more time apart since I had started helping with the pick-up and drop-off trips. Linna had recently moved into a spare room in the main building at my father's directive, a development that I had expected would thrill her. She only complained about the change, though, grumbling about having to move all of her things. I tried not to take it personally. We still met at the treehouse most nights to talk through everything, but I could tell something was shifting with her. She was restless, bored. Even the romance with Kent had lost its sparkle a little, it seemed.

This, though, would be something new. A road trip. A shared responsibility. Adulthood. It wasn't that I thought one afternoon in the car would satisfy her need for excitement, but I was convinced it would remind her of what she kept missing: There were so many ways to be happy within this life, if she was willing to look for them, to work for them.

We were set to leave at 8 a.m. on a Friday morning. I woke up at 6 to make sure my chores were done and to ensure that absolutely everything was in place. I knew that this, too, would be a test. Nothing could go wrong.

It was the very beginning of spring, the mornings still chilly but the days already spiking into the eighties or nineties. I shivered that morning as I walked through the kitchen, reminding myself to grab a sweater from my room before the trip. I thought of how I had quietly closed the door behind me and padded across the empty dining hall to the kitchen, careful not to wake my mother. She was finally sleeping, after tossing and turning all night.

I filled a kettle and put it on the stove to heat up, rubbing my arms to stay warm. I couldn't wait for the cup of hot tea, extra grateful that it was the one thing that had never disappeared from my diet. I could still remember the smell of coffee brewing from when I was a child, how it filled the main building each morning. But that was before my father researched the addictive properties of caffeine. Tea was better for all of us, he explained. Just then, Linna skipped into the kitchen, making a face that was something like a silent scream, a signal of how excited she was. It must have been two or three years since she had left the farm.

"I know, I know," I whispered. "I can't wait."

She waited with me by the stove, then poured herself a cup of tea before grabbing a giant carrot out of the fridge, the focus of our current fast. There was a single window above the stove that overlooked part of the gardens, where a rabbit had hopped into view. It was quietly going about its morning, paws wet from dew, nose twitching furiously.

"Think he's jealous?" Linna said, loudly biting into the carrot.

I laughed.

"Trust me, buddy," she said, gesturing toward the rabbit with the carrot. "It's not as fun in here as it looks."

I smiled but shushed her, imagining my father lurking somewhere nearby and punishing us for Linna's jokes by taking away the trip. We couldn't afford that. I filled a mason jar with water and made another cup of tea for my mother. A blip of guilt fluttered across my chest. The weekly drives had become a time that was just ours, but I knew she needed to rest whenever possible on the bad days, to let her body heal itself. She would sleep all day, hiding from the sun, waiting for the worst of the headaches to pass. What good did I really do for her waiting around?

"Let me bring this to her and then we'll get ready to go," I said to Linna.

She nodded, still watching the rabbit.

As soon as I entered our room, I was itching to leave. The air was stale, the walls caked in invisible grime. The one, small window hadn't been opened in weeks, my mother's need to block out the sun outweighing our desire for fresh air.

As I set her drinks down on a side table, I heard a small sound and knew she was in one of her in-between states. Not quite asleep but not lucid, either. She'd mumble things that didn't make sense, talk to shadows like they were people. Unfiltered and childlike. I just nodded, cringing as I reached for the doorknob to leave. "The tea is hot, so just be careful..."

She replied by making the sound again, saying something into her pillow. I couldn't make out what she was saying but could hear the frustration in her voice.

"I'll be back soon," I said, and she gurgled the half word again.

"Get some rest, okay?"

And then I shut the door and walked outside.

CHAPTER 19

Now

I spend the next hour in the park painting Reese a detailed portrait of my childhood while he records on his phone. I start at the beginning, telling him about the farm, the crops, the unparallelled joy of all that open space. Every day, I tell him, I walked outside and saw a thousand miles of possibility. I could stretch and run, build and grow. There is nothing that compares to that feeling, I explain. Not one thing.

"You really felt like you could leave?" he pushes. "At any time?"

The question reminds me of something my mother asked once, and I shrug off the memory.

"Sure," I answer. "For a long time, anyway. That's what he told us. I believed it. I believed him."

Reese nods, waiting for me to go on.

I tell him about Ben and Bertie arriving. I tell him about Jessie, Rhonda, and Kent. I tell him about the fasts, the weigh-ins. And the entire time, I watch him. I watch his eyes fill with alarm, then empathy, then confusion. I watch him wonder how all of us could have been so very gullible, though he knows enough not to say it. It's when I mention Linna, though, that I see something on his face change.

At first, I think it's a coincidence. But eventually, there's no mistaking it. Every time I say her name, he looks away. I wonder what he thinks he will reveal, exactly, when he looks at me. Does he know I know who his source is? Is he worried he's already given away too much?

He's staring at his hands, eyes focused on his notebook, when I tell him about how Linna and I had fought about Kent, how silly it all was to me now.

"Every time I remember it now, I just think... what a waste." I shake my head. "What a fucking waste."

I expect him to press further, but he seems uncomfortable and abruptly changes the subject, asking me about my mother and her headaches. I launch into the details, the whole sad story, but my mind is still on my sister and the book sitting on my lap.

For a long time, never knowing what, exactly, happened to Linna felt like a gift. I could tell myself she was anywhere, safe and happy. I could imagine her writing in a cabin alone somewhere or traveling the world, sitting in bustling cafés, happily observing it all. I could guess that she still loved books, that she still moved through the world quietly, thoughtfully soaking it all in. But eventually, all the imagining became a problem. I realized that all I could do was guess, inserting my memory of who she was into different scenarios. I didn't know what adult Linna was actually like, if she loved yoga or romantic comedies or cooking. I would probably never know. I had taken that possibility away from myself. I had made sure that even if she was out there, somewhere, that she would have every reason in the world to never want to see me again. And then I had discovered Marion Earl.

The world had thrust her words into my path, placed them there so precisely that there was no way I would miss them. There was part of me that knew it was her instantly, cellularly. That first page, that first story. I would find myself pausing in the middle of sentences and looking behind me, the distinct sensation that someone else was in the room with me like a toothpick dragging across my skin. I had read books before that I had loved. This was something else.

It was her signature in the book that had made me sure, though. The bubbly, exaggerated dot on top of the 'i' was a hallmark of Linna's handwriting as a teenager, a thing I would see again and again as I pored over her handwritten stories. I had forgotten all about it until that moment at the bar with Stella, when it was in front of me again. Yes, it was only a small thing. A lazy loop of ink. It wasn't a theory I could say out loud; I knew how outlandish it was. How obsessed I had become. But it was a truth I felt in my teeth, as deep as a cavity. It ached and it grew. By the time Reese came along, with his source and his nods toward their identity, it was an unignorable pain. A thing that needed to be dealt with.

After all these years, Linna's words had found their way to me again. What were the odds of that? What were the chances? It was a sign. I knew it didn't mean she had forgiven me, but I couldn't just forget the stories I had read. I couldn't ignore what she was so clearly trying to tell me. It was a realization as sad as it was comforting, every word pointed to it: She was lonely, too. Maybe now, we wouldn't have to be.

CHAPTER 20

Then

Linna and I climbed into the car mechanically, like we were astronauts preparing for takeoff. My father was watching us so I didn't dare look at her, lest we both broke out into smiles or laughter, pure delight bubbling over.

Seat belt, mirror check, key in the ignition. It was only then that I glanced back at my father. He was leaning on the side of the barn, studying us, a relaxed smile on his face. I felt pride bloom in my chest, his trust in me a gold star.

We weren't even a mile down the road before Linna's hand flew out in front of her, turning on the radio. The station it was tuned to played country music, a little staticky but clear enough to make out the melody. Linna reached to change it, but I swatted her hand away.

"Leave it," I said. I had visions of my father getting in the truck tomorrow and turning on the radio to find it still dialed to a station he would never listen to, evidence that Linna and I had had too much fun.

Linna shrugged, rolling down the window, letting her hand float over the pockets of wind. "If you insist."

I expected Linna to look thrilled, her smile gummy and unrestrained, but her mouth was set in a hard line.

"What is it?" I asked.

"It's stupid. Just something he said to me before I got in the car."

I knew she meant my father. I waited for her to explain or, I hoped, to drop it altogether.

She took a deep breath. "He said to be extra safe, that I of all people should know how dangerous it is out here," she explained. "It felt... I don't know, like he was taunting me or something."

My hands gripped the steering wheel, blood draining from my knuckles. "I'm sure he didn't mean..."

She snorted. "Come on, Rin. He was definitely talking about her. You know he was."

We rarely discussed Linna's mother or the car accident that killed her. When it did come up, it was only on Linna's terms. I let her guide the conversation, end the conversation. I let her set the boundaries.

"Maybe," I admitted. "He's right, though. You should see how people drive..."

She turned her face toward the window without replying.

Linna and her mother had been living on the property for almost two years when it happened. We'd spent every day together since they arrived, begging our mothers to be done with chores early, running through fields together, acting out imaginary plays, laughing about nothing. Linna felt like a sister to me right away, as much a part of my genetic code as anyone else—more, maybe.

"It's like I always said," my father would tell us. "Discipline creates a world where there's still room for magic. And you, my girls, are magic."

He was right. A friendship like this, a sister who came out of nowhere, it felt like the most magical thing I could imagine. When my father told me that he was legally adopting Linna, it felt like destiny. The only possible ending to our story.

After my father shared the exciting news, my mother explained their necessary divorce, something about how it was just a sheet of paper, how she'd give up anything for the good of our family—Linna and her mother included. But it was like I only absorbed half of it, only the parts that really mattered to me. Linna was officially my family. When Jessie and Kent and other kids arrived, I assumed that my father would eventually do the same for them. When he didn't, it only seemed to confirm what I already felt, that Linna was special, and so was our bond.

It was maybe a year after the adoption when the accident happened. Linna's mother and my father had gone out to run an errand one morning when a drunk driver T-boned the passenger side of the car. My father had asked to speak to Linna alone at first, to tell her the news, but she grabbed onto my hand and insisted that I go with her. We did everything together, so why wouldn't we do this, too?

"She's gone," he had said. "There was nothing anyone could do."

It was nighttime, hours after he had originally said he'd return home. It wasn't unusual for a trip into town to take longer than expected, but when he had returned without Linna's mother with him, we knew something was off. He explained that he had spent all day with the police, recounting the accident. I scanned his body for injury, but he looked untouched, calm. He told us the paramedics on the scene said that sometimes this happened. One person walks out of the accident without a scratch and the other never has a chance. "Totally random," my father said. "That's what they think." He didn't have to spell it out for me to understand his meaning, even then. My father was too important to be the one who didn't make it.

"Ten in the morning," he added, shaking his head. "Can you believe the evil of this world? The addiction to that poison. This, girls, is why we're here. This is why we live like we do."

I kept waiting for Linna to speak, even though I was afraid to see her face, her tears. But she remained silent next to me, her nails digging into the top of my palm, pinching me.

"This is exactly why I insisted on the adoption. Why I went through all that paperwork," he went on. "So we can keep you here, safe."

I was so thankful that Linna could stay, that my mother's willingness to divorce him was worth it, it took the air out of me. I waited for Linna to say the same thing, or to wail, maybe, to scream, but she stayed quiet.

"Where is she?" she finally said, her voice steady.

My father stared back at her.

"Well, there's the Christian tradition of heaven, if that's what you want to believe... or the Buddhist principle of reincarnation—"

"No," Linna interrupted. "Where is... where is her body?"

"No need to worry yourself with that," he said, his face pinching with irritation, just slightly. "She's at peace."

"I can't see her?"

I felt her nails dig deeper into my palm again, and I bit the inside of my cheek to distract myself from the pain.

"No, Linna," my father said, more sternly this time. "Little girls aren't meant to see things like that."

* * *

I stared at my hands on the steering wheel and remembered the notches that Linna's nails had carved into my skin, the scabs for weeks after.

"I still don't understand why I couldn't see her," she said, after almost ten minutes of silence. "It's like he stole her away from me."

Something in me lit up at this, activating an urge to fix the sadness I heard in her voice, to systematically eliminate it altogether. "We were so young. He was protecting you."

"He was protecting something all right," she said.

I didn't reply, didn't push. I knew better than to pull her into a conversation that I didn't want to have. This day was supposed to be the opposite of the last few months, an opportunity for her to see that there was more than enough freedom available if she really wanted it bad enough. Discipline reaps rewards.

I could feel Linna's eyes boring into the side of my head from the passenger seat. "He's started weighing people, you know."

"What?" I asked, like maybe I didn't hear her correctly.

"To make sure everyone is following the moderation fasts."

"Oh," I said, my mind focused on individually freezing every muscle in my face. "Who told you that? Kent?"

It was just one word, but I could hear how sharp I sounded.

She didn't take the bait. "I overheard Jessie and Maura talking about it, actually."

"Huh," I said, like this was a new development I was only mildly interested in.

Part of me wanted to tell her what happened that day with my father and Rhonda months earlier. I wanted to tell her that I had started going back to the closet early in the morning when everyone else was asleep, stripping off my clothing and standing on the scale naked, clawing for that same high. I wanted her to understand that this was a good thing, this discipline. That it was good for me. I felt focused, on track, each day filled with purpose.

But how could I begin to explain to her what I knew she wouldn't understand? That sometimes, when my mother was so sick that she couldn't leave her bed for days, when everything felt out of my control, it was the only thing that worked. It was the only thing that made it feel like I could breathe.

It was perfect driving weather. Perfect anything weather, actually. The sky was a giant sheet of cobalt blue, the sun shining uninterrupted and proud. It was warm now, but the breeze felt as sharp and cool as it had that morning. It was the kind of day that felt illegal to not enjoy. I refused to let it slip through our fingers.

On the way back from the farm store, the radio station was finally crystal clear, a song about two women named Mary-Anne and Wanda blaring through the speakers. I turned up the volume, listening to the lyrics. I glanced over and could see Linna was doing the same, tapping her fingers against the window to the rhythm. A smile crept across her face then, sheepish and small, the kind that burns off any lingering tension. I could tell we had moved on, the conversation about her mother and the weigh-ins dissolving into nothing.

I grinned back at her then rolled down the windows, letting the air whip through the truck. I had forgotten to tie my hair back, and it kept flying across my eyes, blocking my vision, but I didn't care. We were together, flying down an empty highway, happy.

When we got back to the farm, my father was waiting for us, and I was glad I had insisted on turning off the radio as we pulled off the highway, just in case. He was leaning on the side of the barn again as if he had stayed frozen right there for the entire time we were gone. He waved at us and I could feel Linna's joy freeze over the second she spotted him. I waved back, then rolled up the windows as I pulled into the parking spot.

"That was great, huh?" I said, turning to Linna, taking my time as I shifted into park and took the keys out of the ignition.

I hated how needy I sounded, but I was determined to end the trip on a good note. There was no reason to sour the day. We needed to bottle this feeling and remember it.

"Yeah," Linna managed. "I had fun."

"We can do that every week now," I said, excited.

She hopped out the passenger side door without replying. I figured she hadn't heard me.

The trip had taken most of the day and my whole body felt sore, clenched with adrenaline for the entire drive. We were a few hours from sunset, so I knew my mother would still be in bed. I wasn't ready to go back to the room and its stale air, all that darkness, so I climbed into the treehouse instead. I laid back on the quilts, the soft, familiar weave comforting me as a strong breeze snaked through the window. I put my hands behind my head and closed my eyes, Linna's and my laughter echoing in my head until I fell asleep.

When I woke up it was dark. While I suspected that I'd missed family meal, walking into the silent dining hall confirmed it. I tiptoed around the picnic tables, then quietly opened the door to our room. After bad episodes, my mother would sometimes be awake at odd hours, her body conditioned to sleep during the day and be alert at night. But I found her asleep now, her hands nestled under her face, cupping her cheek.

It was a mistake, that I touched her. I stumbled while pulling on my pajamas, my fingers accidentally brushing against her calf as I braced myself on the foot of her bed. Her skin felt wrong.

I cleared my throat, hoping to wake her, but she didn't move. A wisp of panic curled into my chest, tightening. I coughed louder, but again, she stayed completely still and painfully quiet. My heart was pounding in my ears with thick, heavy thumps.

"Mom..." I said, raising my voice as much as I could manage. I felt a deep and sudden stab of grief for my childhood, hearing the voice of my younger self in this plea, remembering all the times I had gently woken her up in the middle of the night to tell her I had a tummy ache, a bad dream.

When she didn't stir, I moved closer, cautiously putting a hand on her shoulder to shake her. I reminded myself of the many logical reasons she would be sleeping so deeply, how sometimes she was so tired now that when she did finally fall asleep, it seemed like she had shut down every nonessential function completely. It was her body's way of healing itself, my father had explained. But as soon as I touched her, the full weight of my palm resting against her skin, I knew.

CHAPTER 21

Now

In the moments I am able to stop thinking about Linna, it feels almost good to tell Reese what happened to my mother. I take my time recalling the story, charting the downward spiral of her health almost clinically. I tell it to him honestly, no detail spared, even at my own expense. It feels like my responsibility to paint the full picture for him, to describe her pain as accurately as possible. I had been in such denial when she was sick, so convinced my father could fix her. This is what claws at me the most now, what keeps me up at night. I will never have the luxury of knowing if real medicine would have helped her or not.

"The worst part is that I blamed her," I tell Reese, zipping up my jacket to my chin. The sun has started to set over the park now, tangerine light splicing through the trees. Everything has cooled. "For not trying harder to get better. I thought it was all her fault. That if she just followed the rules a little more, she'd be miraculously cured. I actually *told* her that."

Reese stares at me thoughtfully before his eyes briefly flash to his phone, which sits on the bench between us, recording the conversation. We both watch for a second as the recording app's timelapse ticks by.

He looks up. "I'm sure you understand by now that this wasn't your fault."

I snort. "Well, I certainly didn't help things."

"You were seventeen, Catharine."

"Exactly. I was seventeen. Almost eighteen. An adult, basically," I insist. "I knew better."

Reese lets this settle for a second.

"The thing is... these types of extremist leaders have a way of making sure you interpret every success as their responsibility, like you couldn't have possibly felt that good without them," he says. "But when it comes to failure, it's the opposite. It's all yours, every time. They make sure of it. If you always blame yourself, then you can never blame him. It's residual trauma. I've seen it in so many victims."

I bristle, shifting my weight on the bench. I had been wondering how long it would take before the word *victim* was thrown around. It feels wrong. Hadn't he just heard what I did? How I acted?

"Sure," I manage, deciding not to push back. I don't need him to insist on outlining all the ways I had been royally, clinically fucked up. "Makes sense."

He seems pleased with himself for a beat, but then his face hardens. "Do you have any idea how he did it?"

I'm confused. "What do you mean?"

"I mean, it had to be poison, right?" he offers lightly, looking deep in thought. "Slow-dose antifreeze or something, maybe..."

I blink at him, the rest of my body frozen in place. His words are trickling through my brain slowly, like they're arriving there one at a time. Poison. Slow-dose. Antifreeze. What is he talking about?

"That is..." he stumbles. "That is what you're saying, right? That he killed her. That he was responsible for her death..."

I know I should pause here and process what he's saying, formulate some intelligent follow-up questions, especially given that he's recording all of this, but I don't.

"What? No," I snap instead. "He should have taken her to a doctor, yes. But poison...no. It wasn't like that."

He tilts his chin to the side. "It wasn't?"

The question sounds patronizing and loaded. He's trying to make me feel crazy.

"I mean," I correct, softening my reply. "No. That just doesn't make sense to me."

I expect it to irritate Reese that what I'm saying isn't supporting his line of thought. That he will realize he missed something and feel stupid, but he looks content. Relaxed. Smug, even. "What about Ben and Bertie then?"

What is he saying? That my father killed them, too? Stirred anti freeze into their iced tea amid all the homeschooling and farming? It's ridiculous and clichéd. I think of the photo in my entryway, Linna, Ben and Bertie, and me smiling. I think of the tomato fields, the treehouse. Reese doesn't understand that those years were different. My father was different then. What happened later was different, too.

"They were elderly," I reply, my voice smooth, calm. "They died of old age. It happens."

Reese frowns, then holds up a finger as he digs into his *New Yorker* tote bag with the other hand, emerging with a notebook. He flips through to a page that's paperclipped with two loose sheets of paper. From what I can see, they are photocopies of birth certificates.

"Benjamin Abramson was born in 1945 in Scranton, Pennsylvania," Reese reads, side-eyeing me as he flips to the next one: "Bertie West was born in 1949 in Salem, Oregon."

I do the math quickly, my skull vibrating with new information.

He beats me to it. "They were only in their fifties when you knew them."

That's impossible. I almost say it out loud before thinking better of it. I knew they had retired a little early, that Ben had received a massive payout following a work accident and they had used the money to move to Florida. I remembered that. But fifties? It doesn't compute.

"How old did your father tell you they were, exactly?" he pushes, gently.

"I don't remember," I stumble. I must look pathetic, processing all of this in real time.

The truth is that I don't remember him ever saying anything about their ages. All my memories of Ben and Bertie feel fully formed and wholly my own. Sacred. I close my eyes and think of Ben's sun-spotted hands, Bertie's bright white hair cascading from under a wide-brimmed straw hat. I could only see them as I always had, loving grandparents gone too soon. People who kept me safe, who required nothing of me. It was the only truth I could access. Anything else felt wrong, scratching my skin like sand.

I can tell Reese senses my discomfort and, to his credit, he doesn't say anything for almost an entire minute. I know because I watch the timer on the recording app as I try to steady my breath, the numbers dissolving into new ones in an instant.

"Look, I know this is a lot," he finally says.

It's nearly dark now, and I'm shivering. The temperature must have dropped ten degrees since I left for my run, and my sweat has crystallized into a thick, salty crust on my back.

"It's fine," I offer. I try to make my voice neutral, but it comes out robotic, forced. "I guess it makes sense."

I know it's what I need to say. What he needs to hear. It's important he knows that I'm different now. That I've reflected on all those years there and I finally get it. I see everything for what it was. The more defensive I am, the more it looks like I'm defending my father.

"Still doesn't make it easy." He shrugs. "Look, it's late. We can wrap this up. Circle back later this week, maybe?"

He stares at me, pleading. As in: Can we *please* keep talking? Will you *please* go on the record again?

I hesitate and twist my face into a grimace. It's a look that says maybe I have changed my mind. Maybe this has all been too much for me. It's such a small shift in control, but it comforts me.

"I can ask again," he tries. "My source. I can…I can see what I can do."

I nod, and he seems encouraged by this, though his brow is furrowed in thought.

"It might help if I tell them what you told me today," he says eventually, slowly, like the idea is occurring to him in real time. "Play them the interview. You've both lost people you loved. Maybe the rest is unimportant."

I picture Linna listening to our conversation, seeing how much I've changed. What I've learned. She might be able to trust me again.

"Sure," I agree. "Do that. Whatever helps."

I wait for him to hit the button on the phone and end the recording, the interview, but he is stalling. I raise my eyebrows, waiting.

"Just…I need to ask, before we go," he starts, cautious. He's choosing his words carefully. "Your mother, Ben, Bertie…it's horrible. Those losses…I can't imagine. But…"

Spit it out, Reese.

"I know from experience that it can take a while to accept the extent of the lies," he says. "It's a lot of loss to process. Grief."

I bristle at his poor choice of words. I know he's referring to his experience of interviewing people like me. Victims. I know he thinks he's close enough to it to understand. But he's wrong.

"But you do know that he hurt people there, right?" he asks. "More people than just your mother?"

I answer instantly, reveling in the shift. Now I'm the one who knows something he doesn't. "Yes."

CHAPTER 22

—

Then

The room felt like it had halved in size since I had found my mother, and I needed air. I should have walked out and told someone what had happened immediately, but it felt like the least I could do to stay there for a while, to sit in the quiet with her. To remember how selfish I had been. But after an hour, I couldn't breathe. I kept thinking about her body, if decomposition began the precise second someone dies. Had her skin cells already started to shrivel and rot while I had been weeping on the floor? It felt like a grotesque flaw in human design that there wasn't some sort of in-between period where the body stayed still and unchanging, reverent. It made me angry.

I grabbed a stool from the corner of the room and placed it under the window, then climbed on top and reached for the lever. My breath wouldn't stop hitching in my chest, tiny hiccups for air leaping out of me uncontrollably, the aftermath of so much crying. It was a childlike sound, blubbering and weak.

The window was blocked by two heavy layers of fabric, salvaged from an extra velvet curtain that had once hung on the stage in the dining room. It was only when I pushed them to the side that I felt something stiff in between the sewn-together layers of material. I glanced from the curtain to my mother, my mouth forming the question for her before I remembered.

I yanked on the curtain and caught the bundle of fabric in my arms as it fell, the small tension rod coming down too, then pulled a small pair of scissors from my mother's sewing kit. At first, I had the impulse to tear the fabric to shreds to get to whatever was hidden inside, but something whispered at me. *Be careful.* I glanced to my mother again, imagining the words floating from her consciousness.

Slowly, I undid each neat stitch until I was able to fit my hand inside the pocket between the sheets of fabric and wedged a gallon-sized plastic bag out of the small opening. I flipped it over in my hands, studying the contents—a handful of carefully folded, stapled papers and cash. More of it than I had ever seen before.

I glanced at the door, paranoid, then walked over and sat with my back against it. Not quite a lock, but it was something. Slowly, I opened the bag, taking the items out one by one. I flipped through the papers first, my eyes flying over words and numbers I had never seen before, my brain moving too quickly to process any of it. On all the documents, there was my mother's name, jumping off of the paper. And then there was an envelope, heavier than all the rest. I opened it to find a spare car key inside. My mind was folding in on itself, trying to make sense of everything. I started counting the cash and stopped after a thousand, overwhelmed.

I stared at the papers spread out in front of me, the supplies for an elaborate board game that no one had bothered to explain to me. The room felt like it had halved itself again and I knew I needed to get out, to find Linna.

I rehung the curtains and returned everything to the plastic bag, stuffing it under the oversized hoodie I'd thrown on. It felt imperative that I keep it all close to me, protected and hidden away. By the time I got to the treehouse, all I knew was that I wouldn't have to be alone with it all soon. That was enough.

I was only on the second rung of the ladder when I heard them, their voices hushed. Linna, of course. And Kent. I realized I hadn't even thought about our flashlight rule, that there was only one glowing from the window. But our code was for wanting to be left alone, not so she could bring someone else to the treehouse. It was a place that was exclusively ours.

"She's not a child, Linna," Kent said, and I tensed reflexively.

"I know, but it's like she's stuck at eight years old, still romanticizing all of it. The gardens, the driving, the rules... him," she replied. She sounded exhausted. "I don't know if it's just that she's stubborn or that she's actually that naïve. I know she's not dumb. She's always been smarter than me."

"You're the smartest person I know," he insisted.

"You wouldn't say that if you really knew Catharine."

For a single moment, the adrenaline coursing through my body softens and I am soothed by Linna's defense.

"At the end of the day, it's not about intelligence. It's a choice," he said. "Some people prefer ignorant bliss."

Kent sounded like so many of the people my father had warned us about, the ones who weren't cut out for this life, their reasoning slippery and poisonous.

"You call this bliss?" she scoffed.

There was movement then, the wooden floor of the treehouse creaking above me. I clung to the ladder, frozen.

"I mean..." Kent's voice drifted down, the tone lower now, warmer. "In some ways, maybe."

I heard the unmistakable sound of kissing then, so intimate and unrestrained that I had the urge to close my eyes, even though all

I could see was the wooden rung in front of me, my now-white fingers clinging to it.

"I wish everything here felt this easy," she said.

I felt the urge to vomit. My mother was gone and now my sister was, too. This is what it felt like. Unsurvivable loneliness. I wanted to be away from myself, detached from my body. Anywhere but there.

"We can have this all the time when we leave, you know," Kent said.

I clenched my teeth so hard at the word *leave,* I heard my back molars snap together.

"You and me," he went on. "Our own bed. Our own apartment. Our own money."

I felt something inside me click into place then, an intricate lock finally finding its key. I thought of the plastic bag nestled against my stomach. All that money. They wanted to leave. And so had my mother. That's what the Ziploc was for, wasn't it? All those documents. The cash. I thought of the arguments my mother and I had had over the last year, the cryptic questions and lessons I had been so irritated by. It all came together in one violent wave.

I couldn't leave fast enough, but I forced myself to climb down as quietly and quickly as possible. As I stepped off the final rung, the bag slid out of my sweater. I rushed to grab it and silently hide it away again, but they had heard me. Their voices went quiet, and I felt the blood drain from my face.

"What was that?" Linna said, her head popping out of the opening at the bottom of the treehouse. She was holding a blanket across her bare chest, her curls spilling out around her head in every direction. It only took a second for her to spot me.

I could have run or tried to hide, but what was the point? It was already humiliating enough. Why couldn't this be as embarrassing for her as it had been for me?

She stared at me for a minute, her expression a mix of anger and confusion, and I met her gaze. Defiant. Maybe it was her turn to feel small, I thought.

"Is someone there?" Kent said from the other side of the treehouse.

Linna quickly replied, her eyes still on me. "No," she said. "Must have been the wind."

I should have felt thankful, maybe, that she spared me the awkwardness of Kent knowing I had been there. But it bothered me, this small way she had protected me was as if she were magnanimous and mature, staring down at me from up there. This was the very issue, I thought. That she thinks she knows what I need, exactly how I should be saved. She thinks she knows, and she's wrong.

I gripped onto the bag under my sweatshirt, making sure it stayed in place as I turned around and began the walk to my father's cottage in silence.

CHAPTER 23

Now

Two days later, Reese texts me that his source is finally willing to see me, and I feel like I have won. All that vulnerability, finally, has paid off. I am overwhelmed with relief and unfazed by his condition that the whole meeting will be recorded. Audio only. "Fine," I text back instantly. When he asks if I can meet them today, I tell him I can be at his office in an hour.

I stare at myself in the mirror as I swish mouthwash around, remembering something Stella once told me about mantras. Every morning, she said, you were supposed to stand in front of the mirror, look yourself in the eye, and repeat the same thing.

"You say it every day," she told me. "Whether you want to or not. Whether you believe it or not."

"What's yours?" I had asked. "What do you say?"

"I have everything I need," she said. "I thought about it being something about love, how I'm open to it, or waiting for it. But you know... I don't want to spend each day reminding myself that there's something I'm lacking, a blank spot waiting to be filled. A better version of me believes I'm already whole. I want that version."

There was a wisdom in what she had said, an earnestness. I had thought about how I already fell asleep every night listing the ways I would apologize to my sister if given the chance. It wasn't so different of a practice, really. But it also illustrated what was maybe the biggest difference between Stella and me. She needed to believe she was whole to improve herself, whereas I had to remind myself that I wasn't. Every bit of self-improvement I hoped to find relied on me remembering why my sister was out of my life. The lack of something was the whole point. Her being back in it now feels like a miracle.

This is why I know I will keep talking to Reese, why I keep putting myself into situations where he unsettles me, poking at my weakest spots. Reese is how I'm going to see my sister for the first time in a decade, so I endure the discomfort. I fantasize about the moment I will be able to tell her that I have spent years of my life reading her words. That I am sorry. That I understand. That I am lonely, too.

I order the Uber and, as I'm waiting, I return to the photo of the four of us, focusing as hard as I can on Ben and Bertie. Their faces are obscured slightly, shadowed as they lean into each other, but it's clear these are people who are closer to middle-aged than elderly. Could they be my grandparents? Sure. On death's doorstep? Absolutely not. I still can't believe it took me until now to see it. Until Reese.

My phone pings to let me know the driver has arrived and I set the frame back on the shelf, my eyes drifting to Linna's paint-splattered face. For the first time in years, I think of her and feel hope instead of shame. I was a different person then. So was she.

* * *

The Uber drops me off in front of Reese's office building, and as I squint through the giant sheets of glass encasing the lobby, I see he's already waiting for me. The glasses are back today, and he's wearing a button-down. With his rumpled sleeves rolled up and the shirt slightly untucked in the back, he looks like a dad who's had a long day.

He greets me with a polite, forced nod, any trace of playful friendliness gone. "Ready?"

I don't hesitate, his formality making me overcompensate. "Yes."

He swipes his ID card across the sensor and presses the up button on the elevator bank. When we walk in, he hits 18 with a knuckle and I consider saying something casual or vaguely flirty as a way to ease the tension. But his palpable anxiety has rubbed off on me, poking a hole in the calm, measured mask I've been creating for the last hour.

We're at floor 12 when he finally breaks the silence.

"There's one thing you should probably—"

A tinny ding cuts him off and the elevator stops abruptly, the doors opening to reveal a woman in her fifties or sixties. She and Reese exchange friendly, professional smiles and nods. I glance up at Reese, waiting for him to finish his thought, but he stares straight ahead, silent.

When we exit on his floor, there's a blinding neon sign hanging over the front desk with the logo of the website he works for. When it launched a decade ago, some major media investor called it "like *The Atlantic*, for people with short attention spans," and the descriptor stuck. When I asked Reese during our second meeting at the bar how he got the job, he said that they liked a viral tweet of his and things "went from there." I laughed until I realized he was serious.

I follow him as he waves at the receptionist who gives us both a polite hello. I imagine she knew to expect me, one visitor among many at the office that day for her to keep tabs on. It feels odd to imagine such a pivotal moment in my life cataloged in some stranger's calendar, like it's a reminder to take out the trash.

I don't have long to focus on this, though, as Reese weaves through the office. With each step I take, I feel like I'm watching myself play a part in a movie. I take a deep breath and remind myself to stay present, that I know this feeling and it will pass.

"I thought everyone was remote these days..." I mutter to Reese, feeling self-conscious of all the eyes shifting my way.

Reese doesn't hear me, continuing his swift path toward the back of the office. He finally slows down when we approach a large conference room that spans the width of the floor, separated from the rest of the space by one seamless glass panel.

I see her hair first, curls springing in different directions. There are small streaks of gray peeking through now, but I'd know that hair anywhere. She's wearing an oversized denim jacket with patches lining the back, but is facing away from me, gazing toward the large bay of windows on one side of the room, opposite the door. When she hears Reese and me enter, she swivels the chair and stands up to greet us.

My throat pinches with tears. "Linna."

CHAPTER 24

Then

It must have been almost 2 a.m. by the time I got to his cottage, but the lights were still on, the glow spilling out the windows into all that pitch-black nothingness like a jack-o'-lantern.

I remembered the last time I had been here, my driving lessons almost complete. I could still recall the look on his face when he had opened the door, irritation mixed with simmering rage. Now, it was the middle of the night. I knew how angry he would be if I woke him up. But what choice did I have?

He answered the door after just one knock, looking as awake as if it was the middle of the afternoon. I waited for him to greet me, to yell, even, but he just stared, his face blank aside from a hint of annoyance. Immediately, I felt self-conscious of how I must look, my face swollen from crying, exhausted and disheveled from walking across the property.

"I—" I started. "She's—"

I rubbed my throat with one hand, trying to massage the words out of me.

"Spit it out, Catharine," he said.

"She's gone."

For a moment, he looked irritated, like maybe I was being intentionally vague.

"Mom, she's. . . ." I started explaining again, but at the word *Mom,* I felt a sob crawl out of me. The second I said it, I wondered if that word would ever feel the same to say. Would I ever think it and not feel it slice through me? No, I realized. Never. My hand flew to my mouth, stifling the sound. I had never been emotional around my father. It wasn't that it was against the rules, but it felt indulgent and weak.

He softened then, his gaze falling. "Oh no," he said. "I see."

I could feel snot running down my face and into my mouth. I couldn't believe my body contained so much liquid, so much salt. I felt like an ocean, the depths unknowable.

"Shh," he said. "I know. I know. You're safe now."

He opened the door wider and I had to look down, the light from inside momentarily blinding me. The floors were so light a shade of wood that I couldn't imagine walking on them. I stared back at my own feet, the dirt caked between my toes, under my nails. Linna and I often laughed about how useless our sandals were in the dirt, how the soles of our feet were stained black by the end of each summer, whether we wore shoes or not.

"Come," he gestured inside the room. "You need to rest now."

I gingerly walked past him, taking in the small but immaculate space. It should have felt sterile to me, maybe, but instead I felt like I could finally breathe. I thought of the cinderblock walls in our room, stained with years of dust and grime, nothing ever totally clean. My stomach turned as I remembered her body still there, alone, and me here, safe.

"She's in our room," I said quietly, my arms glued to my side. I was afraid to touch anything, to dirty it. "Her body."

He nodded somberly. "Of course. I'll take care of it."

I didn't know what he meant. I wasn't sure I wanted to know. "Okay."

I followed him as he disappeared into the kitchen, unsure what to do with myself in the spotless living room. I watched him turn a bright red knob on the gigantic stove and place a sage-green kettle on top.

"Tea," he said. "Times like this call for tea."

I nodded, my eyes traveling over the rest of the room. It was fanatically organized. There was a stainless-steel contraption in the corner, the body of it dotted with knobs and spouts and grates that all looked vaguely scientific. There was a tiny mug hanging on a hook above it, like a coffee cup for dolls. There were so many things in front of me that for a split second, I forgot my grief, my mind filling with only practical thoughts, logical questions. I always knew the cottage was newer than the rest of the farm's buildings, but this was something else. A whole other world right under my nose, all this time.

"You'll stay here while I handle things," he interrupted my thoughts.

My head snapped toward him. This was the first time I had ever been allowed inside the cottage in my whole life. And now I could stay there? Alone? It felt like too much.

"But I'm not usually allowed—"

"It's fine," he cooed, cutting me off. "You're my daughter. I trust you. And you trust me, too. Right?"

His eyes were directly fixed on mine, unblinking. He meant it. For the first time all evening, I felt the ache of my sadness move to the background, just for a moment. I was not alone.

"I trust you, too."

"Good," he said. "We have to. It's just you and me now."

A chill ran down my arm like a shard of glass trailing along my skin, not quite poking through. I remembered my mother's cold body, curled into itself. Then the money, the papers, the key. Linna and Kent in the treehouse, what they had said about me. I realized my father was right.

CHAPTER 25

Now

I didn't expect Linna to be happy with me. She might even be mad. She'll certainly have questions. I've prepared for all of this. I would have a lot to say to me, too, were I in her shoes.

But the look she's giving me now is ice cold, discomfort wrinkling across her forehead in a way that scares me. She looks older than I imagined she would, and it makes me realize my own age. I'm not a kid anymore, and neither is she. I used to find it so easy to remember the two of us running through the garden together, telling stories, laughing about everything, but standing here in this room, I can't see that version of us at all.

Her brow furrows deeper and I feel myself mirroring the expression in confusion, though I realize that it probably wouldn't look like it to anyone else, my muscles frozen in place, my forehead perpetually smooth. But of course Linna wouldn't get Botox. She probably has a sticker on her laptop that says, "Fuck your beauty standards." I smile again at the thought, but her expression doesn't change. I'm still the only person here who seems even remotely happy about this reunion.

I glance at Reese again, prepared for him to look slightly confused, or expectant, like he's waiting for her to give me a piece of her mind, maybe. And yet, he, too, looks unsteady.

"Linna," I start again, ready to launch into the apology that I imagined would come later, after there were hugs, or at least some tears. "I don't know how to tell you how sorry I—"

She lifts a hand, stopping me, and for a second I think she's going to wave off my apology, tell me, to my relief, that she doesn't need it. I hope she'll say something like, "We were both different back then," or "I never blamed you," or "I know it was his fault, not yours." I'd take any of those, gladly. But she doesn't say any of that.

"Catharine," she says, her chin tilted down, like she's trying to remind me of something.

Her voice isn't right.

I look at Reese again and it's only now that he looks expectant, like he's one step ahead of me. I don't like this, how everyone seems to know something I do not.

"What?" I say, my voice high and panicked. I take a deep breath, steady myself.

"Catharine," she starts, each syllable falling out of her mouth slowly. "It's Holly. I'm *Holly.*"

She says this so carefully, I half expect her to spell the name out for me. H-o-l-l-y.

"Holly," I repeat back to her, painfully aware that everyone in this room does, indeed, know something I do not. The image I had of my sister dissolves in front of me, and in its place, a memory of Linna and me emerges. We're sprinting through a half-grown garden, a voice looping behind us, breezy and young. *You two are going to kill me, I swear,* it says, laughter mixed with exhaustion.

"Holly," she says again, her voice soft and warm. "Linna's mother."

CHAPTER 26

Then

I ignored Linna for nearly two weeks after my mother died, and it was convenient, really, that she seemed to interpret my silence as grief instead of rage. I knew she thought I needed space, peace and quiet to process the loss of my mother all on my own, the very same thing she had needed when her mother died. Maybe she was right. But by the time I returned to my regular routine, where Linna's and my paths would cross in the dining hall or during chores, both of us avoiding eye contact, my grief had already become something else entirely.

That horrible night, alone in my father's cottage, I had sat in a corner and cried so hard my body ached from the effort. For days afterward I laid in bed motionless, sorrow marching across my body with virus-like precision, laying claim to everything. It was a sadness that felt untenable, motivated, like if I didn't find something for it to do, it would bore a hole right through the center of my stomach. I knew I couldn't function with that feeling. But anger? Anger was a different thing entirely. Anger, I was familiar with. By the time I thrust myself back into the normal patterns of the farm, it was as if I had agreed to a bargain deep within myself.

I left the sadness buried and hidden, and I spread the anger out in front of me like a map.

I thought sparingly of the bag of money and documents, never quite allowing myself to linger. That night, before going to my father, I had hidden the bag in a secret compartment in the floor of the stage, a space where campers would once have stored costumes for quick changes in productions, my mother had explained to us. When we were younger, Linna and I used the compartment to hide our favorite things, small treasures from around the farm. It was our secret place for a stretch of time, a childish game we soon forgot about once we had the treehouse.

I knew there was risk in putting everything there, but I wanted it all away from me. Away from the treehouse, where I couldn't obsess over it, I told myself. I could only use it as motivation, a reminder that what my father had told me that night in the cottage was correct: It was only him and me now. In the moments that my mind did flash to those documents, my mother's name sprawled across the front of so many of them, rage boiled up through me like steam. For so long, I had been focused on keeping Linna here and keeping her happy that I had missed what was in front of me. That my own mother was intent on leaving me, too. That this place—that I—wasn't enough for her in the end, either. I couldn't imagine anything more selfish. It felt like a slap in the face. Loss upon loss upon loss.

By the time the day of the funeral arrived, it had been two weeks since my mother had died. Part of me was relieved that there would be an official occasion for everyone to exercise their grief publicly instead of directing it all toward me. Linna may have ignored me since the news had spread, but everyone else stared in my direction like I was a broken thing, the loss oozing out of me and poisoning their worlds. The burial, I thought, was their chance to acknowledge it once and for all. And then, I hoped, to leave it behind.

The funeral was an hours-long event in which my father talked about my mother as if they had never separated at all. He told the entire story of their relationship, skipping over the part where they had divorced and he had married someone else, instead praising her for how her sacrifices had benefited the farm. I nodded silently through the awkward, yet kind condolences from everyone.

"I'm so sorry, Rin," Linna said after everyone else had left, the first words she had spoken to me since that horrible day.

I was staring at the ground, eyes fixed on the pile of dirt that I knew marked the spot where my mother was buried far, far below, but I lifted my chin to meet her stare. "Thank you."

"I wish I had said something sooner... but I... I don't know," she stumbled. "That night, the treehouse... all of it... I figured you'd want space."

"I know," I managed. "It's okay. I'm okay."

She scanned my face, as if confirming this for herself.

"Can we talk?" she asked. "Or just hang out? We don't even have to say anything. We can just sit in the treehouse and be there. I miss you."

I felt something crack in my chest. For the first time all day, I wanted to cry.

"That sounds good," I said.

She stood up straighter, a weight lifted off of her shoulders. "Okay," she said with a weak grin.

"I just have to..." I muttered, gesturing toward the final pile of dirt. "You know, the burial process."

It was my job to shovel the final bits of earth onto the grave. It had been Linna's job with her mother, too. I couldn't remember who had done it with Ben and Bertie. My mother, maybe.

"I remember," Linna said quickly, her smile gone. "I'll see you soon."

It was just my father and me left there then. We had spent a lot of time together since my mother died. I had wanted to avoid Linna and everyone else, all those pitying half smiles. He had let me tag along on supply pick ups and drop-offs and other chores, giving me more and more responsibility. But he rarely spoke of my mother. I interpreted his avoidance as a type of reverence, or maybe not knowing what to say. Now, he stood opposite the gravesite, staring at the ground, smiling down sadly. He broke the silence first. "You know, there's something beautiful about it. Death."

I stared at my feet, the white tips of my sneakers muddied with soil.

"It's quiet," he went on. "It says everything with so little, changes it all with just one silent wave of its hand. I respect that."

I reached out for the shovel, anxious to keep myself busy.

"The thing about your mother," he said, eyes still fixed on the grave. "Is that the more she tried to make me believe her strength, the more obvious her weakness was to me. It was painful, really, to watch. But in the end, the disease sensed it, too. It knew that she had her doubts and it took advantage of that."

My mind flashed to the bag of cash, the car key, the documents.

"I mean, we both know she could have left. Right? Of course, she could have. But it was worse than leaving, what your mother did." He shook his head. "She thought she was the exception. That this place and everything we do, how we live... that she could have all of that and be in the real world, too. Deep down, she thought she could have both. That there was some safe, balanced middle ground somewhere."

It dawned on me then that my father didn't know the true extent of my mother's doubts, her desire for something different. He thought she was wavering, unsure, but he didn't know what I knew. He hadn't found what I found. That amount of money could turn the farm around. I opened my mouth ready to reveal it all, then snapped it shut. Did he really need to know? Did he really need to think even worse of her? Maybe not. The secret sank back into my stomach like a rock.

"That's the problem with that world, Catharine," he went on. "Everyone thinks...just a little of this, just a little of that. Just one day off. One moment of indulgence..." He laughed bitterly, trailing off. "It's never just one day, one thing. Out there, there's no such thing as halfway. The second you say yes to any of it, the second you consider it, you've already lost."

I nodded, relieved that he wasn't asking me actual questions. That I wasn't being forced to lie for her or expose her. Protectiveness for my mother had risen in me without my permission, instinctive and fierce. Where was all that anger I felt before? I wondered. Where had it gone?

"It's a miracle, really, that she never corrupted you," he went on, seemingly unaware of any reaction I was having to his words. "Maybe this is the one way she listened to me. I mean, I tried to tell her so many times—whatever you do, don't force Catharine to choose between the two of us."

I blinked.

"I think in the end she saw it, though. Maybe it's what finally made her let go. She saw that you are so much more cut out for this world than she ever was."

I felt dizzy, something in me recoiling and blooming all at once. Here was the one person on Earth who looked at me and saw something other than a pitiful, lonely girl.

"There's no surviving this place without commitment," he said. "It's not easy. We know this. But if you choose to commit to it again and again . . . it's everything. You can have everything."

I thought of my now-regular weigh-ins, breath catching in my chest as I waited for the number on the scale. I knew what it felt like when it was good, when I saw what my commitment meant. I knew the way it changed my day, my stride, my posture, the way it supercharged it all with pride. It was a gift, an assurance that I had made the right choice again and again. A reminder of what discipline really feels like. It felt like soaring. Like peace.

"Yes," I agreed. "You're right."

He smiled, satisfied. "You belong here, Catharine. Always have."

I took a deep breath, imagining it filling me up from my toes to my fingertips, just like my mother had taught me, the memory making me miss her before I could stop it. And I did miss her. I knew that. Even through the sting of betrayal, I felt it. Her absence was a dull ache that pulsed silently through everything, unignorable. But she had made her choice. Now I had to make one, too.

I exhaled. "I know."

"It's more important than ever that we're sure everyone here is as committed as we are," he added. "It's the only way we'll rebuild. Doubt is a sickness, Catharine. It spreads."

I nodded dutifully.

"So if there's anything you're not telling me . . . anyone that you might suspect is harboring the same desire for that world . . ." he started. "You'll be honest with me, right? Trust and honesty are the only way this place will shine again. I know you want that, too."

I felt my face flame at the mention of honesty. I thought of the money again. I decided that I would bring it to him after I met with Linna. I would present it all to him and tell him the truth, which was that it scared me. That I knew he could use it for something important. He would be thankful. He would never doubt my commitment to this place.

"Yes, of course," I said.

He smiled. "That's my girl."

He started to walk toward the main building, his boots treading across the very bottom of the gravesite. I cringed at his mistake, and when I shoveled the final small pile of dirt onto the grave, I put it on top of the deep, ugly print his foot had made, making it disappear.

CHAPTER 27

Now

I roll the word around my brain like a hard candy.

Holly, Holly, Holly. Linna's mother.

"I remember," I manage, bracing myself on the table, then slowly sliding my body into a chair. My mind whizzes through my childhood, racing to spot Holly in the corners of each memory. "I remember now."

"It's been such a long time, honey," she says, her voice full of what seems to be a controlled, cautious empathy as she sits down across from me. To her, I realize, I am a fragile thing, or maybe something to be feared.

I stare at her, taking in all the features I had registered as my sister's. The curls. The height. The slight gap between her two front teeth. It was all Linna. She looked older than I had imagined, yes, but not *old*. Not old enough to be her mother, or mine. Still, I know this person. Every time she speaks, a fuller picture of her comes into focus, an image of something and someone I had put to rest long ago.

"You died," I announce, the words coming out before I can craft them into something less crass. "He said you died."

Her eyes stay fixed on her hands as she picks at a cuticle. "That's what he told you," she says, her tone matter-of-fact, bitter only at the edges. "Figures."

I blink, wait a beat for her to explain, but I am impatient.

"So after the car accident... you just... you left?"

For the first time in years, I think of my mother's neat plastic bag of items. The urge to walk out of one life and into another. I had known it so well.

Holly frowns, then shakes her head. "No, that wasn't... it wasn't like that."

"How was it then?" Now it is me who sounds bitter.

My eyes flash to Reese and his face is unreadable but placid. He already knows this story, I realize.

"Well, it—" Holly starts, but Reese cuts in.

"Sorry, I just... I'm going to press record now. Cool?"

We both nod, though I have some instinct to say no and protect myself. Look where it has gotten you, I think, letting someone in even the tiniest bit. I know I have already allowed myself too much. But I need to know now. I need to hear her story, the truth. I had envisioned this would be a chance to apologize to my sister for how I acted that summer after my mother died. I decide that, in a way, this will be a penance, too. I will argue and question on Linna's behalf. I will ask what makes a mother leave a daughter like that.

"You look so much like him, you know," Holly says to me, changing the subject. "The resemblance is unbelievable."

I don't know what to say to this, if I should thank her or be offended. But then it dawns on me that this is the only person I have talked to in years who knew my father, too. Who remembers him fully, the good and the bad.

I shift my weight to my opposite hip, recross my legs.

"You look like her, too," I manage, though I know that should be obvious given our interaction so far, my embarrassing mistake.

"Really?" she says, her eyes welling with tears.

I'm confused by the emotion until I realize that the last time Holly saw Linna, her daughter was still a child. Of the two of us, I'm the only one who knows what Linna looked like as an eighteen-year-old, an adult. I suddenly feel with gripping clarity that if she knew where Linna was now, she wouldn't have agreed to meet me. We're both missing the same person.

I clear my throat, uncomfortable with her tears. I make my voice sound professional and cold. "So, the car accident..."

She swallows, then nods rapidly, like she's coaching herself to begin. "Right. Okay, yes. I know you must have so many questions..."

Her face is so creased with obvious guilt that I feel nauseous, unprepared for what she's about to reveal. I wait.

"There was no car accident," she said.

By now, I know this feeling well, the experience of coming to terms with one lie only to realize there are more, more, more, and yet it takes me by surprise, anyway. I grip the armrests of my chair until my knuckles are milky white, fix my expression into something neutral. "So then... what?"

"I think it might help if I start at the beginning..." she says, then stares at her hands again. "If I explain how things escalated... or, fell apart, I guess. I don't know."

I picture a small Linna standing next to me, her nails slicing into my hand.

"I think it'll be useful, Catharine," Reese interjects. "To hear each other's full stories. I think... you'll want to hear her out."

My eyes slash toward Reese, where he is perched at the head of the gigantic table like some powerful referee. Does he really think it hasn't crossed my mind that he allowed me to believe this was my sister? That he *knew* I thought it was her. He must have. And he used it against me, made me determined to be here, to give up parts of my story. I feel a spike of relief that, little does he know, I still held so much back. But I don't want to argue.

For a moment, I allow my embarrassment to finally creep into the room. I'm humiliated at how completely I had believed that this would be my sister, that she would be some mysterious author. What was I thinking?

I shake my head, brush off the shame. I remember that it's Holly who has to explain herself here.

"Fine," I allow. "Go ahead."

Holly takes a deep breath. "He let me fall in love with the place first."

Immediately I know what she means. Here is one single person who knows the contours of the home I cherished, the one thing I never wanted to leave behind. I hope she doesn't see it on my face.

"Before you fell in love with him, you mean?" I clarify. "Before you two got married?"

And he divorced my mother. And he adopted Linna. And you left.

She blushes so quickly I almost miss it. "Yes," she answers. "When we met I was young—nineteen, a teen mom trying to make ends meet. Linna was barely out of diapers, and my shifts at the health food store were hardly enough to cover our rent. I woke up every morning waiting for my life to take shape, resenting the ways it wasn't how I wanted yet."

Her words sound so much like something Linna would have said that it makes me inhale sharply. I hear the air whistle through my teeth.

"I looked at every man who walked in those doors as the person who would take my life and turn it upside down," she went on. "And then one day, there he was. Smiling at me, asking questions. He came in every week for almost a year before he even brought up me and Linna moving to the farm. By that point, I was waiting for him to ask me. He had painted a picture of a place where everything was easier."

A dark current has entered her voice, and I glance at Reese to see if he's clocked it, too, before remembering that he's probably already heard this. Still, he looks riveted. It disgusts me a little, the excitement. I am less attracted to him than I have ever been.

Her eyes well with tears again, and she shifts her gaze to something slightly behind me. "You know, we used to wonder how much you girls would remember about those years. We'd watch you and Linna playing together, laughing, and say—do you think they have any idea how good they have it? Do you think they'll grow up and thank us for it?"

"You and my father?"

"No." Her eyes shift back toward me now. "Your mom and I."

My mind zooms backward, a VCR rewinding loudly. I try to picture my mother and Holly close, talking. Laughing. Friends. I can't, and that discrepancy between what I remember and what she's telling me makes me feel itchy. I don't dare say anything; I refuse to reveal another thing I have misremembered, or missed entirely.

"We made sure your days and minds were only full of the good stuff," she said, a half smile teasing at the corner of her mouth. "But I guess that didn't work."

"I remember," I correct her, annoyed.

I remember chasing the coolest parts of the day, picking tomatoes at dawn, bringing each to my nose and marveling at the smell, all at once familiar and astounding. Linna taking a bite of one like it's an apple, then saying, "It's so good it seems impossible." I remember sitting on Bertie's lap, memorizing the movements of her fingers as she taught me how to braid my hair. I remember watching my mother laugh in the passenger seat, her face turned toward the clouds, her cheeks flushed with color.

"I remember enough."

She shakes her head. "That's not what I mean. We thought the good stuff would be sufficient. We hid you from anything bad. We hid it so well that I think we started to hide it from ourselves, too. We learned to ignore it. Or at least I did, anyway."

I stay silent.

"I ignored it until it was all on top of me."

CHAPTER 28

Then

There were nearly two miles between the gravesite and the treehouse. For the entire walk, my emotions alternated with each step. My left foot struck the ground, and I was shattered, unspeakably sad. My right foot struck and I was filled with purpose, channeling every bad thing into more effort, more discipline. I was lost at sea (left). I was using it for something bigger (right). I was directionless (left). I belonged there (right).

By the time I got to the treehouse, my body was covered in a thin film of sweat. It was an unusually hot night. The daytime humidity had lingered, and now it hung in the air like a low-lying cloud. But when I got to the top rung of the ladder, I paused, looking around the space. I was surprised to find all the quilts and blankets were pushed aside. Linna sat in the center of the bare floor, her long legs crossed beneath her and the contents of the Ziploc bag spread out around her, winding like a crop circle.

For a split second, I was tempted to start at the beginning, to go all the way back to the moment I had opened the door and found my mother there. How I had reached for the curtains and found the bag, how I had felt nothing but fear. I wanted to tell her how everything she was staring at in awe had only ever caused me pain, how I now understood what had to be done with it. But instead, I listened to the thing inside of me that pushed me toward calm.

"It's nothing," I said, my voice casual, answering the unspoken question that hung in the air.

Linna laughed. "Nothing? Rin, there is twenty grand here. Do you know how much money that is?"

I steeled myself so I wouldn't physically react to hearing the number. Twenty thousand dollars.

I rolled my eyes. "Do you?"

Here was the Linna who I had seen in the treehouse the night my mother died, looking down at me like I was a child.

"It's enough for...for anything," she said, more quietly this time.

"For anything?" I quipped. "Or for your own apartment with Kent?"

She looked embarrassed, though not entirely surprised. "You did hear us talking then? That night?"

I huffed. Did she really think I was this dumb?

"I'm so sorry about that," she added. "I feel horrible."

I brushed her off. "Trust me, I had more important things to worry about at the moment."

Her flush of embarrassment darkened then, her cheeks a shade closer to maroon than pink. Her forehead was dappled with sweat, and she swiped at it quickly. "I know."

I couldn't help it. I wanted her to feel bad, to know how terrible that night had been for me. I wanted her to realize that though she spoke to me like she knew better, she hadn't been there for me in the moment I needed her most. Instead, she had made things worse. I wanted her to know that she didn't know how to save me at all.

"So this is why you wanted to talk to me, then?" I ask, remembering her words at the funeral, how kind she had been. How much I had missed her. I mimicked her words. "*We don't even have to talk... We can just sit here.*"

"I wasn't lying," she replied, sheepish. "I do miss you. Of course I do. I've wanted to talk to you ever since that night. But the money...the way you wouldn't look at me, how you were spending so much time with him...I was frozen."

I don't reply.

"That night, after you found us up here..." she went on. "I went after you. Told Kent I had to go. Ran to the main building. But when I got there, I saw you hide something in the stage. I could see how nervous you looked. I was worried about you. When I saw what you had hid...I panicked."

"And then you took it." I finished her thought.

I had considered going back to check on the money dozens of times but had always managed to convince myself that it was safer and easier to forget about it. Realizing that Linna had had it all this time made me feel ridiculous. Naïve.

"I was worried he'd find it," she whispered.

I shook my head, ignoring her as I picked up the contents of the bag item by item, placing them into a neat stack.

I half expected her to grab my arm and stop me, but she just watched me gather everything, pulling her knees toward her chin. I wondered if she was doing the math again, adding it all up. "We could do whatever we want with this," she whispered. "Go wherever we want."

I am newly grateful that Kent got in the way and I wasn't able to show her any of this the night my mother died. Who knows what she could have convinced me of then, in the midst of my darkest moment.

"It's not yours to do something with in the first place, Linna," I spat, now stuffing the items back in the bag haphazardly, crumpling everything as I went. It was a breezeless night, the air warm and rotten. I felt like I was suffocating.

"I know, but—"

"It's not even mine," I finished, "It's all hers. *Her* escape plan. *Her* money. She wanted to leave me so badly she had a whole secret go bag just waiting there, hanging over us as we slept."

"No." Linna shook her head. "That's not true."

I felt myself unraveling, exhausted from the day, from everything. I felt all those steps to the treehouse pounding through me again, muscles aching.

"Come on, Linna. Just stop," I started. "I mean, I get it. Why would she want to stay here? I was horrible to her, anyway. I left her there that day...drove away with you. And I mean, what a joke, right? Because you don't even want to be here either. I must have seemed like the most selfish, pathetic thing in the world to her. Of course she wanted to be done with me. Who could blame her even a little bit?"

Linna's eyes were full of tears. She shook her head.

"No. Catharine, listen to me," she started, pushing back her emotion, her voice stern now. "The papers...the documents. All of this is for you. Not her. Not *just* her, anyway. It's all for you, too. She wasn't trying to leave you, she was trying to protect you."

I paused, the plastic bag now full between my hands. I stared down at it.

As if sensing my confusion, Linna reached forward, grabbing the bag, then fished out the small piece of paper with "social security card" scrawled on the top, my mother's name below, placing it flat on the ground. She kept digging, pulling out another one, placing it down next to the first. I inched forward, noticing my name for the first time. I remembered how quickly I had gone through the contents of the bag that night, how anxious I had been to get it away from me. I had missed so much.

"I thought... I thought maybe you knew," Linna whispered. "That you were saving it, waiting for the right moment..."

I considered asking, "For what?" But I knew what Linna hoped. It was the same thing that I did. She wanted us to want the same things.

Linna took a large chunk of stapled papers from the bag. The car registration, I remembered. She flipped to the second page, then pointed to a small section of type. My name again. The truck was in my name now.

"When did she..." I tried. "How..."

"I don't know," Linna said. "The papers are dated from right after you got your license. Maybe she snuck out. He's been distracted..."

It was possible, maybe, but it didn't make sense.

"I don't understand."

I felt adrift again, a sea of darkness swallowing me up.

"Maybe she just couldn't do it herself," Linna suggested, her voice soft. "She couldn't get herself to leave."

My thoughts flashed to my father, the way he had talked about my mother only an hour earlier. How he had reminded me where I belonged, of what was worth it and what wasn't.

Linna looked tired, sad. "Maybe she thought you were stronger than her."

Maybe I am, I thought.

"You know what? Why don't you just take it and leave, Linna," I said. "Take it to wherever it is you and Kent want to be and just *go*."

Linna didn't reply. She seemed chastened, unsure of herself.

"Do you even know where that is?" I pushed, sensing a weak spot. "Where, exactly, is this perfect place? Paris? Timbuktu? The moon? It's just like you, Linna. All this dreaming and no commitment. You're ready to pack your bags and you don't even know where you'd go."

For a moment, Linna said nothing. She looked small and ashamed, and I felt as guilty as I did victorious. But then she spoke, her voice barely above a whisper.

"Somewhere cold," she said. "I want to go somewhere cold. With seasons. Snow. I want that. I *need* that."

I blinked at her. My arms were sticky with sweat now. Everything around me seemed damp. Had it always felt this miserable up here? This claustrophobic and suffocating?

The mere thought of snow felt so satisfying, so instantly refreshing, that I almost agreed with her out of pure instinct. *Yes. That. Me, too.* But I couldn't do that. Not now.

Doubt is a sickness, Catharine. It spreads like a disease.

"Why don't you just admit it?" I pushed. "You're not cut out for any of this. You never were."

"And you are, right?"

I wanted so badly to hear a note of jealousy in her voice, but I found none.

"So what if I am," I countered. "What's so wrong with that?"

"That's what he told you, right?" she asked, her voice low and warm.

I didn't say anything.

She continued. "He wants you to think that it makes you special."

I felt my neck grow hot with shame.

"Rin," she insisted, scooting closer to me while I instinctively moved backward. "You are special. But it's not because of this place. It's not just because he says so. It's not because of whatever rules you follow. You know that, right?"

I had the urge to put my hands over my ears and rock back and forth like a child, tune her out. *Doubt is a sickness.*

I forced myself to sound calm, rational. Unbothered. "If you want to leave, Linna, you should just leave."

"I would never leave now, not after your mom," she said. "No way."

I clenched my jaw, swallowed back tears.

"You were there for me when it was my mom...and now I'll be there for you. Even if you're mad at me. I'll wait."

I was awash with relief and fear. I didn't know how to exist without Linna, and I didn't know how to exist alongside this Linna, a person who so desperately wanted something different.

"I'm not going to keep you here forever," I said.

"Not forever," she agreed. "A few more weeks. A month, maybe."

I hadn't realized how imminent her departure was. Before now it had been an abstract, a daydream. Now it was something that was happening. Linna was leaving.

I brought my knees to my chin then, too, matching her position. I rested my cheek there, face tilted away from her.

"Fine. A month. Whatever you want," I said. "But I'm giving him the money. All of it. I'm telling him the truth."

"Catharine," Linna said, slowly. "You're not yourself right now. Just give it some time. See how you feel about it in a few weeks."

"I already decided this, Linna—" I started to push back, but she cut me off.

"What do you think he's going to say when he goes through all this?" she offered. "Sure, you can tell him it was all her idea, but do you think he'll really believe you? Trust you? Do you think he'll ever let you leave the farm again?"

I flinched, but quickly brushed her off. "I don't know…"

I knew I sounded unsure.

"Just give it a month," she said. "See how you feel."

I didn't want to argue with her anymore. I was so tired.

"Fine."

After, we sat in silence for another half an hour, two mirrored images of each other on either side of the treehouse, the weight of the day sinking in. Everything had changed.

"I just don't want to be hungry anymore," Linna said, finally. "I don't want to be constantly fantasizing about gobbling it all up in secret. Life, food. Any of it."

"I understand," I said, and I did.

CHAPTER 29

—

Now

"How bad could it have really been if you married him?" I hear myself ask Holly. "Let him divorce my mother…let him adopt your daughter?"

I stop short of the last part: Then left her there.

Still, she looks ashamed, the judgment in my words curving her spine, sinking her shoulders.

"You excuse a lot when you define your life by how different it is from everyone else's," she said. "I told myself that, of course, it wasn't supposed to feel as comfortable as my life before. Of course it was going to be an adjustment."

That's how you know it's working. My father's words echo inside me, booming. *The effort means you're changing.*

I stare back at her.

"And…your mother," she says. "I don't know what she told you, but by that point, they were already separated, basically. It wasn't working. The divorce was what was best for— "

"I know," I interrupt her. "I know all of this."

I feel suddenly protective of my memories, on edge. It's a new experience, hearing someone recall something from my childhood like this. Not my version of events, but theirs. For a moment, this had comforted me, but now I am panicked. Memories being mine and mine alone had made them malleable and convenient. When I was the only one with them, it was just as easy to convince myself that something never happened as it was that only my version of events mattered. This is different. It feels dangerous, capable of burning down everything.

She looks away from her hands, studying me. "I always knew there was part of her that still loved him. But when we talked, she mostly seemed relieved to have some distance from him," she muses. "But you made things hard, I think."

I bristle.

"Not hard," she corrects herself. "That's not the right word. She loved you more than anything. And you loved it there so much..."

I stand and walk over to the credenza at the end of the room, pour myself a glass of water from a glass pitcher, then drink it down in one go.

"I'm so sorry, by the way," she says. "About your mother. Reese told me. It's horrible, what he did to her... to all of us."

I gulp the final bit of water too fast, some of it spilling out and dribbling onto my chin. I turn away from the table toward the wall, wipe my mouth. I am grateful to have an excuse to hide my face. So Reese has really told her about everything, then. All his little theories.

"Thank you," I reply politely. "It was a long time ago."

I feel warm, my upper lip blooming with sweat. I fill the glass with water again and sit back down to redirect the conversation. "But I'm not sure what that has to do with why *you* left," I say, then hammer home my point. "Why you left her there."

"Right," she says, placing her hands flat on the table.

She pauses for a second, then begins. "It started with Ben and Bertie. I watched them turn in his mind from these amazing people, the ultimate believers…to threats. He saw how much you loved them, I think, and it scared him. Made him feel unimportant."

My mind jumps to the conversation with Reese in the park and I try to push it away, to access all the memories I have that tell me she is wrong about this.

"Bertie, maybe, he could have handled," she goes on. "All women were handle-able, to him, I think. But Ben was different. And they were a unit. You remember, I'm sure."

I think of the photo of the four of us in front of the barn, all of our smiles toothy, honest. I remind myself: Ben and Bertie were happy. We were happy. It was good then. Of course it was. Why else would I have held on to it for so long? Why would I have fought for it so hard?

Holly seems to sense my unease. "They loved you, too, you know," she says. "I think they would have stayed no matter what. Just for you…to make sure you were okay. No one could have convinced them otherwise."

She's trying to comfort me, maybe, but this doesn't make me feel better in the least. I take off my jacket, the leather feeling stiff and constrictive. At once, every item of clothing I'm wearing feels wrong, pinching me, reminding me that it is all only a costume.

"I wonder now if he was using them, too. Testing everything on them. Strange teas and herbs, weeks-long moderation fasts then days with nothing at all. If maybe that's why they…" Holly says, then stops herself.

I want to scream, but I keep my stare blank, my body still.

"In the end, maybe it doesn't even matter." She shakes her head. "What I know for sure is that *I* said yes to all of it. I was the guinea pig gladly. I felt proud, even, to be the person who got to try all of it first. Can you believe that?"

It's clear that Holly isn't just sad now, but angry. She has picked a cuticle so deeply it's bleeding now. I watch her press the sleeve of her jacket into the wound.

"Stupid girl," she mutters. "Stupidest fucking girl in the world."

I must cringe because she looks at me and apologizes. "I know I'm not allowed to say that. To blame myself. But it's the truth. I'm ashamed of how gullible I was, the choices I made. It eats me from the inside."

A better person would tell her now that no, she shouldn't blame herself. That I, of all people, understand. I say nothing.

"By the time I left, I don't think I had eaten a real meal in three weeks...maybe a month," she says. "I was delirious. Out of my mind. I wasn't thinking straight."

I close my eyes, a move that I imagine might read as empathy, but I am trying to remember. I do my best to picture Holly with sunken eyes, collarbones jutting out of her tanned skin, and I can't find it. I consider that maybe she's lying, and I hate myself for it, because I can feel what she's saying is true. I stare at the wall of glass behind her, the city beyond. I imagine placing the few remaining good and pure memories of my childhood on the edge and kicking them off into oblivion, one by one.

"I journaled a lot over the years trying to figure out how I could have been capable of it. Thousands and thousands of pages. I wish I knew."

All my senses sharpen at once. "You're a writer?"

Holly laughs. "God, no. The journaling was just, I don't know... processing. Atonement. I'm a massage therapist now."

"Where?" I push. "Where do you live?"

"Texas," she offers. "Austin. For about five years now."

"And before that?"

I can feel Reese staring at me now, wondering what exactly I'm doing.

"New Orleans. That's where I ended up...after. It's a great place to disappear."

Marion Earl lives and writes in the mountains.

Maybe I really had imagined it all.

I take a moment to absorb all of this, everything she has said. It feels like she is telling the truth. Again, I feel shame crawl up my neck. I am dizzy with how wrong I have been, about so many things.

Holly clears her throat, as if resetting the conversation. "Look, I know Reese said you weren't ready to meet me yet, and I got that," she starts. "I really did."

My gaze shoots toward Reese. He told her I *didn't* want to meet? He delayed this on her end, too? I watch him fiddle with the lid on a cup of to-go coffee, long gone cold, and it dawns on me: He had let her believe that I knew she was alive, and he had let me believe that she was my sister.

"I understood if you thought I was horrible, if maybe you were protecting Linna all these years...hiding her from me," she says quietly. Her mascara has caked into the creases of her eyelids. "I would understand."

A wave of disquiet swirls through me. Linna.

I know the questions that are coming next.

"I need a break," I announce and stand.

Reese stands up too, and for a second, it looks like he's about to try to convince me otherwise. My eyes cut his way. Don't you dare.

"Great idea," he agrees instead. "Let's regroup tomorrow."

I walk out the door without saying goodbye or looking back. I'm a mouse running through a maze, zigzagging with pure, primal focus. I move through hallways and elevators and streets without stopping to think or rest and eventually, I'm in my apartment again, safe.

I crawl into bed with all my clothes on, the careful items I had picked out earlier now clammy with sweat and city grime. My brain begs for sleep, but I'm fixated on how right Holly was: that knowing your decisions were influenced by things that were bigger than you doesn't make them lighter or easier.

In the end, we have to live with the choices we make.

CHAPTER 30

Then

My father didn't talk to me outside of chores for days after the funeral. So much time passed that I had begun to wonder if he had forgotten about our conversation, the way he had implored me to help him rebuild. And then one night, I woke close to dawn to a loud knock on my door followed by a thin burst of bright light.

I sat straight up, startled, nearly slamming my head against the cinderblock wall, trying to orient myself. The entire room had felt foreign since my mother died, her twin bed silently removed, without explanation, along with her body. Rhonda and Stacy had come to me in the days after and offered me a spare bed in the bunkhouse, even though I was already aware there was extra space if I'd wanted it. Years ago, my father had built a dozen sets of bunk beds and lined them up in the long, ranch-style building. At one point, the bunkhouse had been a bustling hub of activity. A giant slumber party. Now, only a handful of the beds were occupied.

No, thank you, I had told Rhonda and Stacy. I needed the alone time. I needed to think. With my mother gone, there were only eight of us now. Linna and (I assumed) Kent leaving would leave six—and that was if Kent's departure didn't inspire Rhonda, Jessie, and then Maura and her mother to leave, too. *Doubt is a sickness, Catharine. It spreads.*

So, I spent most nights alone in the room my mother and I had shared, doing these types of calculations, trying to figure out how to ensure that things got better now instead of worse. It's why I was relieved when my eyes adjusted to the light, and I realized that the presence at my door was just my father, his forehead adorned with a headlamp.

"Catharine," he announced. "Come with me. I need your help."

I sprang out of bed and slid my feet into a pair of sandals in one fluid motion, as if I had practiced it. I was ready.

Still, I had to rush to keep up with my father, who was walking at an impressive pace through the main building, then out the door, then toward his cottage. I was still drowsy, trying to wake myself up with the movement. I jogged to keep up. "Coming!"

It was officially spring now, and a heat wave had blasted through the middle of the state, leaving the air unseasonably sticky and thick. I was drenched in sweat from the walk by the time we arrived at the front door. It may not have been my first time there, but I felt a thrill at walking inside this place again, once forbidden and mysterious. I held my breath as he unlocked the door and opened it, a burst of freezing air whooshing toward me. Air conditioning.

I tensed only for a minute before I remembered that I wouldn't be here too long. Air conditioning, my father had explained to us many times, circulated disease, but it did so slowly. It was fine in small doses, my father had told me before I started doing the farm store pick ups and drop-offs. An hour here. An hour there. It won't hurt you. It's the prolonged use—the addiction to the comfort of it, he had said—that causes the real damage. Here in this ice cold, pristine room, my mind was swimming. What made this different? What made him different? Immediately, I hated myself for the questions. Questions were weakness, a path to a loophole, a way to get out of hard work. Didn't I remember?

I followed my father into the living room, my eyes traveling over the furniture I had seen weeks ago but hadn't fully absorbed. I stared at the couches, white and completely spotless, each layered with thick pillows. We hadn't had a sofa at the farm for a long time, not since the one in the dining hall started stinking of mold. Even before then, it was old and torn, perpetually moist with humidity. These couches looked like two clouds having a conversation with each other, both floating on top of a thick, plush rug. I knew I should have been more comfortable there than anywhere else on the farm, more physically at ease, but the wrongness of it rubbed against my skin. I was not made for places like this.

He briefly disappeared into the adjoining kitchen, then reentered the room with a glass of water and gestured toward one of the clouds as he sank himself into the other. "Sit."

Delicately, I perched myself on the edge of the couch, almost hovering, hesitant to let my weight sink into the plush white cushions. I looked around the room, taking in the art that lined the walls, the bookshelves full of books with uncracked spines and unfamiliar titles. I had seen all of this on the night my mother died, but my senses had been dulled by grief. I had missed so much. I had missed how everything in the room rippled with newness. I couldn't think of even one thing I had owned in my life that wasn't a well-worn hand-me-down, and here was a room of objects that belonged to only him. Envy thumped through me before I could think better of it. I looked at my filthy feet and the truth was clear to me: I was not a person who deserved all of this. I could feel my father's eyes on my face, watching me.

"It's astonishing," he said. "Same nose, same eyes."

He meant the two of us, I realized. I had heard this before, how much we resembled each other, but I'd always had trouble seeing it myself. The comparison made me feel uncomfortable, awkward. This time, there was something else: A spike of disgust, unmistakable. What was wrong with me? I made myself smile.

"Not totally the same, though. Not quite. There's something else with you... an edge." He squinted toward me, then shrugged, shaking the thought away. "It's like looking in a funhouse mirror."

Again, I felt the urge to recoil at his words, even though I was fairly sure he intended them as compliments. I chalked up the reaction to discomfort, a result of being in an unfamiliar place.

"Do you remember what we talked about, Catharine?" he asked. "After your mother's burial?"

The sudden change of subject was jarring but welcome.

"Yes."

"Great," he said, kicking his feet up so they rested on the edge of the couch, placing a pillow under his neck. "I've decided what we need is some sort of a protocol. A system."

I was lost. "A system..."

"Yes," he answered. "I mean, officially."

"Oh," I stumbled, trying to hide my confusion.

"It's like everything else here, Catharine," he explained. "You know the aphids? The pests?"

I thought about them, those microscopic creatures that created so much extra work for us when they struck and multiplied, ruining entire crops at lightning speed. "Yes."

"When they show up, what do we do?" he asked.

I wracked my brain. This felt like a test I had to pass. "I mean... insecticidal soap..." I tried. "Pyrethrin... neem oil. Whatever kills them."

"Right, yes, good," he replied, sounding slightly frustrated. "But before that, what do we make sure of?"

I was drawing a blank, panicking.

"We tell everyone else," he continued, answering his own question. "We make sure everyone knows the extent of the infestation. We make sure everyone knows what to look for, and we stay in constant communication. Teamwork. Right?"

I felt silly now, young. "Of course. Yes."

"And we always get rid of them before they take over everything," he finished. "Yes?"

Goosebumps crawled up my arm and I swatted at it instinctively, the thought of thousands of aphids running across my skin making me squirm. "Yes."

I could see where this was going now.

"We need that here, Catharine," he said. "If we're ever going to build this back up... make it all it's supposed to be, become all *we're* supposed to be, then we need to eliminate the aphids."

I felt the word *eliminate* trigger an alarm in my chest, a siren screaming through my veins. I pushed maturity into my voice and sat on my hands, which had started to sweat despite the chill in the room. I wanted so badly to match his tone, a cool matter-of-factness, but all I felt was a low, rumbling panic. "I see."

I was starting to suspect that the conversation with Linna had twisted something in me, pushed me toward some weaker version of myself. Someone with questions instead of self-control. I had felt so smug after that night in the treehouse, determined. She thought she had a month to convince me to leave, and I was sure I had a month to convince her to stay. It was the only thing that mattered. But her words had stayed inside me. *He wants you to think this place makes you special.* There was an imperceptible crack inside of me, and I was spinning to find it, to fix it.

"Can you help me with that?" my father asked.

I opened my mouth to reply, to say yes, of course I could, but I couldn't get the sound to come out.

"It's you and me now, okay?" he reminded me. "You and me together."

I nodded, still unable to talk. Yes, I wanted to say. Yes, I know. What was wrong with me? Why was I freezing like this now? I knew what was at stake.

He let his words linger for a while, adjusting himself on the couch and taking long sips of water.

"You know that I'm not naïve," he said, his voice smooth. "I know doubt when I see it, Catharine. I can practically smell it on her."

My heart was beating so hard that I could feel it in every part of my body, blood pumping through me in one violent whoosh after another. He meant Linna, of course. He wanted me to tell him that she wanted to leave.

I opened my mouth again, coaching myself through what I knew I had to do. Maybe this is what will change her mind, I thought. Maybe this is the only thing that would.

"Kent," I said. "It's Kent. He wants to leave."

He studied me, and I sat up straighter, as if owning what I had revealed, proud.

"Huh," he remarked, then lowered himself back on the couch so his eyes were fixed up at the ceiling. He cradled his skull with his hands. "Fascinating."

"And soon," I added. "He wants to leave soon. It's all he talks about."

"Is that so?"

"Yes."

I shifted uncomfortably on the couch, waiting for him to reply.

"Thank you for telling me, Catharine."

A tide of relief washes over me, leaving room for only a microscopic prick of guilt. This is what needed to be done, I reminded myself.

"This will change everything for the better. You can feel that, too. Right, little one?" my father asked, eyes still turned upward, unblinking.

"Yes," I said. "I can feel it."

CHAPTER 31

Now

Reese waits less than twenty-four hours before he texts me.

> Thanks for yesterday. That was really powerful.

I ignore it, then turn on read receipts. At least now he will know for sure that I am ignoring him. Maybe then he'll understand.

Six hours later, he texts again:

> Would Tuesday work for another meeting?

An hour later:

> Holly is anxious to keep talking.

I laugh out loud. Oh, Holly is the anxious one. Sure, Reese.

Thirty minutes later:

> Look, if this is about what she said... about how I told her you weren't ready. I can explain. I think what's happening

> here is really important. This story is really important. It needs your voice, Catharine.

I roll my eyes. What a crock of shit.

I get a small, sour burst of satisfaction imagining him staring at his phone, all those unanswered texts stacking up, crushing his ego. I want him to know that I am weighing whether I want to keep doing this, to remember that I could still back out now. I could say it's too triggering. That I'm too upset by it. That I'm horrified by what Holly did, leaving Linna there like that. None of it would be a lie.

I expect the texts to continue, but my phone stays quiet for the rest of the day. Part of me is disappointed by this. At the very least, the texts were a distraction, a way to ignore exactly how meeting Holly had unmoored me. It frightens me how sure I had been, how I had looked at her face and still missed what should have been obvious to me. I battle waves of nausea each time I recall how I had said it out loud, so confident. *Linna.*

I think of *Lighthouse* and Marion Earl and the way I had peppered Holly with questions about her job and where she lived, still deluding myself with a version of the paranoid fantasy I had been entertaining. I remember the subtle glances and phrases from Reese that made me so sure that Linna was his source, and that Linna was the author I so loved. I was wrong, though. About all of it. It's clear to me now that my gut instinct is a thing that cannot be trusted. A dangerous and easy liar. It's been a long time since I have intimately known that particular shame, and now I'm sinking in the thick ooze of it.

Seeing Holly in that room made it impossible for me to ignore just how much I had deluded myself. It meant that it was more likely than ever that I would never see my sister again. But the worst part, maybe, was that I should have known. I had assumed Reese's source couldn't have been Holly because she was dead. My father looked us in the eye and told us so. But he had lied. Of course he had. How many podcasts have I listened to by now that spelled out what he was? A narcissist. A sociopath. A manipulator capable of anything. I should have *known.* And yet, I had let myself divide portions of my childhood into good and bad. Before and after. Until yesterday, I would have sworn it: He was good, once. It was all good once.

I imagine trying to describe the gardens to Reese again, the tomatoes, the feeling of collective energy, the way my father championed it all. The way it made me want to hold on and fight for it, the mistakes it forced me into. Oh, you poor thing, Reese's look would say as he laughed. What was it Holly had said about herself? You stupid girl. You stupid, stupid girl.

I feel exhausted, but find myself pacing my apartment, restless, going back to the photo of Ben, Bertie, Linna, and me again and again, fixating on small details. Each time, I expect something sinister to appear in the background, like it's a faded Polaroid in a horror film, an image that reveals a ghost. I only see the barn, though, its wood long faded to gray, its roof speckled orange with rust. I have the urge to walk into the street and show the photo to passing strangers, thrust it in front of their eyes, ask them what they see. I need someone to confirm to me I am not mistaking it, that each of us really does look happy.

I make myself remember when it was taken, using the greenery and wardrobes to try to place an exact month and year. I remember the short-lived painting classes, which means it was taken after Holly "died," but before Ben and Bertie did. Linna was just starting to act like herself again, emerging from a cocoon of grief. I would have once described it as one of the happiest times of my life, years and years before it all went bad, before things changed.

All that time, it had already been happening. Holly and my mother had been talking about it, like friends. There were so many things that I never saw.

I know it should maybe comfort me that they tried to hide it all from us, at least when we were young. It would mean it wasn't all my fault. But then I think of Linna, the ways she had gently warned me. The ways she loudly warned me. She always knew. I think of Holly and me both searching for Linna, imagining where she could be all these years. I think of us finding nothing, nothing, nothing. Convincing ourselves of signs that never existed. I think of my father standing in a golden sea of trees, telling me what he did and who he was. I think of what I chose to listen to and what I ignored.

The clock on the oven flashes 10:48 p.m. and I force myself to put the photo back on the shelf, then take myself to the bedroom to put on clean pajamas. I opt for the softest pair of shorts I own and an old tank top. Comfort clothes. I want to disappear into my bed and sleep for twelve hours without moving. I take out my contacts and put on my glasses, wire-rimmed and crooked. And then there is a knock at the door, loud, repetitive bangs reverberating through my apartment's paper-thin walls.

I figure, at first, that it must be a mistake. Someone who meant to go to 3A instead of 2A. But then there's another knock. It's not aggressive, but insistent.

"Coming," I yell from the bathroom, searching the hamper for a robe, a sweatshirt. The knocking continues and I groan as I scramble, throwing on a stained hoodie. I expect to find a guy in a bike helmet expectantly holding out a bag of Chinese food. The words "wrong apartment" are practically falling out of my mouth when I open the door a crack and see Reese there instead.

"Oh," I say, staring back at him, crossing my arms across my braless chest. He has the irritating glow of someone who is just beginning their night out. I am pretty sure I have a pimple patch somewhere on my face.

"Hi," he says, his eyes quickly giving me the once-over. A small smile flashes across his face, a nanosecond of arousal, before he seems to think better of it. A mask of seriousness falls over his features.

"How did you get this address?" I ask, tightening my folded arms around my chest, straightening my posture.

"Sometimes I really am good at my job, you know," he replies. His tone is serious, but his gaze is playful. There's something else, too, about how he's standing. There is a slight, nearly imperceptible sway in his stance, a lack of balance. He moves to lean on the vestibule wall and jolts slightly, like he misjudged the distance. "Plus, I told Stella I wanted to send you something. A surprise."

The last word exits his mouth slowly, with effort. Reese, I realize, is a little bit drunk. I study him and think of how I must seem to him now—messy bun, mismatched socks, ratty, barely there pajamas. Before now, he has only seen me in carefully curated ensembles, sparkling with hair and makeup and effort. Right now, to him, I am a woman who is off her game. He'll assume I haven't had time to prepare for this. Maybe that's why he had a drink or two or three before he came here. It didn't matter if he was a little loose, a little off. He would still have the upper hand. I open the door a little wider and lean against it, loosen my arms. I relax.

He stuffs his hands into the pocket of his jeans, then shrugs a little. "Is now a good time?"

"It's 11 p.m., Reese," I say, deadpan.

I can't just fold immediately. Obviously.

"Right," he says, like he's just remembering this. "I know. You're right. I was just out, and I knew you lived nearby and I thought . . . I needed to explain. To make sure you understood everything before you just disappeared off the face of the earth."

So he is worried. Good.

I stay silent for a few moments, like I'm really considering what he's saying, then I open the door wider, gesturing lazily for him to come inside, like I'm exasperated. Too tired to push back. So he will think he has won.

I'm grateful that my apartment is always impeccably clean, everything in its assigned spot. There are a couple of photos of me with friends on the wall, enough to make my life seem full despite our relationships amounting to the occasional email, empty promises to get coffee sometime soon. There's a snapshot of Stella and me, too, on a girl's trip to Charleston. There is a vintage dish that holds my keys and wallet, a well-watered, healthy plant sitting on a stand. I look like a person who has a life, who hasn't made the thing that happened to them when they were a kid the only thing that matters. I zoom out and see us both there and I realize that what Reese is seeing is someone who is dynamic, soft and strong in all the right places. Imperfect in the most inoffensive way possible. This kind of thing is catnip to guys like him, who say they prefer women who don't wear makeup or shapewear, that what they're really attracted to is *confidence*. Please.

Reese walks around with the kind of cautious yet curious saunter that all men perform when they're in a woman's home for the first time. He stops at the fridge and seems to scan the half a dozen or so Save the Dates that are stuck to the front. I've collected them over the years. Women I took spin class with for a few months. Women I met up with for a drink to gossip about the media industry. The weddings have come and gone but I've left the invitations. They all seemed to prove that I was someone trustworthy, normal.

By the time Reese spins around, I'm already sitting on a barstool at the counter, comfortable. He stands on the opposite side, the kitchen island in between us, then places a palm on the marble countertop.

"I met Holly about two years ago," he starts, like a confession.

For a moment it feels ridiculous, as if he is revealing that he cheated on me, like he's about to follow it up with, "it meant nothing, I swear."

"She reached out to me on Facebook, actually," he says. "Said she saw an article I had written about an extremist group out in California, that she briefly lived in a community in Florida in her early twenties that she now realized was probably a cult."

I force my brows together as far as they will go, try to look worried.

"If it wasn't for her persistence, I probably would have ignored her. You'd be shocked at the number of messages I get just like that," he trails off, shakes his head. "As much as I wish I could investigate every slightly woo-woo yoga studio owner, I just can't. I don't have the resources."

I wait for him to continue, silent.

"But what Holly was talking about was different," he goes on. "Brutal. I mean, what she was talking about was serious... murder, potentially. Intense abuse. And I believed her."

How generous of him. I nod solemnly.

"And once I started looking into it, trying to find Linna... well, I got a little obsessed," he admits. "I spoke to people who spent weeks on the farm—though never longer than six months—and they always told me how great it was. Crunchy, sure. Unpleasant? Yeah. But evil? Not so much. But here was Holly with a darker version, telling me about a daughter she couldn't find. No trace of Ben and Bertie, either. Or your parents. Or, for a while... you."

At this last bit he lifts his chin and stares into my eyes. It feels like a monologue, rehearsed and stilted. I don't say anything.

"I even went down there, you know," he adds. "To Florida."

The room starts to spin, but I force myself to push whatever internal button it is that controls my composure. "Oh?"

"Yeah," he says. "I had to cross-check real estate records for months before I found a property that fit Holly's description. But I found it, found him—or at least, the version of him who bought the property. As it turns out, the man loved a fake name."

He pauses then, staring at me. I don't blink. "Makes sense."

He uses a hand to push back his hair, which has fallen over his forehead.

"You know what my friend told me when I went down there?" he asks, with a chuckle. "He said there is more space than you could ever imagine between Tampa and Miami and Orlando. A million miles of nothing. He called it the Bermuda Triangle of happiness. Where people go to die."

I nod. I'm sure I look bored. It's not like it's anything I haven't heard before.

"And sure, at first, it felt a bit like that. But after a day or two of driving, I don't know..." he goes on, staring at me. "That boundless, wild kind of open space...the repetition of the landscape. The way you had to really pay attention to note the subtle ways it changed. The sunset burning over all that land...it wasn't exciting, maybe, but it was beautiful."

I don't expect this from him, and my genuine surprise means I don't stop myself before I reply instinctively. "I know."

"Right." He smiles at me, lowers his voice. "Of course you do."

Maybe it's just the buzz, but there's a note of familiarity in his voice that feels new. I think of how Stella had asked about us after she saw us at the bar, and I had told her we were friends. Maybe he really believed that, maybe that's why he's being so candid now. Maybe he feels a little guilty. That would be fine with me.

"But it's the craziest fucking thing. I got to the place, and do you know what was there? A Sam's Club. Massive. Second biggest in North America. Just opened. Enough parking spaces to rival a theme park. It's a shame, really...all that untouched land, spoiled."

I feel a rush of heat to my face and my mouth waters, a physical precursor to vomiting. I fold my hands in front of myself and press my wrists to the countertop, the stone cooling my skin. I repeat the information to myself internally: The farm is gone.

After so many years, I had figured as much. I knew it was safer that way, if it all disappeared. But this was something different. All this time, Reese had listened to me talk about the farm and he had known. He had been there and he had said nothing. It feels like a violation. I want to pummel him, to scream, but I focus on staying neutral, guarded. "I see."

Reese narrows his eyes toward me, assessing something. "Turns out, it had been abandoned for years by the time the state seized it. Looted in places. Burned down in others. It was just a pile of debris and weeds when they sold it to Sam's Club."

I try to remember the last image I have of the farm, a snapshot of beauty, but all I can see is color. A slow-growing pool of ruby red tinted golden in the evening light.

"Are you upset?" he asks. "I know it must be complicated for you...to know that it's gone."

I tense at the thought that he can read my reaction. "Oh, so *that's* why you didn't tell me any of this?" I laugh, pivoting the conversation. "Just looking out for my feelings, huh?"

"I couldn't tell you everything," he replies. "You know that. That's not how this process works."

I stand up and walk around the island, grabbing a glass from the cabinet and filling it with water from the tap. I expect Reese to trade places with me, to make more room in the crowded galley kitchen, but he stays put. When I turn around, we are less than two feet apart. His eyes dart upward, like he was just looking at my legs, my ass.

I make my eyes travel over his face before I ask the question, linger on his mouth for half a second too long. I watch his pupils dilate.

"What about lying to me? Is *that* part of the process?" I say, trying to push a different button. "Doesn't exactly seem like the pinnacle of journalistic standards."

He blushes. "I didn't lie."

I snort.

"I delayed things a little bit...about Holly's willingness to meet, sure. But I didn't *lie* to you about anything," he says, then pauses. "Well, except once."

I raise an eyebrow.

"I did lie once."

My eyes go wide, waiting. But he just laughs.

"The book," he mumbles, looking at his feet.

My mouth goes dry. "The book?"

"Light..." he snaps his fingers, searching for the name. "Light... light something."

I stare at him, unblinking. "*Lighthouse.*"

"Yup," he nods. "Never read it. Not one word. But I knew it was popular. I remembered seeing it everywhere a few years ago, all those girls reading it on the subway...I don't know. I wanted to impress you." I try to recall the particulars of our conversation. What was the word he had used again? Remarkable. He had said it was remarkable and I had just believed him, given the word some magical meaning.

It is such a small and boring series of lies, but it makes me want to cry instantly. It is a final, needless kick to the ribs. How stupid I have been. I can't bring myself to say anything else.

"I understand if you're angry…I get it. I will admit that I am not totally myself around you. This is usually…not me. Typically, I *am* the pinnacle of journalistic principals, I promise you." He pauses, glancing at me, as if checking that I had clocked just how closely he had been listening to me earlier. His eyes fix on the ground again. "I just…I thought we had some sort of…"

His words are gently slurring together now, soft around the edges. It almost pains me to stay silent, to make him say it, but I wait. Eventually, he gives in.

"Connection," he finishes.

His gaze meets mine now, and though his cheeks are flushed, his eyes are bright and hopeful, sharp blue. It is the look of someone who is finally sure of something. I don't say anything. I imagine he will interpret my silence as an agreement.

"And honestly, Catharine?" he goes on, after taking a deep breath. "You made me nervous."

I snort again. "Nervous? Why? Because of this *connection* you speak of…"

He grins, unfazed by how I mocked him. In fact, he looks almost charmed. "No." He shrugs. "Well, maybe. But it wasn't that simple."

I swallow.

"It just made it easier to tell, I think," he says. His words are clearer now, crisp and careful.

He's so close to me that I should be able to smell the alcohol on him, but instead I inhale and smell bergamot and cedar, the faintest hint of an expensive cologne. Instinct tells me to bury my face in the warm place where his neck meets his shoulder and inhale deeply, but I redirect the energy into my question, pushing. "To tell what, Reese?"

"When you were hiding things," he answers. "Calculating what to hold back and what to give me. Protecting something. You, him, someone else... I didn't know. I still don't know, even after everything Holly told me... especially after everything she told me. But I could hear the wheels turning in your brain all the time, no matter what. Whirring. Every second."

I steady myself against the counter.

"Now, too," he says. "Right?"

Right.

CHAPTER 32

Then

The night after I told my father about Kent, he knocked on my bedroom door again, flinging it open, his headlamp dissecting the room with a now familiar beam of blinding light. I reacted slower this time, though, exhausted from the lack of sleep the night before and the day of paranoia that followed.

I had left my father's cottage that morning just as the sun was rising. I didn't know what my father would do with the information I had given him. The language he had used had been so definite, so clear and full of determination. Eliminate. Destroy. But I knew my father. Even in his most furious moments, there was never physical violence. I couldn't imagine him hurting Kent but, beyond that, I wasn't sure of anything.

My father had become harder to predict since my mother died, his moods erratic, his schedule unpredictable. It was why I followed Kent around the entire next day, crouching behind tall patches of grass and watching him as he went through his daily tasks. The entire time, I kept zooming out and seeing myself hiding there, wanting to laugh. What was I expecting, exactly? My father to jump out from behind something and scare him? Hurt him?

Commit some horrible act? By the end of the day, nothing had happened, and I felt ridiculous. I realized I had been delirious with exhaustion, my thoughts peppered with paranoia and fear, irrational. Of course my father wasn't going to do anything to Kent that he couldn't handle. I thought of my younger self standing in front of bowls filled with cow manure, shame oozing from my pores. I had survived, I reminded myself. Kent would, too. Even if it was the worst-case scenario, it would be a wake-up call for everyone, I concluded. For Linna, too. The best-case scenario was that my father would forget about what I had told him entirely.

When he stood in my bedroom doorway that next night and announced that it was time for a new moderation fast, I was relieved. It was as if our conversation about Kent hadn't happened at all.

"Water only," he said. "That's what needs to happen now, Catharine. That's what will flush out the doubt and weakness in this place."

I tensed, my stomach curling around itself instinctively, remembering hunger. There had only been one water fast before, just after Crystal and Bianca left. It was a tool to remind us that we are stronger than we think, he had told us. But it had made everyone miserable, unable to complete even the most basic of chores. We lost an entire crop of strawberries that month because people kept passing out in the fields when picking, too weak to keep going in the heat.

"Oh," I said, the skepticism evident in my voice.

"What?" he snapped, walking into my room, standing over me. "You don't think they need it? That you need it?"

I shielded my eyes from the light.

"No, no," I insisted. "It's not that. It's just... last time..."

"Last time, what?" he pushed, his knees bumping into the edge of my bed. I scooted backward, toward the place where my bed met the corner of the room. I looked up at him, and it was the first time I realized how much thinner he had gotten recently, his eyes sunken into his face, shadowed by sharp cheekbones. "Last time, it was hard? Is that what you're trying to tell me?"

I swallowed. The lack of sleep was dulling my reaction time, making me choose the wrong words. I knew what he was saying. The difficulty was the point. It was what weeded out people who were weak.

"We *need* hard, Catharine," he went on. "One hard reset. Back to what's important. You want that too, don't you?"

I nodded rapidly. For a second, I let myself picture who I would be after the fog of deprivation passed but the satisfaction of dedication remained. I imagined myself in that small closet, my body perched on the glowing scale, every cell ringing with pride. I would remember how I had held all that hunger in my hands and used it like my father taught us to, as a tool, a gift. "Yes. I do."

He smiled, though his eyes were fixed somewhere behind me now, drifting. "Ten days this time. That's what we need."

My face fell. Ten days. It had only been five the last time, and it had wreaked havoc on all of us. Logically, I knew that humans could survive for weeks on end without food. Years before, my father had gone through an obsession with survival stories. We read *Robinson Crusoe* and *Hatchet*. We studied edible plants. We learned to start fires. But I couldn't imagine ten days with nothing but water. It felt impossible.

"Yes," I agreed, forcing belief into my voice. "You're right."

"Excellent," he said, turning to leave, his last words floating over his shoulder as he walked out the door, not bothering to close it behind him. "We can let everyone know tonight at family meal."

The room was dark again then, the rapid shift in light disorienting me. Ten days. The thought of all those hours without any food made something rise up in me, greedy. I calculated how much I could steal from the kitchen tonight, how much I could stuff into my body before it all began. Weak thoughts. But then I remembered how quickly he had forgotten about Kent, how fast he had seemed to change his mind. Maybe this would be like that, too, I thought. Maybe by tomorrow it wouldn't be ten days but five or six, instead. Something more manageable. I told myself all of this until it eventually lulled me back to sleep, all the while completely ignoring the last thing he had said, the way he had so casually used *we* as if he had been doing it all along.

That night, our usual picnic table felt as if it could collapse from under me as I ate, slowly bringing each bite of food to my mouth. No sudden movements. I could tell Linna was watching me intently from the other side of the table, curious. I had to admit that was something about our relationship that had seemed to soften since our conversation after my mother's funeral. All our secrets were finally on the table. It felt like the first time we had fully relaxed around each other in years.

"What's up with you?" Linna asked me, pushing her glasses up her nose. "You're being weird."

I concentrated on a piece of wilted spinach on my plate, stabbing it repeatedly with my fork and failing to skewer it. "Just tired."

She nodded, but I could tell she was still watching me, skeptical. She was about to say something, but before she could speak, three short claps rang out behind me. I turned to see my father standing on the stage, his eyes wild and red-rimmed.

Linna shot me a questioning glance. I shrugged to indicate I wasn't sure what was going on, but my body barely moved, my joints icy.

When we were children, my father used to give daily announcements and lectures from the dining hall stage, but it had been years since he had stood there proudly. It felt silly to give a speech to eight people, he told me a year prior. I looked around the room, my eyes traveling from Rhonda and Stacy at their table to Maura and Jessie at theirs. "Where's Kent?"

Linna's eyes were fixed on my father, alert, but she shrugged. "Probably still working. Why?"

"No reason." I shook my head, but the motion was too quick, too forced. I could see her notice my fear, the one secret that I had not shared crawling under the surface of my skin.

She started to speak, but my father had begun talking.

"What this place needs," he started. "Is a reminder of what is necessary."

I saw Rhonda nodding out of the corner of my eye. Her shoulder bone was sharp and angry under her skin, soft cotton draped over the tip of a knife. When had she gotten so thin?

"Knowing your full potential and worth is as simple as understanding that the boundaries you have put in place for yourself are imaginary. What is necessary to be your highest self isn't comfort, but the opposite. Pushing past the ideas of what, exactly, you need to be satisfied... that is what changes everything."

I watched his eyes fall on Linna. "I think that some of you have forgotten that."

A single word clanged in my mind: No. No. No.

Finally, my father's gaze lifted from Linna, then traveled lazily across the room. "I know Kent certainly had."

I turned again toward Rhonda, who had wrapped two matchstick arms around herself now. When I glanced back at my father, he was looking at me. He winked.

I felt something acrid and sharp turn over in my gut, guilt or pain or something else. There was no time to investigate the feeling. It was something rotten, and so was I.

"That's why he chose to leave today," he added. "When I confronted him about his gluttony for that world... well, ultimately, he said there was nothing for him here anymore. We agreed."

I could see Linna's chest rise and fall rapidly in my peripheral vision, but I didn't dare make eye contact.

"So," my father started, hands steepled together. "Anyone else, then?"

He scanned the room, as if being careful to account for each one of us. There were only six of us now, all women. In the past, I would have imagined a scene like this would horrify my father. So many people gone. The only other man on the property gone now, too. How would anything get done? But he looked pleased with himself. Satisfied. Relieved, even.

I watched Stacy reach for Rhonda's hand, a small acknowledgment of her loss, but Rhonda jerked away. Her chest was splotched red, the color curling up her neck. It felt cruel and intimate to witness her reaction so plainly on display, and worse yet to find no trace of grief. But I understood. I knew what it was like to claw for sadness only to find a thousand layers of shame.

The floor creaked as my father walked to the edge of the stage and sat on it, his legs dangling over the side, like he was a character in a musical about to burst into song. He was only five feet away from us now, and though my body was twisted to see him, one leg on either side of the bench, it was Linna who was facing him directly. She sat completely still, her hands folded neatly in front of her, nails carving into the tops of her palms.

"Catharine came to me last night and expressed her worry over our commitment as a community. I can't help but agree with her. Kent had been here since he was a child and yet had no connection to this place, no appreciation. What does that say about the rest of you? I'm beginning to think that maybe none of you are grateful," he continued, now walking around the room after hopping off the stage and standing next to me. "It's exactly why we decided we need to get back to basics—a water fast."

I could feel the eyes of everyone in the room on me now, not just Linna but Rhonda and Jessie and Maura and Stacy, too.

"I—" I began, but the words were lodging in my throat, blocking my airway. I brought my hand to my neck and pawed at it. I needed water, air. I needed my mother. My gaze went toward her old spot, at the table with the other mothers, expecting to see her there, a safety net. I felt as if I was sitting side by side with a version of myself from the not-so-distant past, the one who said that one day I would regret pushing her away. I thought of the money, the car registration in my name, all the conversations we had had over the past year, the ways I had ignored her when it was clear she was trying to prepare me for something. I realized it was possible my mother had imagined this exact moment, and I had looked her dead in the eye, intent on running straight toward it.

My father went on. "Who knows? Maybe we're wrong." He shrugged, strolling past the tables where the rest of the women sat. "But there is only one way to find out. Water fast begins tomorrow morning. Ten days."

No one made a sound, but I could feel the collective fear in the room, the vibration of it hovering around us.

"That's all," my father finished, his voice bright and assured.

Slowly, Rhonda and Stacy started to get up, then Jessie and Maura, too, dirty dishes in hand. I stayed put, processing what had just happened, Linna's eyes still locked on me, steeled.

My father had looped back around to the stage at this point, standing on the spot where he had begun the announcement. "Oh, and one more thing," he added, causing the rest of the women to freeze where they were. "There's going to be no mistaking things this time. We're going to know exactly who committed and who didn't at the end of this."

He went behind the tattered velvet curtain, reappearing a second later, his hand wrapped around a clear glass square. The scale from the closet, no longer a secret.

He placed it on the center of the stage, then glanced toward Linna.

"Commitment is nothing without accountability," he said, then waved at the scale. "Well?"

Finally, Linna looked away from me, her gaze meeting my father's. Pure defiance. I imagined all the words she had been storing up for this moment, the precise way she would strike.

"I'll go," I offered, hoping that volunteering would distract my father from Linna, or give her a chance to leave or calm down or do anything that wasn't this.

There was a pause as my father considered this, but then he nodded. "That's my girl," he said. "Never afraid of a little discomfort."

My face flashed red as I absorbed the compliment, knowing how much worse it would make all of this. I would look like a suck-up, eager to be the center of attention. But at least it wouldn't have to be Linna up here first. I climbed up the few stairs to the stage and walked across, standing in front of the room.

I took a deep breath and exhaled before stepping on it, already knowing the number that would appear, having snuck into the weigh-in room three times in the last twenty-four hours. I thought of how I had lied to Linna months ago about the scale, somehow imagining it wouldn't all get back to her, that she would avoid this. That maybe it was a tool that only I needed. I stared at the ceiling as my father announced the number to the room. There were two golf ball–sized holes in the metal roof, jagged imperfections of mysterious origins that had been there for as long as I could remember. I knew the exact spot in the room to place the buckets during storms.

"Always room for improvement," he remarked at the number, telling Stacy to jot it down. "Right?"

I was still staring at the ceiling, but a cloud had passed above now, and for a moment it was easy to imagine that something had miraculously filled the gaps. Two marshmallows. Some cotton balls. A pair of crisp white socks. That just beyond all the hard edges was something softer.

"Catharine?" my father pushed.

"Right," I heard myself agree. "Always room for improvement."

I looked down at Linna and she was still staring, but now a single tear hovered in the corner of her eye. I watched as it fell and raced down the bridge of her nose and felt the rotten thing inside me burn.

CHAPTER 33

Now

It's obvious that Reese thinks he has surprised me, or maybe that I'm supposed to be flattered by how well he understands me. I half expect him to lean closer, grab my hand, and say, "I see you, Catharine. I see all of you." The cliché of it nauseates me, but in a way, I am thankful.

I can spot clearly now the root of Reese's attraction to me. To him, I am a product of a wretched place. A thing to figure out or mend or soothe. A way to make himself feel big and capable. I imagine telling him just how broken I am. He doesn't mind broken, he would say. But what he would really mean is that he likes it. It excites him. It makes me interesting, and him brave. Normally, I'd have no patience for this. But now, I see some value in it. He wants so badly to crack me open and to see the mess inside that he's becoming desperate for it, needy. I decide I will make him beg.

"You really expect me to keep talking to you if that's what you think of me?" I try. "That I'm some calculated, cold monster? Come on."

"I don't think that. I think..." he starts, then shakes his head. He actually blushes. "I think you're brilliant."

I laugh.

"I mean, scary as hell, just to be clear," Reese adds. "But brilliant."

I don't react, determined not to let the instinctual warmth from his praise reflect outward. "Still trying to impress me, huh?"

He smiles. "Actually, I'm beginning to suspect that may not be entirely possible."

I hear myself laugh again and as I do, I realize it's genuine. He's not wrong.

A moment passes before either of us says anything, but eventually he takes a deep breath and tries again. "We're not really that different, you and I."

I silently cross my arms and wait for him to explain.

"I do it, too. Studying people. Learning them. Making note of what they want, what they're scared of. What turns them on."

We're still standing in the kitchen, each of us leaning against a parallel countertop, our toes almost touching.

"I become obsessed with learning the thing that's causing them to share or hide something. It's all I think about," he adds. "Every conversation, every moment, always drawing a detailed map of them in my head as I go."

A chill shoots up my back, a physical acknowledgment of truth, of recognition, but I say nothing.

"It's exhausting, isn't it?" he asks.

For only a second, I imagine how easy it would be to give in now, but I steel myself. I need it to feel like he has earned something in the end, like he is painstakingly knocking down my walls, like he will do and tell me anything to make it happen.

"Isn't that all kind of just part of your job, Reese?"

He makes a sound between a laugh and a sigh, clearly exasperated, then steps toward me. I flinch, but don't move aside as he reaches into the cupboard above me for a glass. "May I?" He fills it from the tap behind me before I can reply, and as he does, his arm brushes the soft, bare skin of my hip where my sweatshirt has inched up.

I realize it's the first time we have touched, skin on skin. Usually, there is nothing I love more than this moment. That first line crossed. All that anticipation buzzing inside one single gesture, every nerve electrified and alert, waiting. I can feel my body react to the sensation before my brain does, my pulse ragged. My breath hitches in my throat slightly, and because he's so close, I know he hears it. He lingers then, slowly drinking his water, him facing the sink and me leaning into the counter. I know I could lean an inch to the left and it would be done, but I luxuriate inside the moment instead. It is almost better than sex, this hovering, the way it can go on forever. The way it can be used.

Suddenly, he places the empty glass in the sink, then steps back, but his hand skims over my hip again before he does, then stays there, his thumb gliding over the ridge of my hipbone before his fingers lazily travel upward, toward the bunched hem of the sweatshirt. They linger there for a moment before gently tugging the fabric down, covering the exposed part of skin. Then he steps backward and stares, both of us acknowledging the intimacy of the moment but not speaking. He crosses his arms over his chest, then nods to himself, like he's made a decision.

"You should listen to something."

He reaches into his pocket and pulls out his phone, then taps and scrolls until he finds what he's looking for.

"It's one of my first interviews with Holly," he says.

I'm disappointed. "What difference will that make to me? We talked. She told me her story."

"Not all of it."

A sharp wave of pleasure passes through me then, knowing that he's revealing something. I will not be embarrassed or surprised again. I have learned my lesson. I will know everything there is to know. I will take no chances.

"Look, I know what it means to tell the truth, to put it all on the table," he goes on. "It's fucking terrifying. It feels like losing something. I get it. So, this is me putting it all out there. I want you to trust me."

He looks directly at me now, confident. Assured. "No more games."

God, men love those three words, don't they? They think there is nothing sexier. I feel the warmth from the moment earlier simmer off of me and dissolve. I also see an entrance. A space to insert the tiniest bit of hope, a taste of my whole story.

"I have way more to lose here than you, Reese."

I've already lost so much, I think but don't add, afraid to lean toward melodrama, however true it may be. I watch his gaze sharpen, hungry for something.

"*This* is why your story is important," he says, pointing toward the phone, the recording. "Your whole story. There are too many questions without it."

Then he hits play, fast-forwarding to the part he wants me to hear, skipping ahead ten- to fifteen-second increments at a time. When I hear my mother's name, I make him stop and press play.

We listen.

Holly: Lisa started sneaking me food when I'd get really weak, lethargic from the lack of calories I was taking in during the fasts. He was so distracted with building the place up that he'd disappear for long stretches of time, leaving us to take care of the kids. At first, she'd only stay for a few minutes, dropping off some bread she had made earlier that day, a salad, a fresh juice. But then she'd stick around for a bit, and we'd talk. She told me about her own story, about what it was like when they had first moved there, what he was like. And it was... comforting, weirdly.

Reese: How do you mean?

Holly: She said that he used to be different... lighter, happier. That, in the beginning, he believed in more of a gray area. They used to go into town on dates, she said, eat at restaurants. Share a bottle of wine. Now, there was none of that. He had gotten a little lost, she said. A little confused. Creating rules he couldn't even stick to himself. And then there was the matter of Catharine.

Reese: His and Lisa's daughter, correct?

Holly: Yes. Linna's best friend, too. They were inseparable. It was part of why, even when it got worse and the fasts got longer, I thought... could I ever really take my daughter from this life? Could I do that to her just because I couldn't handle it? Because I wasn't strong enough?

Reese: It must have been complicated.

Holly: Not as complicated as it was for Lisa.

Reese: How do you mean?

Holly: The thing was... he was obsessed with Catharine.

Reese: Oh, I didn't realize—

Holly: No. Not like that. Not in a sexual way. I know

that's what people assume, but it was something different. It was like she was this extension of him, this malleable thing he was determined to shape. That's what Lisa said. He doted on her. Had all these plans for her. He was nice enough to Linna, too, but with Catherine it was different. It was obvious. Lisa said that this whole place...the farm, the business, the community...to him, it was all a gift for Catharine. Something to leave behind, for her to carry on.

The tape goes quiet for a second, and I can feel Reese's eyes on me as I take in what Holly had said. I wonder if it's obvious to him how unsettled I am, how sick I feel. It is as if I am underwater, everything around me muted and blurred. The pause stretches on and Reese opens his mouth to talk; I expect him to ask me if it's true, if I had noticed my father's obsession with me, too. Instead, his tone is matter-of-fact, explanatory. "I was letting her fill the silence," he says. "The more you talk, the less of the story you get." He seems proud of himself. I nod and try to look impressed instead of nauseous.

Holly: Lisa and I only talked about leaving once. I was delirious with hunger, even with the food Lisa had been sneaking me. Miserable. Depressed, I now know. I was so unlike myself that I was barely taking care of Linna. I'm ashamed of that, but it's true. It was the only time I asked Lisa if she ever wanted to leave. She said she thought about it all the time.

Reese: Really?

Holly: Yeah, it surprised me, too. Because I knew she loved it there. But then it was like she knew she had to correct herself, to explain. She said that the only way she could make sure he didn't get out of control was if she was there. This place still had so much good to offer, she said. So much joy. She could help him avoid all the bad stuff. Bring him back to how things were before, a more balanced state. And then there was the other thing. He would get over *her*, she said. Forget about her within a week or two. He had already done it once, she said. But Catharine? No way. He would never, ever let her go. Not a chance.

Reese stares at me as I listen to this, and I have the thought that I am going to be sore tomorrow. I am tensing every muscle, freezing it in place so as to not reveal even a sliver of what I feel. I stay calm and still by imagining myself in various situations of intense danger. Locked in a car that's driven off of a bridge, water silently lapping at my feet, then my ankles. Trapped under rubble after a natural disaster or an explosion, carefully conserving my air. I tell myself the only way I survive is if I stay calm. I measure my breaths. Inside, I am melting into panic, but I force myself to be still, clearheaded enough to see a path to daylight and safety.

Holly: She said that even if she left, even if she disappeared in the middle of the night, if she took Catharine with her, it wouldn't matter. He would find them. He would find Catharine. And if forced,

Catharine would choose him. He had made sure of this, he told her. Everything was engineered so Catharine stayed, so she would carry it all on if something ever happened to him.

Reese: And you don't know what happened to her, either? To Catharine?

Holly: No.

Reese: What was she like? What do you remember about her?

Holly: She was sweet, creative. Smart as hell. But she had this way of watching you . . . of watching Linna, really. Keeping careful tabs on her.

Reese: Jealousy?

Holly: Maybe a little, but it was more complicated than that. It was like she tied her emotions to Linna's. If Linna was unhappy about something, Catharine was devastated by it. I mean, just absolutely leveled emotionally. Sometimes, I thought it was sweet. Girlhood friendships can be intense like that. Other times, it frightened me a little. It reminded me so much of what Lisa said.

Reese: How do you mean?

Holly: The way Lisa said that Catharine's father would never let her leave? I always kind of thought that Catharine would never let Linna leave, either.

CHAPTER 34

Then

I knew that Linna would be at the treehouse later that night. I knew that there would be one flashlight shining, a physical symbol of what I already understood: She wanted me nowhere near her. But I ignored it, climbing up the rungs anyway, desperate to explain to her that I was only trying to help.

When my head poked into the treehouse, I had to immediately duck, dodging an object flying through the air. I looked to my left. A pillow. The room was in chaos. Art ripped off the walls. Every dusty trinket on the shelves turned over, every book flipped upside down. The ground was so cluttered that there was barely room for me to sit.

"Linna," I whispered. "What are you doing?"

Linna laughed. I could see now that her face was streaked with angry tears, but she didn't look at me, continuing to page through books and push aside blankets.

"What am *I* doing, Catharine?" she said. "How about what are *you* doing? A ten-day water fast? Have you lost your mind?"

"It wasn't like he said," I pushed back, panicked.

For a second, her anger disappeared into something practical and fierce. "He lied?"

I felt lost again, unsure whether to undermine him, expose myself, or both.

"Well, no," I managed. "Not exactly. It just isn't as simple—"

"Right." She laughed, then continued her tirade, turning over every item in the treehouse, pawing at it all, searching. "You know what? I don't have time for this."

My voice was so small. "What are you...are you looking for something?"

She didn't answer me, and I quietly sat in the corner, watching her whirl around, frantic. "Can I help?"

"I think you've helped enough, don't you?" she spat.

"I'm sure Kent knows you're going to meet him out there soon," I offered, imagining Kent setting up an apartment for the two of them, patiently waiting for Linna. "That's probably the only reason why he left."

Linna stopped then, throwing down the box of knickknacks she was digging through. "You can't be serious, Catharine. Honestly. After all this time."

I was lost. "I don't..."

She was crying again now, frantic. "Kent is gone, Catharine. *Gone.* Do you understand what I'm saying?"

She was hysterical now, I realized. Irrational. I tried to sound reasonable, unemotionally reminding her of the facts. "He left, Linna... just like he said he would, just like he told you. It's not like he's..."

I didn't want to say dead. It felt so theatrical, so extreme. Hadn't she been there in the room with my father? Hadn't she listened to him explain? When confronted with a hard choice, Kent chose to leave. It made sense.

"He is, though, Catharine," she said. "I can feel it."

I tried to make my voice sound soothing. "I think maybe you're just a little overwhelmed..."

She shook her head. "He said he'd leave me a letter. He said if he ever left, if someone ever told me that he just walked out of here...I should know that there would be a letter. I would know he was okay."

"I'm sure it's here somewhere, then..." I offered, casually picking up a notebook that had fallen on the ground next to me and paging through it. "It must be."

Linna was sitting on the ground now, her body still, her hands combing through her hair, pressing on her forehead. "It's not. He's gone. Your father did something to him. I'm sure of it."

The way she had separated us by using the mention of *my* father hurt me. It was like she had stripped away our sisterhood. I laughed lightly, my way of signaling that this all felt so melodramatic, so overblown. "Linna, really, listen to yourself. What you're implying is insane."

"Insane?" She shook her head. "You have to know by now that he's capable of anything. You must."

My skin prickled. "He *cares* about us, Linna. That's the root of everything."

Linna laughed, the sound shrill. "Please."

I wanted to prove it to her. "What about your new room? The main building? He wanted you to be more comfortable. Happier."

"Is that what he told you?" I didn't reply. I had assumed as much. The main building rooms were coveted. Linna went on. "He gave me that room so he could *watch me*, Catharine. The more time I was with you, the less I'd be with Kent. Or anyone else. Easier to control. He knows that."

I blew air out of my mouth. "Don't be ridiculous."

"You know what," Linna replied. "I shouldn't even be talking to you right now. You're just like him. Maybe you always have been."

I felt the blow of the insult, the cruelty in her tone. It wasn't the comparison to him that hurt me the most, but the implication that she no longer knew me. That our relationship was something else now, that I was.

She sat up then, staring at me intently like she had in the dining hall. "I need you to be honest with yourself for a second, Rin, and really think about what this place is. Not what it was, or what it can be, but what it actually is in this very moment. What he is."

I tried to do what she was asking, to access the very first thing I felt, and there was no denying it anymore. The shape of it had seeped through that deep crack inside of me. It felt wrong. It all felt wrong. The way he had lied to me and manipulated my words, the scale placed in front of the room, the look on Rhonda's face when he said that Kent had left, the way skin hung on her bones. Wrong, wrong, wrong. But how could I explain to Linna that I could never trust my first instinct? If I did that, I would give in to every impulse I had, every craving. I would want and want and want until it was all I did, until the weight of it crushed me beneath its feet. I could never trust myself like that. It would kill me. I was thankful she hadn't actually asked a question, that I could avoid trying to make her understand any of it.

"Kent is fine, Linna," I insisted again, trying to sound as warm as possible, as comforting. "Leave tomorrow. Go find him. Take the money... it will all be fine."

I hoped the offer of the money would distract her, or maybe pacify her. It would be an olive branch, a reminder that I wanted her to be happy.

"You really think this is all about Kent?" she pushed, ignoring the mention of the money. "And nothing else?"

I shrugged.

"The fasts, the weigh-ins...it's not normal, Catharine," she went on. "It's getting worse."

I avoided eye contact, busying myself by looking through stacks of quilts and behind old pillows, half-heartedly helping her search for this letter she was so intent on finding. "It's just one hard reset..."

"How many hard resets do we fucking need, Catharine?" she said. "When will it be enough?"

However many it takes, I wanted to say, but I just shrugged again.

Finally, I looked at her and saw the anger was gone, only sadness left in its wake. "If you stay here, it will grind you down to nothing. He will. I'm sure of it."

She sounded paranoid now, a lovesick girl blinded by grief. Gently, I repeated the offer. "Take the money, Linna."

"I don't want the money," she said, but she sounded tired. There was no fight in her voice now. "It's yours."

"I'm not going to use it, anyway," I insisted. "Take it. Build the life you want. Please."

She looked at me like she was gauging how serious I was now.

"I couldn't," she said, but it sounded half-hearted, weak.

"Yes, you could," I forced myself to say. "Of course you could."

It hurt me to push her like this, but it was the only thing that lessened my shame. This was my fault, I realized.

"Keep half," she relented. "Promise me that. Keep half of it hidden away from him somewhere. Just in case."

I thought of my mother then, the driving lesson where she had told me that my mind would change one day, whether I liked it or not. I didn't want to fight with Linna anymore.

"Fine," I agreed, telling myself I would deal with the money later, decide whether I was going to give it all to my father, after all. What difference would it make to him if he never knew the full amount, the original sum? Linna would be long gone by then. It wouldn't matter. "Go find Kent. Go be happy. I'll be happy here, too. I'll be good."

My voice broke on the last sentence, and I could tell it activated something in her, too. I wondered if she thought this was me admitting something, telling her that I knew it had all gone bad but I was too scared to say it out loud. She stared at me like I was a lost, broken thing. She stared at me like she was desperate.

"You can't bully yourself into being happy or good, Catharine," she whispered. "You can't hate yourself until you get there. It doesn't work that way."

Why not? I wanted to say. Why does it matter how I get there so long as I do? I closed my eyes and thought of myself in the weigh-in closet, all that bone-deep pride ringing through my body, the way I had fought for it. I had the instinct to protect that feeling, to wrap my arms around it. That feeling was mine. I had earned it.

I laid back, lacing my hands behind my head, then stared up through the leaking skylight. I watched a star blink, then two.

"You'll miss some of this, won't you," I said, so quietly I wondered if she'd heard me.

Linna sighed, and I closed my eyes, pretending to fall asleep. I didn't want to argue anymore. I just wanted to be here, to remember a time when it was this simple. I wanted to press pause, to freeze us both in place. So much time passed before she eventually replied that I nearly missed it.

"Sometimes I worry I'll miss all of it."

CHAPTER 35

Now

By the time the audio recording of Holly's interview finishes, it's almost one in the morning. Reese tucks his phone back in the pocket of his jeans, then looks at me expectantly.

"You get it now, right?" he asks.

I think of the way Holly had spoken about me in the interview, like I was a manipulative child, sharp and calculated. These were qualities I'd believed I fought hard for, acquired with age and experience. To imagine myself as somehow ruined from the very beginning, powerless against my father's influence, disturbs me deeply. No wonder she was suspicious. No wonder Reese was. "I get it."

I walk toward the living room and I feel Reese's eyes follow me. I need to move around. I need for him to not be staring at me, dying to know what I'm thinking. I strum my nails over the raised design on the outside of my water glass, a soothing, repetitive motion, a satisfying sound. I need to think.

I can see it on his face so plainly, pity mixed with disgust, curiosity sprinkled over all of it. He's wondering: What kind of darkness, exactly, makes a person like me?

"So why don't you just ask me, then?" I say, finally.

"Ask you what?" he replies, his voice light. He stands, turning to face me, then reaches up to stretch, revealing a long, tanned torso. A second passes, then two. I'm sure he feels me watching. He strides toward me, his movements smooth and confident.

He's sober now, I realize. More sober, anyway, than when he got here. Instantly, I begin to doubt my perception of him for the entire night. Was it possible that he had not been that drunk at all? Had I miscalculated something? I think of how I had expected to smell alcohol on him but didn't, the way he had so shamelessly and, at times, effectively, flirted, how his words had swayed between slurred and crystal clear. Is it possible that it had all been an act?

No more games. When did any man ever mean exactly that?

I steady myself.

"About Linna," I answer calmly. "About what happened. Whatever you think I did to her."

This seems to pique his interest, but he remains light, breezy. His expression is so open it almost reads as amused. He lowers his voice, like he is talking to a child. "I know you didn't hurt her, Catharine."

I close my eyes. I don't know whether to feel relief at this remark or wild, all-encompassing guilt. I'm still considering this when Reese speaks again. "I mean, you clearly loved each other."

I look at him and he's standing by the shelf with the photo of the four of us at the farm, gesturing toward it casually. When had he noticed that? When he first walked through the apartment? Had he just been saving the observation for now, for some dramatic, targeted reveal?

"We did," I reply, not letting myself react to his acknowledgment of the photo. "I still love her."

"What I *can't* figure out," he adds, "is why you won't tell me what happened to her, then."

He manages to make this sound like a fact-checking exercise instead of an accusation, which would almost impress me if it didn't unnerve me.

"I told you," I say, my voice barely above a whisper. "I don't know."

He nods at me, then turns toward the photograph, inspecting it. It feels like another violation, like he has forced himself into a place where he doesn't belong. "What happened to *you*, then, Catharine," he tries. "How did you get here?"

How did you become this? he means.

"Why don't we start there?"

I nod and begin to carefully pull out another set of memories, leaving so many others behind.

A couple years ago, Stella and I had both taken weed gummies and I let it slip that my mother had actually died when I was young. I backtracked quickly, explaining to her that it was just easier to lie to people about it, to say we weren't close. People asked fewer questions that way, I said. They pitied me less. I expected Stella to shower me with sympathy, but instead she looked almost relieved.

"That explains it," she said. "The commitment issues, the obsession with independence . . . it all fits."

She was psychoanalyzing me, I realized.

"Trauma makes us who we are," Stella explained. "It's the only way we understand ourselves, each other."

Her reaction had fascinated me, how swiftly she had boiled down everything about me to one tragic event. She hadn't even thought to ask what happened next, or considered that maybe that wasn't the only loss I had experienced, the only trauma that shaped me.

"Thank you so much for telling me," she had said.

It was almost remarkable how much the revelation had seemed to endear me to her, how much closer our relationship felt afterward. It had unlocked a new level of trust. It taught me how to say something true without being honest, and that there are benefits to that. Protection. It would be the same with Reese, I decided. I would tell him one more horrible thing, and he would assume that there was nothing else to tell. It wouldn't even cross his mind that the story could get worse.

I look at him, his finger hovering over the record button. I nod, and he taps the screen.

"You were wrong," I begin. "I did hurt my sister."

True.

"It was the worst thing I ever did."

Also true.

"It was why I finally left."

Not quite.

CHAPTER 36

Then

I felt Linna's absence as soon as I opened my eyes, the room hushed except for distant, intermittent birdsong. I sat up slowly. It was dawn, the treehouse dimly lit but clearly neat now, everything in its proper place. She must have tidied it silently, long after I had fallen asleep. There was only a single sheet of paper on the floor now, her messy handwriting scrawled on the front.

Thank you. I love you. -Linna.

I wondered if she was thanking me for the money or for letting her go. Maybe both. It wasn't like she had explicitly told me that she would leave that night but I had felt it, its unspoken weight hanging between us. It had been almost a month since my mother's funeral. Kent was gone. Everything had changed. It was time for her to leave. Finally, I knew I had to let her.

I curled myself back into a ball and ignored the sounds of chatter and commotion now coming from the main building, people starting their chores early, beating the heat. I was so tired. I closed my eyes and reminded myself that it would be easy enough to explain to my father why Linna had left. It turned out that it was just as he had suspected, I would say. Linna was just like Kent after all. She wasn't committed. And no, I didn't know when exactly she had left, I would answer him honestly. I felt sleep drag me back down then, my body calmed by the idea of simultaneously pleasing my father and giving my sister more time to go far, far away from here.

A few hours later, I woke feeling rested, sure of what I needed to do. As I trudged through the gardens to his cottage, I tried to tell myself that this was a fresh start. An opportunity. I would feel the sadness of losing Linna like I felt the hunger. I would hold it in my hands and use it as a tool.

I knocked on the door with confidence, considering that maybe this new state of things should feel like a relief. Yes, my mother was gone. My sister, too. But so were the voices saying I should want something different. Even half of the money being gone should have made me feel lighter. I knocked again, louder. I could already sense that I was kidding myself; that there would be no relief to be found. I felt so alone it seemed unfathomable.

I knocked once more, harder this time, my knuckles aching from the effort. At this, a voice sounded from the back of the house.

"I'm coming," my father's voice boomed, coming out like a groan.

Soon, the door flung open, my father standing there in a bathrobe. I had seen him look tired plenty of times before, especially lately. I had seen his eyes rimmed with red, bloodshot and swollen. But what I was looking at now was something different. He looked browbeaten, bone-tired. A shell of himself.

"Did I ask you to come by today?" he said, audibly annoyed. He turned and walked toward the kitchen, leaving the door open behind him. I took it as a sign I should enter.

"No," I said, talking to the back of his head, straining my voice so he could hear me from the kitchen. A moment later, I heard a buzzing sound, an unfamiliar mechanical hum. I talked even louder. "I just... I wanted to let you know that Linna is gone, too. She left to be with Kent."

I sat on the couch and waited for him to reply, but he said nothing. A few minutes later, he entered the room with one of the miniature white mugs I had seen before, held between his thumb and pointer finger. Steam rose from the mug and the scent wafted toward me, earthy and warm.

"Coffee?" I asked, trying to keep my tone curious instead of accusatory.

He rolled his eyes, like I was an idiot, a child. "Decaf," he said. "Decaffeinated. Obviously."

I hadn't known before then that this was an option, that there was a type of coffee that was safe. A spring of jealousy went through me. It smelled so good. But maybe I hadn't been listening close enough, I reminded myself. Maybe he had mentioned this to us once and I had simply missed this detail somewhere along the way.

He set the cup down on the table between us and took off his glasses, massaging the spot between his eyes. "What do you want, Catharine?"

I had made a mistake by coming here, I realized.

"I just..." I started. "I just wanted to tell you about Linna. That she left. That's all."

"Right. And now you've told me."

I stood to leave, tears stinging behind my eyes. I knew my father could be harsh; I had seen how he acted last night, but this felt unreasonably cruel. Purposeless. He knew how close Linna and I were. We were sisters. She was his daughter, too. Hadn't he said that once? Where was the man who had brought Linna here, who looked at us and saw the magical thing that connected us?

Where was the person who had brought me tea when my mother died, comforting me? "I can go..."

"Wait. Catharine," he said, raising a hand to stop me. "I'm sorry. I just had a late night. I'm exhausted."

I should have felt comforted by the apology, but something about what he said sent alarm roiling through me. I sat back down, processing this.

"Well, that," he went on. "And I already knew."

A single hair rose on the back of my neck like a pinprick. A warning.

"I already know that she left," he added. "I saw her last night."

"You did?"

"Pure coincidence, really, that I spotted her out there in the dark," he mused. "I was running."

I had seen my father jogging across the property many times, his white tank top tinged yellow with decades of sweat stains. It was what helped him think, he said. But at night? It didn't make sense.

"I couldn't sleep," he added with a shrug, as if anticipating my question. "Like I said."

"Oh," I said again. "Right."

He broke out into a big, rolling burst of laughter. "She had a backpack slung over her shoulder like she was going on some sort of a mission... crouching through the grass. It was hilarious, really."

I felt dread start to build, the feeling wrapping itself around my legs like a jellyfish, stinging the whole way up.

"She told me she was just on a walk, but come on. You saw how she looked at us last night, didn't you?"

Us. The word was a piece of paper slicing under my nail.

"I don't know, I—"

"Please. You saw that defiance. That doubt. It was dripping off of her," he went on. "Disgusting, really."

I couldn't be there anymore. I stood up again, thinking I might be sick. "Actually, I just remembered I was supposed to wash the—"

"Sit," he said, and I did, too nervous to push back.

He crossed his legs, resting the cup of coffee on his kneecap. "Really, it was just instinct that I thought to look in her bag. I had had *such* a long night already, and I almost ignored the hunch but gosh, am I glad I didn't."

I locked my teeth and lips together, prepared to swallow down the bile that was rising. I glanced at him, hoping he couldn't sense my fear, but he was staring past me now, his eyes fixed on the window, the gardens beyond it.

"And then I said...hm, a bit strange to go on a walk with ten thousand dollars in your bag, isn't it?" he chirped. "A bit odd."

A scream built in my chest. He had found the money.

"It was a mess after that, really." He shrugged. "The yelling, my god. The whining."

I had to wrack my brain. Had I really slept through something so horrible? Had my body learned to forget my sister, the sounds of her fear, that quickly? I thought of what Linna had told me about Kent, what it meant that he was gone. That he hadn't left her that note. And I had laughed in her face. I had actually laughed.

"Do you know how much ten thousand dollars would do for this place?" he asked. "How many improvements we could make? That's more than someone's brought in in years."

Wait.

"What...what do you mean?"

He was looking at me now, eyes playful. "You don't think people just come here for free, do you? That all this knowledge and community comes with no price? People prove their commitment through a donation first, Catharine. The more people, the more donations. It's exactly why there's no room for dead weight. We need people to come here and know that they made exactly the right choice. People like Kent? Like your sister? Your mother? No, we don't need that at all. They're a liability."

I had never thought about money. About people paying to be here. There were no salaries, no tuition bills, no supermarket checkout lines. I knew we made some money from the farmers markets, the farm stores, but as I looked around me, I realized how naïve I had been. I stared past my father, taking in the freshly painted walls adorned with art, lighting. I thought of Ben and Bertie, Stacy, Rhonda... everyone. They paid for this, I thought. They paid for all of it.

"She kept saying she found it." He laughed. "She really expected me to believe that she just wandered across it one day, like it was a shiny penny. It was absurd. Of course, she had stolen it from us. From someone. It was obvious. And besides, that deception... the way she saved it for herself, her new life with Kent. What utter selfishness. Makes me sick."

So she hadn't told him that the money was mine, or that I had given it to her, or even that it was my mother's. It was a gesture that felt so unearned I wanted to weep, but I kept my eyes fixed on my feet, staring at the half-moons of dirt under my toenails, my sandals hovering over the plush white carpet. I didn't want him to see my face now, to question what was racing through my mind.

"She wasn't angry until I told her about you, though."

I was an ice cube plunging into a glass of lukewarm water then, my insides snap-cracking. "About me?"

"About how you had your suspicions about her. Her commitment to this place."

"I never—"

"Come on, Catharine," he said, rolling his eyes. "We don't have to lie to each other. I knew exactly what you meant when you said Kent. Kent wants to leave. It's that simple. Right. Wink, wink."

I can't breathe.

"I know you, little one," he said. "I understood what you were trying to tell me."

An image of my sister's face then, her disappointment in me bottomless. She must have thought that I sent him after her. That I told him everything.

"She threw a fucking fit at first, screamed bloody murder when I tried to take the bag away, but what did she expect?" he said, setting his coffee down on the table. "That I was just going to let her walk away with it? Take what was more mine than it was ever hers? It's just silly, really."

"What did you do?" I whispered.

His eyes focused on me now for first time since I arrived. "I took the money, obviously."

"I mean…"

He raised one eyebrow, waited. "Oh," he finally said. "Oh, Jesus. You think I hurt her? That we had some brawl out there in the middle of the night? Catharine, really, who do you think I am?"

I was confused. Isn't that what he had been explaining this entire time? Isn't this what he had been telling me? He kept laughing, and the sound was hideous, garish and mocking.

"I thought…"

I was drowning in rage, treading an ocean full of it, pushing it away in useless handfuls. I was tired.

He stared at me for a long time then, carefully, waiting for me to finish my reply. But I felt like I had nothing in me to give him anymore. My world had been emptied out and I had, too.

"Wow," he said finally, his eyes wide. "You don't believe me."

I couldn't reply. I couldn't stomach lying anymore.

He shook his head. "After all I have done for you."

I felt shame swirl into my anger, a familiar sludge, choking me.

"We're done here, don't you think?" he announced then, reaching for his now-empty cup on the table, accidentally knocking it over in the process.

I reached for it on the ground, helpfulness ingrained in me, and he mirrored the motion at the same time. As he stretched forward, the sleeve of his robe inched up his arm, a brief flash of color popping beneath the plush terrycloth fabric. It was quick, but I knew what I saw, what it was. A gash running down his forearm, red and angry and fresh.

CHAPTER 37

—

Now

The day after Reese's late-night visit to my apartment, I get a text from Holly asking to meet.

> Reese gave me your number. Can we talk? Just us?

I don't know what he shared with her already, but what I told Reese during the interview was true: I had hurt my sister, in almost every way possible. The ways I had failed her felt irredeemable, violent. I had never known exactly what happened that night when my father found her, but I couldn't deny that whatever it was had been my responsibility. So, of course, I couldn't have stayed there on the farm after that morning at my father's cottage, I had explained to Reese. Of course I had to leave.

I had watched his face as I told him that part of the story, explaining to him how I had seen the wound on my father's arm and known, without a doubt, that I could no longer participate in his cruelty.

It felt like running full speed into a cement wall, I told Reese, and I'm instantly exhausted at the idea of retelling it all again to

Holly, carefully highlighting specific details to ensure she believes me completely, sharpening the pain and loss she already feels. But I do want to see her again, to have the chance to apologize in person. To see if she actually believes I am different now.

I reply, and we agree to meet tomorrow for coffee.

"It's not your fault," she emphasizes, stirring an iced latte. "He brainwashed you."

I adjust my position in the seat, uncomfortable. I hate that word. *Brainwashed.* It feels both childish and clinical to me, conjuring images of silly girls sitting in the front row of magic shows, eyes wide, ready to be deceived. It makes personal responsibility disappear.

When I don't reply, she insists. "I hope you know that."

I remember Reese lecturing me about trauma, about blaming myself instead of my father. I don't want to argue with her about any of it. "I do.

"It's not your fault, either," I manage, then clarify. "I heard what happened... after. What he did... it's horrible, Holly."

Thanks to the recording Reese played for me, I know the whole brutal tale. The day Holly left the farm, she had been on the third or fourth week of an intense fast, weak to the point of hallucinating. She'd gotten in the car with my father, expecting to be back in an hour, so sure of this that she didn't even say goodbye to Linna.

But he had discovered she had been sneaking food, breaking the rules, and she had been too out of it to push back against the accusation. He had her sign what she later realized were custody papers and then dropped her off at a motel room, prepaid for a month. He had lined the room with tall stacks of chips and candy, dozens of cases of soda. If she was so determined to pursue gluttony, he said, then he would help her do it. She told Reese it was weeks before she emerged from the room, and when she did, she found the motel was full of people like her, everyone missing something desperately, trying to fill the void. That night was the very first time she got drunk, she said. A month later, she had moved to harder things. It had taken her fifteen years to get sober, to feel like she could finally face Linna and apologize. When she couldn't find the farm on her own, she contacted Reese.

"It was horrible," she agrees. "It was."

I realize I don't know which part she's responding to, the fact that she had left or the things my father had done to her. Maybe it's all of it. I don't say anything.

"He could have been lying," she says, her voice hopeful. "About finding her that night."

I smile limply. I considered that once, too. "But the money..."

I can see a version of myself reflected in Holly's tone, the pinch of need behind each word. Some part of me wants to tell her all about Marion Earl, to describe to her just how blinded by hope I had been, too. Look where it had gotten me. I might have never even replied to Reese's first email if my head hadn't been filled with those stories, convinced that all of them were laced with secret messages, hidden codes. Signs that Linna was just fine, that maybe I didn't have to hate myself so much anymore.

"Right," Holly admits. "But the mark on his arm...it could have been from anything. Farm work. Repairing some part of the old barn."

I nod, though my heart isn't really in it.

"Or maybe he wasn't lying. Maybe she did get away. She fought back and hurt him. But ultimately, she got away, and..." She's stirring her latte so rapidly now that the liquid is sloshing over the side of the glass. "And he spun it as him letting her go. That would make sense, wouldn't it?"

This, too, I've thought about, for more reasons than Holly knows.

"She could still be out there," Holly insists while I stay quiet. "We could find her."

There are two teen girls sitting next to us, phones hoisted over pain au chocolats, staging the shot. They switch phones, then take photos of each of other mid-laugh, cappuccinos outstretched in front of them. Throughout this entire process, they don't even talk. They seem at ease, light. Content to just be near each other. I smile. "Maybe," I say to Holly. I'm sure she can hear the lack of confidence in my voice.

"I think Reese is right," she adds. "Our stories are powerful."

I want to roll my eyes, but I don't, just listen. Wait for her to fill the silence. Isn't that what he had said?

"I wasn't sure about going public with it all at first. There was so much darkness, so much guilt. It took me years to even think about everything that had happened, to remember. It's why I drank. I wanted every memory to be a black hole. And then I got sober, painstakingly. Found Reese. Found you. And I was convinced that even if you didn't blame me, or didn't hate me, that I'd still end up dredging up all of this old shit and relapsing. But it's been the opposite. Talking to him, to you . . . even if we haven't found Linna yet, it's still been worth it. It feels like starting over, like I can finally breathe again."

I'm happy for her. I am. I admire how easily she has let go of her guilt. She's practically glowing. But we are not the same.

"I'm so glad you feel that way," I say, diplomatic, and take a sip of my coffee.

"We could find him, too."

I am mid-swallow when she says this, and my jaw cracks on a large piece of ice, hitting an exposed nerve on a worn-down molar. I close my eyes, waiting for the pain to pass.

"Your father," she clarifies, like I don't know who she means. "God knows he's still out there. New identity. New name. New schtick. New people buying it. He's like a lizard. Limbs that regenerate. The man would survive anything."

I run my tongue over where the ice cracked, searching for the sensitive spot. "You're probably right."

A question occurs to me then. "Are you two still... married? Technically?"

She shakes her head. "Turns out the custody papers weren't the only thing I signed that day. I had no idea. It's pathetic, really."

I try to remember what it was like on the worst days, the ones where I was so tired I felt like I could sleep for weeks, food the only thought in my brain. I could have been convinced of anything, too. I was.

"You left," she says, finally. "But what about everyone else? What do you think happened?"

I'm watching the girls next to us again. One of them is talking to the waiter now, flipping her hair, batting her eyelashes. The waiter laughs, touches her shoulder. The friend is hunched, shrinking into herself, tapping through a game on her phone. I can feel the rage slowly steaming off of her.

"I don't know," I answer, shifting my gaze toward Holly again. "I left so quickly. I had to build a whole new identity to survive. Honestly, it was hard to care what happened to him, to the rest of them—other than Linna. She was gone. My mother was gone. Ben and Bertie gone long before them. I had no reason to be there, not really. Afterward, the less I thought about any of it, the more it felt like I dreamed the whole thing. That was easier."

Holly nods knowingly. "I understand."

I wish she would drop this. I run through topics in my mind, what subject to move on to next, but she keeps going.

"But if you *had* to guess. "She shrugs like it's a casual question, but her tone says she isn't going to let this go.

"If I had to guess," I exhale, "I'd say that me leaving scared him."

Holly's eyes light up with interest, or maybe rage.

"He would have spun out, burnt it all to the ground and started over, taken the rest of them with him. Started somewhere new where you or I would never think to find him," I finish, trying to remind her that what I'm telling her is nothing she didn't already think and suggest herself. Nothing new.

It's not that I haven't anticipated this part of things, the kinds of searches that will happen when Reese publishes his story, but we're months away from that. This is the kind of long-form investigative piece that takes years to assemble sometimes, Reese had told me. My involvement meant that every interview he had done prior was different now, each piece of information recontextualized. He wasn't starting from scratch, but it was something close to that. We had months before his story would be done, maybe a year. Maybe he would do a podcast instead, he had mused. Either way, I have time.

"I really expected Reese to find him there," Holly says, her eyes focused somewhere behind me. "To find all of them there, really. Linna, your mother. You, even."

I glance over to the girls again, and the one playing the game on her phone is near tears now, the other pushing her to explain what's wrong, what happened. "Sad video on my phone," she answers eventually, and the other laughs. "Oh, god, is it the one about the golden retriever? Gets me every time." I cringe.

"What do you mean?" I ask, distracted. "At the farm?"

"Yeah," she says. "It's dark but…I thought he'd find bodies there."

Reese told me about his trip to Florida, his theories about the extent of my father's violence. But there hadn't been talk of bodies, of actively searching for them.

"He talked to the police down there," she adds. "And they just laughed at him, asked him if he understood what excavating for a major build is like."

He hadn't mentioned the police to me, either. But, of course, he had talked to them. I don't have time to consider what it means that he didn't share this with me. I think of how his demeanor had shifted at my apartment, how he went from tipsy to sober so swiftly, how I had doubted that he was actually ever drunk in the first place.

"They said if there were bodies to be found, they would have found them. No matter what condition they were in. The types of permits and inspections you need for construction like that…not a chance you just accidentally miss a body or three or five or ten. Zero chance, they said. They laughed him out of the room, basically."

I can picture it. Big, burly men with buzz cuts surrounding Reese, sneering at his outfit, his clear disdain for the place they call home.

"One of the sheriffs actually remembered the farm," Holly adds. "His uncle lived out near there apparently, a long time ago. He said he talked to him and all his uncle could remember was that it was a quiet family. A Christ-focused family. A pretty wife, a nice daughter. Quiet, good people, he said. Didn't exactly help Reese's case."

"Wow." I shake my head, quickly taking this in, then check the time on my phone. The meeting has already run long, and I can sense that it has shifted into something else now. Holly is looking at me again, waiting for something. I motion silently for the check.

"Aren't you going to ask?"

"Ask about what?"

Holly lowers her chin ever so slightly. "Ben and Bertie . . . your mother."

I realize my mistake now, what she's getting at. They had died there.

"Oh," I say, answering the question for her that she hasn't yet asked. "I mean, I saw their bodies, if that's what you're implying . . . I was the one who found my mother."

She shakes her head. "But where did he bury them, if not there?"

"Maybe they just missed the graves." I shrug, the memory of burying my mother rising up from somewhere deep. I can picture the disturbed patch of ground, the pile of dirt. At the time, I had assumed it was my mother's body below my feet. Now I know I could have been burying anything.

"But you never actually saw him bury the bodies there, right? Not Ben and Bertie? Or your mother?" she pushes.

"No," I answer. "I guess I didn't."

Holly seems satisfied enough by this answer, though I suspect not completely. She nods.

The waiter brings the check and I take it and insist on paying, though Holly barely argues. She's distant, her mind clearly elsewhere now.

"Then they could be anywhere, I guess," she says as I sign the check. "He could have put them in a swamp somewhere, fed them to alligators. Linna, too."

The image makes me nauseous. "I don't know, Holly."

I stand to leave, swinging my bag over my shoulder, and hover there, but she stays seated, looking up at me. "Look, I should really—"

"It doesn't bother you at all," she pushes. "The not knowing. You really don't want to find out? To do whatever it takes to find them all?"

I stare down at her, shift my bag to the other shoulder awkwardly. It's such a stupid question. Insulting. I knew them all so much better than she did. I loved them all so much more. I want to say: I was there so much longer than you. You have no idea what that was like. But I don't. "Of course it bothers me. It kills me," I say instead. "I just . . . I can only give him so many years of my life. He's taken so much of it already."

She looks a little guilty now. Good. "I know." She nods, eyes closed. She feels this, too. I think for a second that this will be the end of it, but then her eyes fly back open. She stands so we're facing each other. "Maybe this is how we get it back, though, Catharine. Maybe sharing our story is the start of reclaiming all of it. Letting everyone know exactly what he did, and who he was. Truly holding him accountable, no matter where he is or what happened to him. Reese's story is good. It's fine. But we need to tell the story ourselves, too. Somehow."

I feel the intensity of her words, how badly she needs this. I almost want to tell her everything then and there, sit back down at the table and explain the parts I left out when I told Reese about that last day. But I know I can't do that.

"Don't you want him to get exactly what he deserves?" she asks.

I look straight into her eyes. "More than anything."

We both let this sink in, the comfort of despising the same thing warming the space between us.

"I just need some time," I add, then check my phone again. "I really do have to go now, though . . ."

She nods, and we say goodbye, then hug. The motion is awkward and stilted, and the entire time all I can think is how odd it is that we've done this so many times before and I can't remember it. My childhood feels like a thing I dreamed, a world I made up.

I feel unsettled on the walk home, so I take the long way, gradually comforting myself with the thought that the meeting had gone well. Holly could have been furious with me about Linna, about how I failed to keep her safe, how I put her directly in the path of danger. She could have asked more questions about the end, about my final days and hours there, but she didn't. She believed me. I could feel it in the way she pushed me. She knew that after everything I had been through, I must want nothing more than for him to pay for what he did. She wasn't wrong.

I walk through my front door and my phone pings the second I take off my shoes, a new email from Reese. It's the first time I've heard from him since last night in my apartment.

> Subject: Change of Plans
>
> We're going live with what we have on Monday. It will be a multipart story, staggered releases. An investigation in real time. I wanted to give you the heads up. Let me know if you have any concerns.

My heart races. Monday? It's Wednesday now. Less than a week.

I read the email again and realize he had included a link at the bottom. I click it and it directs to a TikTok. As soon as I open it, my stomach flips. On the screen is Holly, wearing the same thing she was at the café earlier, walking down a quiet path in the park as she talks into the camera. The title text on the video reads: MY CULT STORY, PART 1.

Oh, fuck.

I play the sixty-second clip and it outlines the beginning of everything, all the same twists and turns she shared that first day at Reese's office. It ends with her teary-eyed and determined, that same confidence in her voice that I had heard earlier. "Part two and so much more coming very, very soon. We're going to get answers. For Linna." I look at the right hand of the screen and it has 5,000 likes, 300 comments, and counting. It was posted an hour ago. I can already imagine the internet reporters reaching out to Holly, begging her for an interview. Reese is probably seething. It's his story that's supposed to go viral, after all.

I quickly reply to his email.

Is there even enough for a story right now?

I know he needs proof of everything to get an okay from his editor, enough background information to actually make the piece interesting, even if it isn't the ten-thousand-word behemoth he had initially pitched. He emails back in minutes.

Oh yeah. There's enough.

I want to ask him what this means, what he has, what else he's learned that he hasn't shared. But I don't. Instead, I watch the comments on Holly's video pour in in real time.

Holy shit, is this for real?
I'm so sorry you went through this omg.
How is no one talking about this???
WHERE IS LINNA????
Umm...does this mean this guy still out there? Wtf

* * *

Just when I manage to put my phone down, it buzzes again. I reach for it instantly, sure it must be Reese, telling me more. But instead, it's Stella. She has texted me a link to Holly's TikTok. It now has ten thousand likes. "Sounds a little bit familiar... maybe you should send to Reese??? Btw, what's going on there??" she texts.

I groan, realizing how this is going to be. How much I'm going to have to explain to her.

I feel so naïve now, remembering how I had just sat in front of Holly and nodded as she told me how confident she feels in her story now, how much it needs to be told. How I had told her I needed time, so sure that I would have plenty of it. Time to perfect how I told the story, the twists and turns. The dramatic pauses. The emotional cliffhangers. The parts I held back. I would have time to make sure that people would say, "She deserves privacy," and "Someone else's trauma isn't your entertainment," at all the right points. With time, I could make sure of that reaction. I could guarantee that. But that's gone now. There is no more time. I can't wait for her or Reese or, soon, the police to dig deeper and drag parts of my story to the surface without my permission or my control. I am done being one step behind, done waiting. There is no Marion Earl. No Linna. No Reese and me as some sort of team. No connection. There is only me, the story that made me, and what exactly I will do with it.

I open my call log and press on Reese's number. He picks up almost instantly. "We need to talk."

CHAPTER 38

Then

I had no plan other than distance, as much as I could get. It was all I could concentrate on as I ran out of my father's cottage, grass like sandpaper poking against my bare feet. I had lost my sandals somewhere on the way back to the treehouse and I felt the splinters slice into my toes as I climbed the rungs, then pulled myself into the shelter. I ignored my bare feet, the splinters, the sweat soaking my shirt; there was only so much time before I lost my nerve. I had to keep moving. I had to keep going until I was far away from all of this, until I could breathe.

We had been keeping the money and documents in a pillowcase at the treehouse, tucked between the plush filling and the fabric. It had been Linna's suggestion. My father rarely visited there, if ever. It seemed as safe a spot as any. Still, I knew that there was a chance he could find it. Part of me had even secretly hoped for it some days. Maybe it would be better if he took all the options off the table for me. The thought gave me goosebumps as I reached into the pillow and grabbed for the plastic bag, beads of sweat crowding my forehead.

Quickly, I accounted for the basics—spare key, money, documents, car registration. Before I hustled down the rungs of the ladder again, I looked out from the small window of the treehouse, the one that gave the best view of the farm. It was still morning, the sky a happy, screaming blue. A single, comically small cloud floated overhead.

I shook my head, determined to focus, my eyes scanning the gardens, the main building in the distance. I tried to spot my father, or anyone else who might ask questions or cross my path on the walk to the old barn, but the farm was still silent. I took a deep, greedy breath and imagined the quiet filling me up, too. I was sure I would never know stillness quite like that again.

I passed through the first set of gardens slowly, tomato plants stretching out on either side of me. I had grabbed a crate at the edge of the field and placed the plastic bag at the bottom, picking the fruit as I went, covering it up. I balanced it on my hip, and let the familiarity of the task calm me. It forced me to move slowly, methodically. If anyone found me here—if he did—I would be doing what I had always done. I brought one to my nose and inhaled, trying to memorize smell. He was probably right. Nothing could ever smell as good as this. I threw it in the crate and kept moving.

By the time I got to the barn, my arm was straining from the weight of the now-full crate, but I had made it. No one had stopped me. My father was nowhere to be found. I stood in front of the truck and stared, then glanced back over my shoulder, out the barn doors. The farm still sat silent in the distance. I was alone. I was leaving. I adjusted the crate so it was resting on my hip again and used my free hand to open the driver's seat door, taking a deep breath. I had just begun to lift myself into the cab when I heard his voice drift in.

"Little early for tomato drop-off, don't you think?"

Startled, I banged my head on the top of the truck, hard. When I looked up, my father was leaning into the passenger side window, elbows resting there, smiling at me.

"Oops," he said. "Didn't mean to scare ya."

I stared at him, expecting to find anger or disappointment on his face, but his expression was animated and happy, slashed with a wide grin. It was everything else that seemed wrong. His entire body was covered with a slick of sweat, his eyes wide and barely blinking. It was a look I knew well, an excitement so acute that it verged on sickness.

"Sorry," I said. "Was just trying to get ahead of chores."

He tilted his head to the side, frowned. "With no keys?"

I scrambled. "Was going to pack up first and then go get you. See if you could come with me."

He smiled, this time with no teeth.

"Since you were so tired," I added, for good measure.

He nodded. "Of course. Always so helpful, little one."

A single bead of sweat dripped down the curve of my spine then, tickling me as it fell.

"You know," he said, opening the door and hoisting himself into the passenger seat, staring straight ahead. "I am in the mood for a drive, I think."

I didn't want to get in the car with him. The idea of it made my skin itch. "It's fine, really, I can wait—"

"I said," he repeated, his head slowly swiveling to look directly at me. "I'm in the mood for a drive."

I could tell something was off, even more so than this morning. I looked out the door of the barn, instinctively searching for someone, anyone to come by and notice us. But I saw no one; the farm was still completely still. I glanced back at my father. He looked as exhausted as he had earlier, but his energy was different now. He felt radioactive, off-kilter. I didn't think I had seen him blink once yet. I hesitated.

"So get in the car." He smiled. "And fucking drive, won't you?"

I realized I didn't have a choice.

Quickly, I put the crate of tomatoes in the bed of the truck and climbed into the front. He threw the keys into my lap, and I started the car, driving the familiar route to the farm store. When we turned onto the highway, he pressed the button for the radio, then rolled down the window, smiling as he took long gulps of fresh air. I kept having the urge to scoot farther away from him.

Just before we get to the first turn, a song I recognized came on the radio, the one Linna and I had laughed about. Tears bit the back of my throat at the memory. Was that the last happy day we would have together? My father seemed to sense my reaction and turned the music off swiftly. I remembered the way Linna had prodded me about my father during that drive, asking about his rules, his lies. I had so willfully ignored her.

When I clicked on the turn signal, my father stopped me. "Other way. Take a right here."

"What? The farm store is—"

"I said turn right, Catharine."

For an hour or so, the drive went like that—him directing the turns, eventually winding us down what felt like a long-abandoned country road. Acres of overgrown forest, swampland so thick with mosquitoes that I rubbed my eyes, assuming my vision was blurry. Eventually, we weren't even on a main road anymore.

"Where are we going?" I whispered, cautious.

"You'll see."

In time, the dirt path turned into a barely cleared wooded area, then no path at all. When it was too dense to keep driving, I stopped. Shifted into park.

"Now we walk," he said, hopping out of the car. I hesitated, then watched him walk to the back of the truck, staring at the tomatoes. My heart raced. I took the keys out of the ignition, then quickly walked over, trying to distract him.

"Here," I said, throwing him the keys. A show of loyalty.

He caught them, then stuck his finger in the key ring and spun it around, sunlight streaming through the trees and glinting off the metal. "This way."

We walked for close to an hour, though at times it felt like much more. My legs were so covered in mosquito bites that eventually I stopped swatting. I imagined that at some point they would simply run out of blood.

Suddenly, he stopped. "Here we are."

I looked around us. As far as I could see, there was nothing but shades of brown and green, cypress trees sprouting from shallow, murky puddles of water. It was so humid that even the air in my lungs felt wet. I was drenched in sweat.

"Where are we?" I asked, slowly. "What is this?"

"This is where I come to think, Catharine," he said. "It's peaceful here."

The farm wasn't enough peace and quiet for you?

I nodded. "It is."

"Your mother loved it here too, actually," he added. His hands were on his hips now, his face tilted upward. There was a break in the tree line just above us and the sun was cutting through, turning leaves golden green.

I couldn't picture my mother here. But maybe I hadn't known this about her. Maybe this was from before everything, when she was happier.

"It's why I brought her here to rest, in the end," he said, his voice so light that I almost missed his meaning.

"What?"

"Ben and Bertie, too." He smiled, nodded. "I know how much you loved them. How much you respected them."

My entire body had tensed. A mosquito buzzed closer and closer to my ear. I thought of burying my mother, the way I had imagined her deep below the ground. Was she ever there at all?

"I thought..." I mumbled. "The burials..."

"Are symbolic, obviously." He laughed. "I've always told you that."

I remembered the final shovelfuls of dirt, how it was our job to put them on top of the grave.

"So their bodies are just..." I looked around, my eyes scanning the forest floor, all that dirt and swampy water. My eyes stopped on a dark spot near a hollowed-out log. Water moccasin, as thick as my forearm. I shivered. "They're just out here...they were always out here?"

"Yes. Well...somewhere," he finished my thought. "Everyone has their own section of the forest, their own place to rest. This heat means that by the time I come out here again, any trace of them is long gone. They return to the earth. It's beautiful, really."

I spun around, slowly, trying to recall the way we had walked from the truck. Every angle of the forest looked so similar, an image repeating itself again and again. I was afraid to think about why he had brought me here, afraid to ask.

"Last night was obviously a little less cut and dry." He chuckled. "But in the end, I think they'll be at peace, too. I gave them that."

I swallowed. "Last night? What, what do you mean?"

"After I ran into your sister, it just sort of...clicked." He snapped his fingers above his head, and the sound startled a nearby bird, causing it to squawk angrily. "No more half measures. No more fasts. I mean, look at Kent. Look at your sister. Clearly, it wasn't enough to get rid of the sickness. We needed to start over."

My mind flashed to the quiet of the farm that morning, the stillness of the buildings.

"What do you mean start over?"

He laughed. "I mean start over. Clean slate. The greatest reset of all. You and I will rebuild, just like we were always supposed to."

I stepped backward on instinct. He laughed. "Oh, don't give me that face again," he said. "There's no need to perform outrage now that it's just us. You and me, remember? Think of everything we've been through together. Everything you've fought for. The way you committed to this place, despite your mother's weakness, your sister's gluttony. Despite it all, you stayed steadfast. Every test I put in front of you, you passed."

I could hear my own breathing then, shallow gulps rising out of me. I was scared, I realized. It felt like eighteen years of fear distilled in one moment.

"So they're . . . they're gone," I added. "Rhonda, Stacy . . . Maura, Jessie . . . gone?"

He shrugged. "They never had what you and I had."

I tried to do the math, to remember what time exactly I had fallen asleep. I knew it was early, just as dark had fallen. I thought of the way I had woken at dawn, then forced myself back to sleep, imagining I had given my sister more time. I remembered the sounds I had heard, that hushed commotion, the way I had assumed it was people starting their chores early.

"And Kent . . ."

He nodded. "Doubt is a sickness, Catharine."

I was afraid to ask the next question, but I knew I needed to. I needed to hear him admit it to absorb the full scale of what he had done, and what I had. “And . . . Linna?”

I expected him to nod again, to shrug, to admit that he had lied to me last night, but at this question, he responded differently. A flash of agitation moved across his forehead, discomfort rippling through his posture. For a moment, he said nothing.

“What about Linna?” I pushed again, and at this something snapped in him. His eyes met mine, full of rage.

“The same as the rest,” he answered, gesturing lazily to the hazy swamp in the distance.

It occurred to me then with instant, ringing clarity that he was lying. The way he reacted to hearing her name, the anger pooling behind his eyes. I forced myself to imagine my father finding her in that field, what he would have been like if she had gotten away. It would have made him panic. Act drastically. I looked around at where we were, parsing through what he was telling me. This was a man who had been set off by something. Maybe that something was my sister clawing at him, digging her nails into his skin until he let her go, then running, running, running. A spark of hope lit in my chest, one that would not go out for years to come.

“It’s why I brought you here,” he started again.

I took another step backward, but he was moving toward me now, closing the distance.

“Look at your face, little one,” he cooed. “You look just like they did last night.”

I could feel the terror in my features, pained and pinched. I wondered if they all had stood right here, too. If they were dead before he brought them here or not. I wanted to scream, but who would hear me?

“You forget so quickly that you and I are special, Catharine.

That's the whole point of this," he said. "I brought you here to say goodbye to them. A gift. Because we're going to start over, you and me. We're going to build a whole new system. A better version of the farm. Somewhere far away from here."

"We are?" I heard myself croak. I sounded so stupid, but I couldn't grip on to reality just then. It felt nightmarish and slick.

"We are." He nodded, proud. "I just need to know that you're in it with me. That you're all in."

I nodded, panicked, grasping for the easiest way back in the car, out of these trees. I could feel the welts from the bug bites rising on my legs, swollen and angry.

He beamed at me, proud. The woods were aglow with orange light now, beams slicing through the cypress limbs, reflecting off the swampy pools of water. It was the first time I had thought it was beautiful. I tried to imagine what my mother would think of this place, how she would describe it. I saw a heron glide by overhead, its body long and graceful. It was so quiet. I imagined a goodbye to my mother floating up to it, a note tied round its neck with a bow. A delivery sent to wherever she was in this giant silent expanse of a place. An apology.

"I'm in," I said, lowering my gaze to meet his.

He smiled, his teeth flashing white against the strange pallor of his skin, then crossed the remaining few feet to stand in front of me. "I knew you would be."

At this, he started the walk back to the car. I followed him dutifully.

When we finally got to the truck, he stopped in front of it, waiting for me. "Let's hit the road then, shall we?" he asked. "Lots to do."

I walked up to him so we were close, a foot or so away from each other. "Can I drive?"

He smiled, then pulled out the keys, handed them to me.

I rubbed my thumb over the cool metal, the sharp edges. He smiled, watching me. He looked so proud.

"I always told your mother, there's no mistaking it—that's my daughter, that's my flesh and—"

I heard the sound first. The spurt of blood, the clank of metal against bone. Then, his face, the expression dumbstruck before it was pained. A glint of light coming through the trees, the sun star bursting through Spanish moss, reflecting off the key wedged beneath my father's brow, dug so deep into his eye socket that it had almost disappeared entirely.

I stared at my hand, then the truck behind him, then back at my father, who had started to let out a sound like a squeal, high-pitched and girlish. He lurched forward and I sidestepped out of the way as he fell, a crisp crack ringing through the woods as he hit the ground. Bone on rock. A pool of blood beneath his head growing so quickly it felt cartoonish. Impossible.

"Oh," I said, staring at him there, his body twitching, the movement slowing down with each second before stopping entirely, dirt soaking up blood. "I didn't mean to..."

I trailed off, the words tasting wrong, acrid. I was suddenly certain that it was the first thing I had truly meant to do in my life.

CHAPTER 39

Now

"He was going to kill me," I tell Reese, who is sitting across from me in my living room once again. This time, he is dead sober, his hands clutching a to-go coffee. "I had no choice."

He takes this information in, staring at his hands, then leans back into the couch and stares up at the ceiling. "Fucking hell, Catharine."

"I wanted to tell you before... I don't know, before it all blows up. Before something else happens. I wanted to get ahead of it."

Then he lets out a long burst of air, like a whistle, shakes his head. "This is going to be..."

I nod. I know what he's thinking. A mess. This is going to be a mess. He's not completely wrong. For a little while, anyway, it will be.

"This is going to change everything," he says finally, the words not what I'm expecting. "I mean, I *knew*, I guess. I did. But this... you putting it all out there? This is beyond anything I could have imagined."

I prickle. "You knew?"

He stands. "I mean, sure." He shrugs. "I knew *something* must have blown up in your face back then. Why else would you be so desperate for control now?"

I blink. I expected, at least, for him to briefly pretend to be shocked at hearing another person confess to murder. But he's not even trying to hide it. He's lit up, excited. He's pacing my living room now, chugging the rest of his coffee.

"I mean, I didn't know you killed anyone. But did I think you had it in you? When push comes to shove?" He bobbles his head from side to side, like he's considering his own question. "Yeah. I did."

I recall how he stood in this exact spot days ago and told me that he knew I didn't hurt my sister, that I couldn't have. I think of us in the kitchen, him waxing poetic about the beauty of where I grew up. I think of his hand on my hip. A shudder snakes through me.

"Like I said," I repeat, shifting in my seat. "I didn't have a choice. He would have left me out there with all of them otherwise."

At this, Reese seems to remember the seriousness of what I'm revealing to him. The implications. He stiffens.

"So, no bodies?" he pushes. "To clarify, you never actually saw them out there, when he brought you there?"

"No."

"Then how can you be sure they were actually there?"

"I'm sure," I say. How do I explain to him that I felt them all there that day? That I looked into my father's eyes and saw the truth of what he was saying in every word. For so many years, it was only what he had said about Linna that day that felt different to me. The lie hidden amid all the horrible honesty. A secret code. A hidden message. I had thought I was smart enough to spot it. Now, I see it all for what it was. I would have done anything to believe that I was not alone.

"Could you take me there?" Reese asks. "Take police there? Would you remember?"

"I could try."

He sighs then, relaxing a bit.

"There will be an investigation, you know," he adds, as if I hadn't considered this yet. "I mean, it's clearly self-defense, given all of Holly's statements, but still."

"I know."

"A trial, maybe."

"I know."

I started thinking about how all of this would go almost as soon as I arrived in the city a decade ago. The very first free seminar I attended at the public library was by a defense attorney who specialized in violence against women. After, I began to consider the possibility of exactly something like this happening. An investigation. A journalist. A trial. It was the first time that I contextualized what I did to my father, and what he did to all of us, not as a part of my life but as part of a story. I prepared accordingly.

At first, all the planning felt vital, practical. I spent entire weekends in the library buried in research, understanding similar cases, precedents, media response. It was all a small comfort when I'd find myself remembering that day in the woods. But as the years passed and my life took shape around me, it started to feel more hypothetical, a strange little hobby rather than a real-life safety net.

"That's two seasons right there," Reese interrupts my thoughts. "Minimum. Then there's the aftermath, the media response..."

I must look confused, because he explains.

"Docuseries. Then podcast. Or podcast then docuseries?" He pauses, hand on his hip, considering this. "Whatever. Doesn't matter. Either way, I mean... Jesus Christ, people are going to love you, Catharine."

My eyes go wide, alarmed, like I can't even believe he's talking about this right now.

He smiles at my reaction, looking almost charmed, then leans forward. "You know you're basically made for television, right? You're sharp, funny, charming, attractive. And then you add this on top of everything..."

"By 'this,' you mean..."

He waves off the implication. "I mean, yeah, we get it. Murder is bad. Murder is scary. But *self-defense* is different. And self-defense isn't scary. It's fucking empowering. It's sexy," he pushes. "You're basically the physical embodiment of 'fuck the patriarchy.' "

I grimace. "Stop, Reese. This is ridiculous. You're being ridiculous."

"How?" he says. "You know I'm right. I know you do. You're too smart not to."

"I just told you I killed someone, Reese."

He shrugs. "He was a monster."

I don't push back. He was.

"Soo..." he says, moving toward me, then gesturing in my direction dramatically, as if he's bowing. "That makes you the hero."

I wince. "No, it doesn't."

"This is how stories work, Catharine," he goes on. "Someone has to be the hero. Who's it going to be if not you? Holly? The woman who left her daughter after giving up carbs for a few weeks. Sorry, not a chance."

I'm almost surprised at his cruelty, how casual it is, but I ignore it.

"Write whatever story you want, Reese," I push. "But I don't want to be some trauma porn celebrity. Make the docuseries without me. Do whatever you need to do."

At this, he seems to panic a bit. He stands.

"Catharine," he starts, serious. "Think about the optics of that. A story about women manipulated and abused by a man...told by a man. No. You know you have to be the face of this. I'll do the work. You just sit there, do the press circuit. Have the memoir ghostwritten eventually, whatever. But you have to work with me on this."

I think on this for a second, and now it's me who is pacing my living room. Back and forth, back and forth.

"Do you know how many people this will help?" he tries again. "How many women will listen to your story and see themselves in some way? How many girls will wake up to the horrible situations they've found themselves in? Fight back? Make different choices? This isn't about me, Catharine. Maybe it's not even about you." He pauses for dramatic effect. "It's about *them*."

I stop walking now and close my eyes, as if absorbing the argument he is making, as if it's really hitting me.

"Maybe this is what will help us find Linna," he adds, in a final plea, and I can hear in his voice confirmation of what I know I now believe, too. The sheer improbability of what he is suggesting, the desperation behind it all, is what finally shuts the door in my mind. Linna being alive seems as unlikely as the idea that Reese is in this to fight the patriarchy from the inside. It's fantasy. It's fairy tale. I know that now. There is no way my father would have ever let her go, let her live. Yes, Linna would have fought back, but my father would have won. It was what he did. When cornered, he was a dog with a bone, too. Teeth bared, jaw locked.

Still, it makes sense that Reese would think this is the thing that convinces me, so I meet his eyes now, pensive.

"I want control," I say, finally.

Reese looks surprised. "What?"

"I want to be a producer," I say, adjusting my ask to make sure I was clear. "If we're going to tell this story, then I need to know it's being told the right way."

"Fine," Reese says. He can't help himself. He wants me to agree so badly he'll do anything. "Yes. Whatever you want. That'll be... it'll be great."

I can guess that he's thinking that this detail might not matter, that by the time I get wrapped up in the investigation and trial, I'll forget about this, but I am thinking long-term here. I've been thinking long-term for a while. I will need a fresh start after everything, a comfortable cushion of money to rebuild from. Writing a shitty memoir or making TikToks isn't going to get me there. I need something solid, something real. I stand up straighter. I feel lighter than I have in ten years.

"Okay," I say. "Then I'm game."

"Okay," Reese says. "Great. This is going to be great. This is going to change lives."

I'm sure he means his life, mostly, but that's okay. On this point, we actually agree. This is going to change so many people's lives.

Reese is flustered now, almost sweaty. "All right, Jesus. Okay. There's so much to do. I've got to work. Call people... outline. Call the... police, I guess? I don't know. You'll need... what? A lawyer?"

I shake my head. "I haven't really thought about that yet."

It's an easy lie. I've had a person picked out for this for years, their retainer saved.

"Well, you should," Reese says, heading for the door.

He pauses, just before he opens it, looks back at me.

"What did you do after?" he asks. "After you... after he... you know."

He can't even say it out loud. He looks pathetic, young. A little boy.

I shake my head. "I just drove," I answer. "I just drove and drove and drove."

CHAPTER 40

Then

I leaned down and pulled the key out of his face like I was picking fruit. After, I washed it in a murky pool of water nearby, wiping it dry on my jeans before sticking it in my pocket. It wouldn't be dark for a while yet, but I moved quickly anyway, grabbing the crate of tomatoes from the bed of the truck and moving it to the passenger seat beside me, pulling the bag full of papers and money out, placing it safely in the glove compartment. I climbed into the driver's seat, stuck the key into the ignition, then looked over my shoulder as I backed up the long, narrow path, not bothering to look at my father's body even once. The sky had darkened now, the air electric with the promise of a storm. On the walk back to the car, my father had explained to me how the entire forest turned into a shallow, murky swamp with the slightest bit of rain, the moisture and heat dissolving anything organic in a matter of days. And then, he said, there were the alligators.

The setting sun had lowered the temperature, and I rolled down the window as I made the long, slow, quiet drive back to a main road. I saw not one person, not one house or car or sign of life for almost two hours. He was right; it was peaceful. A great place to think. The breeze through the truck's window felt delicious and all mine. I took down my hair and it was wavy, sweat-soaked, and wild. I let it dry in the wind. Eventually, I was on the highway, driving north, north, north, the sky a frothy orange. I was flying.

I glanced at the passenger seat, the crate beside me. I could smell the fruit from where I sat. I thought of home and felt something inside me ache. I grabbed one of the tomatoes, brought it to my nose, then sank my teeth into it, eating until the juice ran down my arms.

FIVE YEARS LATER

Traveling taught me that morning is different everywhere. Dark and cold some places and sticky-sweet in others. After the first season of the docuseries came out, I put all my things in storage and spent a year hopping from place to place. The Catskills. Northern California. Maine. And then there was Wyoming, the mornings silent and crisp, nothing cutting through the quiet except birdsong and the sound of the wind lazily dragging its way through spruce branches. No one and nothing in a hurry. All that space, always threatening to gobble you up, so vast I thought I'd disappear in it. But all it did was give. It gave me so much that I didn't want to leave. It was this particular and slow unfurling of the world that I decided I couldn't do without.

It took time, though, to find this place. Money, too. Reese was right about a lot of things when it came to the docuseries, but it was the money he had underestimated. It trended in the top ten of Netflix series for six months before it eventually was replaced by another, eerily similar show, one that I had also spearheaded. As it turned out, I had a knack for producing, for shaping the story into something important. Shifting the focus onto women's voices. I suspected Reese thought that Netflix offered me a multiseries contract out of pity after the trial, the media attention, the eventual mistrial (there's only so much you can do without a body, you know?). Poor, sad girl. But I knew it was because I was good at this, telling the stories of other women who had suffered the way I had. Maybe it was a little of both. In the end, it didn't matter. It was more money than I had ever fathomed, enough to buy my dream piece of property. Ensure that this kind of morning was mine forever.

In another life, the one-hundred-acre lot had been a camp where dozens of Girl Scouts bused in every summer to practice survival skills and sing campfire songs, the pristine sky sparkling with stars overhead. The property was dotted with cabins, all hidden deep in the woods, most of them abandoned for years now. It all reminded me of the best days of my childhood, the ones that shined with sunlight and warmth even now, untarnished by my father's evil, still.

It's dawn, and I'm sitting on my porch staring out at the trees, a thick quilt draped around my shoulders. I cradle a mug in my hands and watch the steam spiral upward. Every morning, I sit here with my coffee and remind myself that everything I can see is gloriously, impossibly mine. Each tree, each rock. I get to choose what happens with them; I don't need to wait for anyone to renovate them, to make them into something beautiful. I can do that myself now.

An alarm goes off on my phone, the sound disturbing the still of the morning, and I startle. My coffee sloshes into my lap, and I realize it's gone cold. I need to make another pot before everyone gets here. I look down at the screen.

One hour!

I manage the jolt of adrenaline I feel by reminding myself of what I still have to do this morning. Go over the checklist. Make more coffee. Tidy up.

I walk through the screen doors of the primary cabin, my eyes scanning the large main room. The ceilings are more than fifteen feet high, and the effect is breathtaking. Even now, after living here for more than a year, I find myself stopping to take it in once or twice a day. I designed the entire living space to be wide open, exposed wood beams cutting across the expanse of the ceiling. The focal point is the windows, though. They take up an entire wall, the view only broken up by a massive stone fireplace. Beyond it all is deep greens and sparkling blues, the colors interrupted by the looming presence of the mountains.

A log cracks in the hearth and it reminds me that I need to get more wood ready. It will be in the sixties by lunchtime, but it's still chilly now. And there's nothing more inviting than a crackling fire.

The hour goes by in a blink, leaving just enough time to apply a swipe of lip balm when I hear the first car arrive, a low rumble working its way through the woods. It cost a fortune to put in that driveway. I walk out on the porch and hold my hand over my eyes like a visor as the Suburban rolls into sight. I open the Notes app on my phone, checking off the first arrival. There will be six more like this over the course of the day, ten women in total, but this is the only one that really matters. The driver walks around to open the car door, and I hear a loud squeal before I see her.

"You made it," I say, my grin wide and welcoming as I walk to her.

"Are you sure I'm not in New Zealand or some shit?" Stella says. "I think I've been traveling for seventy-two hours straight."

I laugh. If Stella had been initially disappointed that I hadn't shared my story with her, she had totally forgotten that by now, her bitterness long dissolved. It was an effect likely helped along by how often I invited her to fancy parties and media dinners. She recently went through another bad breakup and was in search of distraction, then meaning, then a mix of the two. It's why I invited her here when someone dropped out at the last minute. I knew it would be good for her.

"I know it's a hike to get out here," I say. "But I think that's part of what makes it special."

She looks around, hands on her hips, then takes a big gulp of air. "You're right. It does feel different here."

We hug, and it's like I can smell the hope pouring out of her.

"Holy shit." She takes in the primary cabin. "How did you find this place? How did you *afford* this place?"

I laugh but start walking, gesturing for her to follow me. "Come on, I'll show you around."

"Let me just grab my bag."

"No need," I say, nodding toward her driver. "Tony will get it."

"Tony?" she mimes as I continue walking.

"He helps out with stuff around here sometimes. There's a lot to manage."

"I'm sorry, are you just casually telling me you have a whole ass butler on staff here?" she says. "Who *are* you?"

"He's not a butler." I shrug. "He's just Tony."

"He's just Tony," she mimics, echoing the tone of my voice, but when I open the door and she follows me in, her jaw drops. "Wow. Wow, wow, wow. Who cares about having a Tony when you have *this*?"

"Well, thanks," I say, offering her a glass of water, which she takes and swallows in one go.

"Jesus, even the water tastes better," she says, collapsing on the couch and sinking into the cushions, eyes closed.

"The rest won't get here until noon or so," I quip from the kitchen, where I'm prepping the welcome snack board—a sprawling spread of meats, cheeses, and crackers, everything as fresh or locally made as possible. "Feel free to get settled and take a nap if you want. Your cabin is the first one after the clearing. Walk toward the woods and take a left. Can't miss it."

She moans. "That sounds like a great idea if I could... only... move..."

"Well, no rush," I say, satisfied that she feels so comfortable here. "You have a while to get settled, after all."

"Thirty glorious days of this," she says, staring out at the view, like she can't believe it. For a minute, I stare with her, taking in all that blue. There's a smattering of happy-looking clouds sitting above the mountains, hovering. I smile. It's a day so perfect it's almost like I engineered it this way. Who wouldn't arrive here and immediately feel like a better version of themselves?

"Honestly, Catharine," Stella says, her tone more serious. "I can't thank you enough for inviting me here. I can't tell you how good this is going to be for me. To recenter myself, realign with my values, turn off my phone. Spend every morning with people who want the same things. What a gift."

"It's nothing," I say, beaming at her appreciation.

"It's not," she insists. "I know you're not running a charity here. And I mean, I see why. Look at this."

I prickle at the mention of money. Pricing the retreat had been difficult for me. I knew I was providing something of value, a month-long residence (with options to extend it to sixty or ninety days, or even longer) for women who were desperate for a return to their confidence, their purpose, their best selves. I had scheduled seminars from other powerful women I had met in the last few years. Even Holly was scheduled to come back and give a talk. There were world-renowned trainers being flown in, developing workout plans for each and every participant. And all of it, every single bit, was going to be set in a pristine, completely private locale. I had spent a fortune renovating the old cabins in just a few months, each one now equipped with luxury fixtures and amenities. I needed to make back my investment, and frankly, I needed to create a career that was multifaceted. Dynamic. Still, it felt odd to put a price tag on it. If I could have had everyone experience it all for free, I would. But that's just not how the world works, is it?

Seeing Stella here, so relaxed already, has reassured me, though. This is why I'm doing this. It's reminded me how much this place will change people's lives. How much it's already changed mine.

"This place made me feel like myself again." I shrug. "I wanted other people to have the same opportunity."

"You've already changed so many people's lives by telling your story, Catharine," she said. "This is just going to be a bigger version of that."

I smile. It's a bit much, maybe, but the validation is nice. I'm glad she sees the vision, too.

"And look, I know you said this is a gift, but I really do understand that being here for free is a big deal. I want to help in any way that I can," she starts. "Just say the word. This month, after this . . . whatever. I want to be part of this."

I was hoping she'd say that.

"Totally not necessary," I say, making a mental note to circle back to this in a few weeks, maybe before HIIT week. Stella hates

HIIT. "But thank you. You're the best. Now why don't you take a nap before you become a jet-lag zombie and scare the rest of the guests?"

"Good call," she says, heading toward the front door, stretching as she goes. "First cabin on the left, right?"

"You've got it."

As I watch Stella bound down the porch stairs, my phone pings with a new email. I pull it out of my pocket and expect a confirmation that another guest's flight has arrived, but when I look at the screen and see who it's from, I stop breathing.

I had started emailing Marion Earl on a whim, really, when I was first planning the retreat. Years ago, at the height of my absurd obsession, I had found an old email address in the deepest caverns of an amateur writers' chat room. I wasn't even sure if it was hers. More than once, I had drafted an email to her only to delete it, no combination of words ever quite right. Finally emailing her now, after everything, felt like an acknowledgment of reality, a thing that would heal me. In my mind, the worst-case scenario was that I would send fan mail, follow up a few times, and simply get no reply. I could easily find another author to fill her spot as a speaker. Yes, there was a time when I would have emailed her hoping for something else, but now, it was simple. I wanted people to come to this place and be inspired, and Marion Earl inspired me. I can finally see that now.

With time, I've come to accept that her words were never a clandestine message, but they were an earnest example of the power of art. Her writing had affected me deeply enough that I had conjured an entire other reality in my head. For years after I met Reese, this had unsettled me. Embarrassed me. But now, I have reframed it as something else. Against all odds, Marion Earl had reached into my dark world and given me hope. The least I could do was properly thank her.

My hand trembles as I click on the message and start reading.

Catharine,

I wanted to thank you for your emails. There are only a few readers who have found this address, and fewer yet who keep emailing after an initial lack of reply. My agent implied that maybe I should be wary of such enthusiasm, but I was never scared of you. It was obvious you had a gut feeling it was me on the other end, out there somewhere, reading your words. I know that feeling, too.

I also wanted to tell you personally, and directly, that I will not be able to attend your retreat as a speaker, despite your generous offers of financial compensation. Please know there is no dollar amount that would change my mind.

I wasn't always as happy as I am now. I live a quiet, joyful life. It's one that has required cultivation, a comprehensive trimming of darkness around the edges. I'm protective of it. We're all protecting something, I guess, aren't we? For better or worse. Whatever it takes.

Thank you for understanding. Thank you for reading.

Marion

My heart is still racing as I pull my attention away from my phone and catch sight of Stella in the distance. She is nearly turning the corner into her cabin now. I imagine her face when she opens the doors, takes in the linen bedding, the pillowtop mattress, the clawfoot bathtub. Everything exactly as I chose it. I will let her have this moment, even if there's something in me that wants to warn her that the next four weeks won't be easy. It won't be all relaxation and reflection and gorgeous views. I called the program a retreat because it's easier, but this isn't meant to be vacation. It's a lifestyle change, something hard-fought. Earned, even. There will be work.

I sit in the rocking chair, the repetitive motion relaxing me, burning off any lingering adrenaline from the email. I desperately want to reply, to ask more questions, but I know I can't let myself get distracted now. There is work to do. Even now, even after everything, it's so hard to remember it. It's so hard to really feel it, deep down in my bones.

It will be worth it, I remind myself again. It has to be.

I wonder if Stella knows it, too. If it's what she'll tell herself when it gets hard, when she feels like she can't push any further. I hope she will.

I hope she'll say it again and again, as long as it takes, a new mantra to replace the old one.

It will all, one day, be worth it.

ACKNOWLEDGMENTS

Writing and publishing a book is an exercise in many things, but, for me, it is a lesson in gratitude above all. Every day that I get to wake up and write books, then share them with the world, is a greater gift than I have ever known. I am thankful to every person who helps make it possible.

Five years ago in Philadelphia, I walked out my front door to go meet Dana Murphy for the first time, crossing Reese and Catharine Streets as I did, and my life changed. For the first time, I considered that maybe a life and career of writing books was possible. It cracked open my heart and lit up my world. Thank you, Dana, for being a remarkable agent and even better human. Your intelligence, humor, and steadfast kindness are unmatched. How lucky am I?

This book would not be what it is without Gabriella Mongelli, who felt as strongly about Catharine as I did from the very beginning. Gaby, your belief in this novel (and in me) has meant everything to me. Your brilliant edits made it sing. Knowing that someone as smart as you were behind *Little One* was a constant source of comfort. All my thanks, forever.

Thank you also to the rest of the fantastic team at Little Brown, especially the talented Peyton Young and the incredible Sally Kim.

Thank you to Katherine Akey, Tessa Keefe, Michael Barrs, Arik Hardin, Ben Allen, Laura Starrett, June Park, Alison Merchant, Chloe Texier-Rose, and Sabrina Callahan, for all your individual talents and the remarkable teamwork that has made *Little One* possible.

Thank you to Katie Greenstreet, for your generous and heartening support of this novel.

Thank you to Becca Freeman, Maddie Higley, Brian Peoples, and Courtney Heath for making *Bad on Paper* happen each week. You are some of the most hardworking and creative people I know. Thank you, most of all, to the listeners, who have graciously welcomed me into a community where I have found so much connection and comfort. Your kindness and generosity are boundless, and I love you all.

Thank you to the writers who have inspired me to keep going. To Ashley Audrain and Amity Gaige, especially, thank you. Your work has meant so much to me that there are small nods to it in this book. Please never stop writing.

To the many friends who have supported me throughout this journey, I am forever indebted. Thank you to Gabrielle Massari, Ayana Lage, and Haley Neer for all the Marco Polos, nonstop texts, and unflinching support. Thank you to Martha Sorren for being the kindest, smartest voice of reason. Thank you to James Cave and Jess Lima for cheering me on and making life upstate so fun. Thank you to Alli Hoff Kosik, Ella Berman, Becca Freeman, Clémence Michallon, and every other author friend who has generously shared their writing journey and perspective with me over the years.

Thank you, always, to Alex Arnold, who was the first human being on Earth to read any version of *Little One*. Alex—I often wonder where my life or career would be if I hadn't met you. How can I ever thank you enough? I am so glad to call you a friend.

To my parents, thank you for a lifetime of love and support. Thank you also for telling every person you've ever met on a cruise ship about my books. Thank you to my brother Grant for always making me laugh. Thanks also to the Romosers, who I am lucky enough to call my family, too. I love you all.

Finally, thank you to Jake. This book is dedicated to you because you gave me the space to believe it was possible. Thank you for doing the dishes. And the laundry. And the yardwork. Thank you for the writing cottage. Thank you for the little notes. Thank you for listening to all my far-fetched old house plans, for always saying yes. Thank you for never making me or my dreams feel small. Thank you for always asking me to watch the sunset on the porch. Thank you for a life so gorgeous I can hardly believe it's mine.

ABOUT THE AUTHOR

Olivia Muenter is a writer, reader, and cohost of the *Bad on Paper* podcast. She lives in an old house in the Hudson Valley with her family. Her first novel, *Such a Bad Influence*, was an instant *USA Today* bestseller.

RAISING READERS

Books Build Bright Futures

Thank you for reading this book and for being a reader of books in general. We are so grateful to share being part of a community of readers with you, and we hope you will join us in passing our love of books on to the next generation of readers.

Did you know that reading for enjoyment is the single biggest predictor of a child's future happiness and success?

More than family circumstances, parents' educational background, or income, reading impacts a child's future academic performance, emotional well-being, communication skills, economic security, ambition, and happiness.

Studies show that kids reading for enjoyment in the US is in rapid decline:

- In 2012, 53% of 9-year-olds read almost every day. Just 10 years later, in 2022, the number had fallen to 39%.
- In 2012, 27% of 13-year-olds read for fun daily. By 2023, that number was just 14%.

Together, we can commit to **Raising Readers** and change this trend. How?

- Read to children in your life daily.
- Model reading as a fun activity.
- Reduce screen time.
- Start a family, school, or community book club.
- Visit bookstores and libraries regularly.
- Listen to audiobooks.
- Read the book before you see the movie.
- Encourage your child to read aloud to a pet or stuffed animal.
- Give books as gifts.
- Donate books to families and communities in need.

BOB1217

Books build bright futures, and **Raising Readers** is our shared responsibility.

For more information, visit **JoinRaisingReaders.com**

Sources: National Endowment for the Arts, National Assessment of Educational Progress, WorldBookDay.com, Nielsen BookData's 2023 "Understanding the Children's Book Consumer"